F
MOR

THE SILENT HARP

BOOKS BY GILBERT MORRIS

THE HOUSE OF WINSLOW SERIES

1. The Honorable Imposter
2. The Captive Bride
3. The Indentured Heart
4. The Gentle Rebel
5. The Saintly Buccaneer
6. The Holy Warrior
7. The Reluctant Bridegroom
8. The Last Confederate
9. The Dixie Widow
10. The Wounded Yankee
11. The Union Belle
12. The Final Adversary
13. The Crossed Sabres
14. The Valiant Gunman
15. The Gallant Outlaw
16. The Jeweled Spur
17. The Yukon Queen
18. The Rough Rider
19. The Iron Lady
20. The Silver Star
21. The Shadow Portrait
22. The White Hunter
23. The Flying Cavalier
24. The Glorious Prodigal
25. The Amazon Quest
26. The Golden Angel
27. The Heavenly Fugitive
28. The Fiery Ring
29. The Pilgrim Song
30. The Beloved Enemy
31. The Shining Badge
32. The Royal Handmaid
33. The Silent Harp
34. The Virtuous Woman

CHENEY DUVALL, M.D.[1]

1. The Stars for a Light
2. Shadow of the Mountains
3. A City Not Forsaken
4. Toward the Sunrising
5. Secret Place of Thunder
6. In the Twilight, in the Evening
7. Island of the Innocent
8. Driven With the Wind

CHENEY AND SHILOH: THE INHERITANCE[1]

1. Where Two Seas Met
2. The Moon by Night

THE SPIRIT OF APPALACHIA[2]

1. Over the Misty Mountains
2. Beyond the Quiet Hills
3. Among the King's Soldiers
4. Beneath the Mockingbird's Wings
5. Around the River's Bend

LIONS OF JUDAH

1. Heart of a Lion
2. No Woman So Fair
3. The Gate of Heaven
4. Till Shiloh Comes

[1]with Lynn Morris   [2]with Aaron McCarver

GILBERT MORRIS

the SILENT HARP

BETHANY HOUSE
Minneapolis, Minnesota

The Silent Harp
Copyright © 2004
Gilbert Morris

Cover illustration by William Graff
Cover design by Danielle White

Scripture quotations are from the King James Version of the Bible.

Published by Bethany House Publishers
11400 Hampshire Avenue South
Bloomington, Minnesota 55438

Bethany House Publishers is a division of
Baker Publishing Group, Grand Rapids, Michigan.

Printed in the United States of America

Library of Congress Cataloging-in-Publication Data

Morris, Gilbert.
    The silent harp / by Gilbert Morris.
        p. cm. —(The House of Winslow, 1935)
    ISBN 0-7642-2761-0 (pbk.)
    1. Winslow family (Fictitious characters)—Fiction. 2. Difference
(Psychology)—Fiction. 3. Social classes—Fiction. 4. Single women—
Fiction. I. Title II. Series: Morris, Gilbert. House of Winslow.
    PS3563.O8742S53   2004
    813'.54—dc22   2004012896

TO DOUG PATEK,
my friend and brother

GILBERT MORRIS spent ten years as a pastor before becoming Professor of English at Ouachita Baptist University in Arkansas and earning a Ph.D. at the University of Arkansas. A prolific writer, he has had over 25 scholarly articles and 200 poems published in various periodicals, and over the past years has had more than 180 novels published. His family includes three grown children, and he and his wife live in Gulf Shores, Alabama.

Contents

PART ONE
April 1915–November 1918

1. Society Rules 15
2. "What's a Home Run?" 29
3. Meeting the President 45
4. A Clandestine Romance 61
5. The Best-Laid Plans 71
6. A Bit of Metal 85

PART TWO
February 1922–October 1928

7. The Reluctant Doctor 99
8. The Camp 107
9. The Woodchopper 119
10. "Grandfather Was a Poor Immigrant" 135
11. A Lord From England 143
12. When the Sun Goes Out 157

PART THREE
March–June 1935

13. Clayton Takes a Fall 169
14. A Knight in Denim 181
15. Love Is *People* 195
16. Out of the Past 209
17. The Promise 225
18. The Trouble With Being Rich 237

PART FOUR
September–October 1935

19. Leland's Secret 249
20. Lunch and a Sermon.............................. 261
21. A Time to Love.................................... 271
22. The Open Door.................................... 283
23. The Bride 291
24. Seana's Rule...................................... 299
25. A Fitting Finale 309

THE HOUSE OF WINSLOW

★ ★ ★ ★

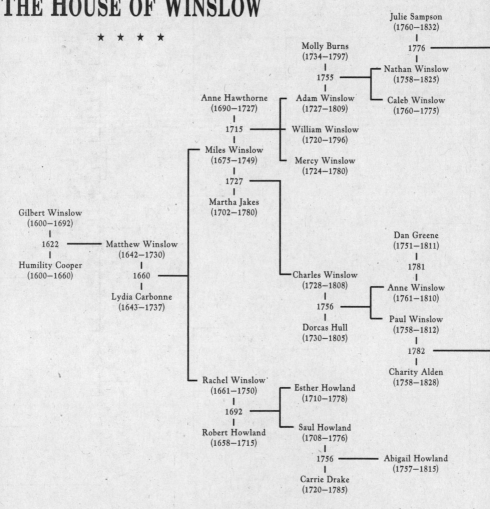

Julie Sampson
(1760–1832)

1776

Molly Burns
(1734–1797)

1755

Nathan Winslow
(1758–1825)

Anne Hawthorne
(1690–1727)

Adam Winslow
(1727–1809)

Caleb Winslow
(1760–1775)

1715

William Winslow
(1720–1796)

Miles Winslow
(1675–1749)

Mercy Winslow
(1724–1780)

1727

Martha Jakes
(1702–1780)

Gilbert Winslow
(1600–1692)

Dan Greene
(1751–1811)

1622

Matthew Winslow
(1642–1730)

1781

Humility Cooper
(1600–1660)

1660

Charles Winslow
(1728–1808)

Anne Winslow
(1761–1810)

Lydia Carbonne
(1643–1737)

1756

Paul Winslow
(1758–1812)

Dorcas Hull
(1730–1805)

1782

Charity Alden
(1758–1828)

Rachel Winslow
(1661–1750)

Esther Howland
(1710–1778)

1692

Saul Howland
(1708–1776)

Robert Howland
(1658–1715)

1756

Abigail Howland
(1757–1815)

Carrie Drake
(1720–1785)

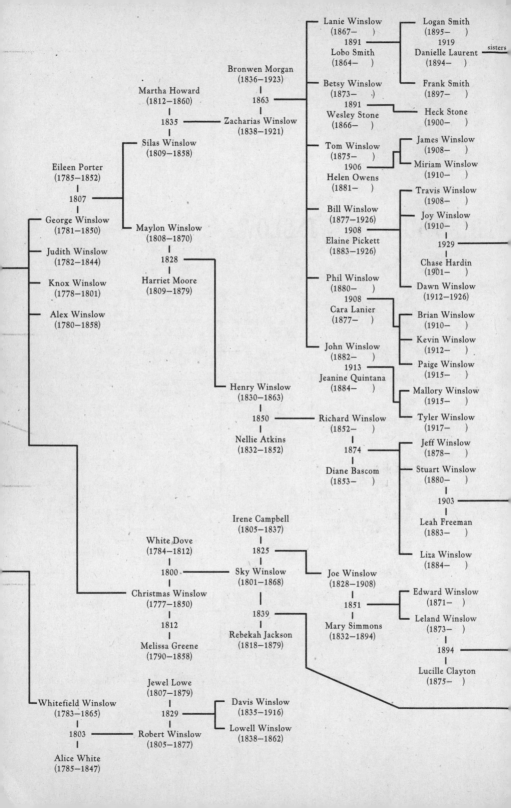

THE HOUSE OF WINSLOW

(continued)

Noelle Laurent
(1888–1915)
|
1909 ———— Gabrielle Winslow
| (1910–   )
Lance Winslow
(1887–   )
|
1918
|
Josephine Hellinger
(1893–   )

Leah Hardin
(1934–   )

Mark Winslow
(1840–1922)
|
1868
|
Lola Montez
(1847–1925)

Cassidy Winslow
(1878–   )
|
1898 ———— Benjamin Winslow
| (1899–   )
Serena Stevens   Elizabeth Winslow
(1881–   )   (1902–   )

Dan Winslow
(1844–1919)
|
1875
|
Hope Jenson
(1846–   )

Peter Winslow
(1879–   )
|
1908 ———— Luke Winslow
| (1909–   )
Jolie Devorak   Timothy Winslow
(1888–   )   (1911–   )

Priscilla Winslow
(1880–   )
|
1907 ———— Kimberly Ballard
| (1908–   )
Jason Ballard
(1874–   )

1861
|
James Rogers
(1827–1861)

Cody Rogers
(1862–   )
|
1886

Marlene Signourey
(1844–1865)
|
1862 ———— Laurie Winslow
(1865–   )

Thomas Winslow
(1842–1922)
|
1877

Jubal Winslow
(1878–1898)

Ruth Winslow
(1880–   )
|
1904

Vance Wickham
(1840–1862)
|
1862

Faith Jamison
(1855–   )

David Burns
(1872–   )

Belle Winslow
(1843–1921)
|
1865

Aaron Winslow
(1873–   )
|
1898

Missouri Ann Ramey
(1892–   )
|
1931

Raimey Winslow
(1904–   )
|
1923
|
Edna Smith
(1905–   )

Locke Winslow
(1924–   )

Bryan Winslow
(1925–   )

Ross Winslow
(1926–   )

Marianne Winslow
(1910–   )

Davis Winslow
(1835–1916)

Gail Summers
(1880–   )

Lewis Winslow
(1874–   )
|
1898

Patience Winslow
(1845–1923)
|
1861
|
Thad Novak
(1841–1918)

Sam Novak
(1866–   )

Charles Patterson
(1866–   )
|
1886

Deborah Laurent
(1878–1927)

Leah Patterson
(1888–   )

Helen Novak
(1867–   )

Ben Patterson
(1891–   )

Sharon Winslow
(1895–   )

Clayton Winslow
(1915–   )

Lee Novak
(1868–   )
|
1890
|
Sarah Madison
(1870–   )

David Patterson
(1893–   )

Maureen Novak
(1893–   )

Corrie Novak
(1895–   )

Isaac Novak
(1897–   )

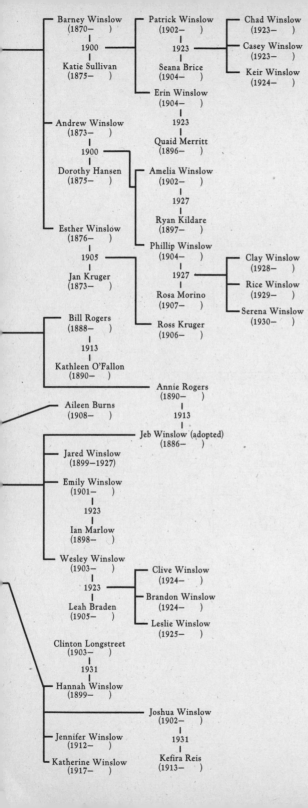

Barney Winslow
(1870–   )
|
1900
|
Katie Sullivan
(1875–   )

Patrick Winslow
(1902–   )
|
1923
|
Seana Brice
(1904–   )

Chad Winslow
(1923–   )

Casey Winslow
(1923–   )

Keir Winslow
(1924–   )

Erin Winslow
(1904–   )
|
1923
|
Quaid Merritt
(1896–   )

Andrew Winslow
(1873–   )
|
1900
|
Dorothy Hansen
(1875–   )

Amelia Winslow
(1902–   )
|
1927
|
Ryan Kildare
(1897–   )

Esther Winslow
(1876–   )
|
1905
|
Jan Kruger
(1873–   )

Phillip Winslow
(1904–   )
|
1927
|
Rosa Morino
(1907–   )

Clay Winslow
(1928–   )

Rice Winslow
(1929–   )

Serena Winslow
(1930–   )

Ross Kruger
(1906–   )

Bill Rogers
(1888–   )
|
1913
|
Kathleen O'Fallon
(1890–   )

Annie Rogers
(1890–   )
|
1913
|

Aileen Burns
(1908–   )

Jeb Winslow (adopted)
(1886–   )

Jared Winslow
(1899–1927)

Emily Winslow
(1901–   )
|
1923
|
Ian Marlow
(1898–   )

Wesley Winslow
(1903–   )
|
1923
|
Leah Braden
(1905–   )

Clive Winslow
(1924–   )

Brandon Winslow
(1924–   )

Leslie Winslow
(1925–   )

Clinton Longstreet
(1903–   )
|
1931
|
Hannah Winslow
(1899–   )

Joshua Winslow
(1902–   )
|
1931
|
Kefira Reis
(1913–   )

Jennifer Winslow
(1912–   )

Katherine Winslow
(1917–   )

PART ONE

April 1915–November 1918

★ ★ ★

CHAPTER ONE

SOCIETY RULES

★ ★ ★

"Now—that ees what I call a beautiful garment!"

Sharon Winslow gazed at her reflection in the gilt-framed mirror, studying the soft white silk empire-style chemise. She fingered the embroidered yoke of organdy lace and ribbon beading. "It is pretty, Lorraine," she admitted, a frown creasing her brow. "But I don't see much point in such fancy underwear. Nobody's going to see it but you and me."

Sharon's petite French maid had not been long in America, and she still thought all things French were better than anything American. At the age of twenty-two, Lorraine Gaban was senior to her mistress by only two years. One glossy black lock of hair escaped the white cap she wore, and her dark eyes snapped as she snorted impatiently, "Ah, but when you have a 'usbund, he will see it, *n'est-ce pas*?" She admired her mistress with some pleasure.

Sharon Elizabeth Winslow was not beautiful in the classic sense, but being tall, slender, and well formed, she still attracted admirers. Her glossy brown hair formed a pleasing widow's peak, and her large brown eyes were expressive. A natural beauty mark graced her right cheek.

Lorraine smiled at her mistress and nodded firmly. "And you will have a 'usbund soon now. Maybe you will meet him at this party—what you call it?"

"It's called a fête. That's French, isn't it?"

"*Certainement!* But what is occasion?"

"My good friend Hannah Astor is getting married."

"*Mais oui, ma'mselle*, I remember her. Such a pretty *jeune fille.*"

"She's marrying Charles Fulton, and then they'll leave on a ship to make the grand tour."

"I hear this man Fulton ees handsome but poor."

Sharon allowed the maid to pull a corset on over the silk chemise, and sucking in her breath as Lorraine tied it firmly, she demanded, "How do you hear such things?"

"Oof! What you think we talk about, the servants? We talk about our employers."

"That doesn't seem very nice."

"Who do *you* talk about?"

"All kinds of things, I guess, but I suppose you're right about Charles. He doesn't have any money, and to tell the truth—and if you breathe a word of this, I'll strangle you, Lorraine!—I think he is marrying Hannah for her family's money. I'm worried about her."

"When you get a 'usbund, be sure he has money. That way you weel know he's not marrying you for yours. Now put on this slip."

Lorraine pulled the slip on over the corset, after which she turned to fetch the dress. Fingering the smooth satin, the young maid's face glowed. "Ees such a beautiful dress!"

"It is pretty, but it cost too much."

"What you care what it costs? It make you look good. Here, put eet on."

As Lorraine made the final adjustments to the dress, Sharon examined the evening gown in the mirror. The top section was cut in one piece with the sleeves, and the sleeves were open from just below the shoulder to the wrist, caught there with decorative embroidery. Red fabric lined the open sleeve of the otherwise black-and-gold gown, and the middle section of the sleeve was braided with soutache in various shades.

"*Magnifique!* You look delicious."

Sharon laughed at her maid's use of the English language. "Not delicious. Pretty perhaps."

"*Non, non, non* . . . more than that. Here, you seet down now, and I will put on your jewelry."

Obediently Sharon sat while Lorraine brought one of her jewelry boxes. "I theenk you should wear this necklace."

Sharon lifted the sparkling necklace out of the velvet-lined case and shook her head. Even though she was accustomed to expensive things, the diamond necklace, which had been her father and mother's gift at her debut, still shocked her. Each carat-sized diamond flashed with cold blue fire as Lorraine fastened it around her neck. Sharon picked up one of the matching earrings and fastened it on her ear. "You know, Lorraine, the price of these baubles would feed hundreds of those war orphans over in Europe. Perhaps some of the ones in your own country."

Lorraine made no comment. The little maid usually bubbled over, but now Sharon saw tears in the girl's eyes.

"Oh, I'm sorry, Lorraine! I know it grieves you every time you think of your brother."

Lorraine's brother had been killed at the Battle of the Marne, just seven months earlier, along with thousands of other Frenchmen. Lorraine had idolized her brother, and when news of his death arrived, she had been completely distraught. Now Sharon quickly rose and put her arms around Lorraine, embracing the smaller woman like a child.

"I'm so sorry, Lorraine." She could think of nothing else to say, and the two stood silently for several moments. Sharon finally murmured, "You may be excused now, Lorraine. I can finish by myself."

"Ah non, ma'mselle, eet's all right." Lorraine dashed the tears from her eyes and began working on her mistress's hair as Sharon selected a ring. "Your hair ees so shiny. Eet has just a bit of red under zee light," Lorraine said, talking again nonstop, as was her habit. She had just finished Sharon's hair when both women turned at a knock on the door.

Sharon called out, "Come in," and the door opened. Her mother, who was about to have another child, entered slowly, obviously uncomfortable with her late pregnancy. "Are you almost ready, Sharon?"

"Yes, Mother. Here, sit down." Sharon jumped up to lead her mother to one of the Louis XIV chairs. "This chair will support your back. How do you feel?"

"I'm fine." Lucille Winslow was thirty-seven years old—too old in the minds of some to be bearing another child. She was a much smaller woman than her daughter but with the same lustrous hair and rich brown eyes. She was still an attractive woman, but the difficult pregnancy had drawn lines on her face. "I wish I could go with you tonight."

"I wish you could too, Mother, but that's out of the question."

"I suppose it is." Lucille sighed as she put her hands on her stomach. "This baby isn't like you. It must be a boy. He kicks like an elephant."

Sharon turned to her maid. "You can go now, Lorraine. You've done a good job on me."

"*Oui, mademoiselle.*"

As Lorraine left, Sharon sat down next to her mother. "What does the doctor say?"

"He says it could be any day. I'll be happy when I can hold my son in my arms."

Sharon hesitated, then said, "You always speak as if it's a boy, but it may be a girl."

"I pray that it's not. Your father longs for a son. Of course, women aren't so choosy. Another girl would be fine with me—but don't tell your father I said so."

Sharon was fearful for her mother's health, but she said no more about it. Before long they began talking about the conflict in Europe, speaking of "The War" as if there had never been another, nor ever would be.

"Things are looking so bad over there," Sharon said. "I'm afraid we're going to get drawn into it."

"No, that will never happen. President Wilson is firmly against it, and the Women's Peace Party is growing. Why, they just held an international conference in the Netherlands this month to encourage nations to stop the fighting." Lucille shook her head. "Besides, it's a long way from America. It has nothing to do with us." She took a deep breath and changed the subject. "There are going to be three eligible young men at the fête tonight, dear."

Sharon sighed at the inevitable push from her mother to discuss eligible bachelors. As she understood her parents, the chief goal in their lives was to get her married well, but it was not that simple. In New York's high society the social lines were clearly written in stone, and they were as massive as the Great Wall of China. It behooved one to know one's place in the scheme of things.

At the top of the social pyramid were the Astors, Vanderbilts, and Morgans. These powerful families ruled as potently as any monarch who ever lived. Their wealth was immeasurable and impossible to expend. As fast as they spent their money, more flowed in.

The next level below these titans were the almost-giants. Not as wealthy as the holy trio, they still had enormous fortunes.

The Winslow family belonged in the level just beneath the almost-giants. Leland Winslow, however, was "new money"—an anathema to the social leaders in New York City. If a person's wealth did not extend back for at least three generations, there was no hope of being accepted into the social stratosphere. Countless parents devoted their lives to trying to break through the unseen barrier to enhance their children's prospects and died without success.

Leland's ancestry was a mixed bag to be sure. It was true enough that the Winslows could trace their ancestry back to the *Mayflower*, on which Gilbert Winslow and his brother Edward had arrived in America. But Leland's father, Joe Winslow, had been a hapless prospector for much of his life. Joe's father was Sky Winslow, who had sired several prominent sons and daughters, but Joe was not one of them, having died penniless.

Joe's sons, Leland and Edward, fared much better. They had begun their lives working as lumbermen in the forests of Oregon. They had inherited their father's spirit of adventure but were wiser in their use of this valuable gift. Not content to remain as laborers, they began to buy up tracts of timber, one at a time. Before long they had bought their own sawmill, and their fortunes grew rapidly. America was hungry for lumber to build the houses and factories that were springing up all over the land. Leland and Edward had caught the tide exactly right and made their millions.

But in the social milieu of New York City, millions did not signify everything, for the social rules dictated that the majority of one's wealth had to be inherited.

Leland might have been content simply to be wealthy, but his wife, born Lucille Clayton, wanted more than this. She herself had come from a prominent family, known for their social connections. It was Lucille who had infected her husband with the importance of rubbing elbows with the Astors, the Vanderbilts, and the Morgans, and the way to do that was through marriage. Most of their efforts where their daughter was concerned had been to this end. Sharon had been carefully indoctrinated throughout her childhood, constantly hearing of the necessity of marrying well.

"Harold Vanderbilt will be there," Lucille now said, "and Jeffrey Astor, of course, and Melvin Morgan. Make sure that you make yourself available to them."

Sharon kept her amusement to herself. Her mother, for all her wisdom, seemed to have a blind spot in this area. "How am I going to do that? A woman can't go up to a man and say, 'Here I am. I'm available.' She has to wait until a man comes to her. Besides that, Mother, you know how

these things are. There'll be a long line of young women
waiting on those three."

"You've been reading too many romances," Lucille
rebuked her daughter, not for the first time. "This is the *real*
world. No knight in shining armor is going to come riding
along to rescue you. You have to work hard to make sure
they notice you."

"I know that's true, Mother," Sharon reluctantly agreed.
She was well aware that she had a romantic streak, and all
of her parents' urgings were not going to change that. She
kept it buried as well as she could, but now a tiny rebellious
thought surfaced as she spoke with her mother. "I'll make
myself available to the 'right men,' as you see it, but what if
I fall in love with the wrong man?"

Lucille's face grew tense at her daughter's teasing look.
"I've tried to make it clear to you—both your father and I
have—that marriage is primarily a financial arrangement."

"But what about love?" Sharon insisted.

"There are those silly romantic notions again!" Lucille
exclaimed. "It's just as easy to love a rich man as it is a poor
one." She rose with difficulty from her chair and took her
daughter's hands. "Now let me look at you and then you'd
better be off."

★　★　★

The Winslows' chauffeur stopped the car in front of the
Astor mansion, joining a line of chauffeur-driven limousines
in the circular driveway. The short, muscular man deftly
opened the door and tipped his hat. "Here you are, Miss
Sharon."

"Thank you, Franklin."

"I'll be waiting to take you home when the party's over."

"I may want to leave early."

"Yes, miss. I'll be watching for you."

Sharon joined the other guests who were steadily

flowing into the massive building. It reminded her more of a railway station than a home. The first time she had been here to visit her friend Hannah, she had been awed by the place and had stayed overnight in a room almost large enough for a game of tennis. Now she passed through the grand foyer, covered from floor to ceiling with paintings, many of them priceless. As she entered the ballroom she blinked at the blaze of light the chandeliers threw over the dance floor. The ballroom was decorated in Renaissance style, with tapestries on the walls and statues by famous sculptors displayed in specially built niches. An orchestra was playing at one end, and the room was full of people, many of whom Sharon knew. She heard her name called and looked to see Hannah Astor coming toward her. She was a plain girl, but with the help of a lovely gown and the skilled hands of her beautician, Sharon thought she looked rather pretty tonight.

"I'm so glad you're here, Sharon. Let's get out of this crowd."

"How many people are here? It looks like hundreds."

"Oh, I don't know. Most of them I could do without. Come on. I'm waiting for Charles. He's making the final arrangements for our departure."

Hannah led Sharon to a relatively quiet corner of the room, partially hidden from the milling crowd by an ornate screen. "I'm so tired!" Hannah exclaimed as she plumped herself down into a brocaded chair. "Getting married is the hardest work in the world. You know, Sharon, by the time you've gone through the engagement, all the preparations for the marriage, the parties, the balls, and finally the wedding itself, a woman is absolutely not fit to be a good wife."

"I'm sure that's not true," Sharon said, although she felt differently. "Are you excited about your trip?"

"Yes, I really am. We went out to see the ship yesterday. It is absolutely *opulent*! There's a Pompeian pool on the deck surrounded by real sand! And you can get anything to eat. Mushrooms and strawberries are grown in an onboard greenhouse, and of course, they serve the world's finest oysters, caviar, and truffles."

"It sounds wonderful, but . . . aren't you worried about those German submarines?"

"Oh, this is a pleasure ship. The Germans are only threatening ships that are carrying munitions or war supplies."

"I wonder how they can tell the difference." Sharon shook her head. "I'd be afraid to travel on a ship these days."

"Oh, don't worry. We're not going anywhere near Germany."

The two young women talked on about the upcoming nuptials and honeymoon plans, and finally Sharon said, "You know, I had hoped to see Margaret tonight, but I haven't seen her yet. Is she coming?"

Hannah shook her head. "I'm afraid not. Her husband is taking her on another trip—back to England. It seems they only just got home from there. They're leaving tomorrow and she simply didn't have time for a party."

Sharon sighed. "Poor Margaret. That husband of hers won't even let her see her dearest friends! I will never forget what's happened to her." The three girls had been an inseparable trio in finishing school. "I still can't believe her parents forced her to marry that Fritz Hoffman," Sharon said. "He may be a wealthy count, but he's a German! He is so . . . so awful."

"Yes, he is," Hannah agreed. "She even cried at her own wedding. You remember she wanted us to help her run away?"

"Poor, poor dear. She's had such a miserable life. At first, I got a few letters from her, but I haven't heard anything lately."

"Perhaps we can all get together again after my honeymoon trip. They should be back home again by then."

"That would be so wonderful." Sharon sighed. "The three of us together again just like at school."

"Come along now," Hannah said. "You have to dance with my cousin Jeffrey. You'll have to forgive him. He's very immature."

Jeffrey Astor was grown-up physically but not emotionally or socially. As soon as Sharon began to dance with him, she saw that he was inebriated. His speech was slurred, his eyes were watery, and he kept stepping on her feet. Her mother would want to hear all about their conversation after the party, but that was just too bad. Sharon was glad to escape from him after one short dance.

She then danced with Harold Vanderbilt, another of the titans—or at least the son of one. He could talk only of yachts, a subject of which Sharon knew nothing and did not care to learn about. The third member of the eligible-bachelor trio her mother had pressed upon her was Melvin Morgan. He seemed jovial enough, but he was in his mid-forties, which seemed ancient to Sharon. Not only that, but his face was always red and he was very overweight.

Before the evening was half over, Sharon was glad to get away. She found Franklin waiting for her, and he led her to the car. "Did you have a good time, miss?" he asked as he opened the door.

"Oh yes, it was very nice. Thank you, Franklin." As the chauffeur got into the driver's seat and edged the car away, Sharon thought, *I wonder how many people would envy my being at a party like this—but here I am bored with it all.* She certainly couldn't tell her parents that the party was boring, so she began to fabricate a good tale in her mind—something that would satisfy them for the time being.

★ ★ ★

Early one morning a week later Sharon was sitting in the library reading, curled up in a chair in the same position she had enjoyed as a child. Engrossed in her book, with the sunlight streaming through the tall windows, the unsatisfying events of the party were the furthest thing from her mind. Hearing footsteps on the parquet floor, she looked up to see her father enter. "Hello, Dad."

"Good morning, daughter."

Sharon watched her father's tall, strong figure make his way across the room. He was picking up some extra weight these days, and his dark hair was now touched with gray, but he still had the bright blue eyes she had always known, and to Sharon he was as handsome as ever. He reached her chair and ran a hand affectionately over her hair. "What are you reading so early in the day?"

"*Jane Eyre.*"

Leland sat down across from her and crossed his legs. "What's that one about?" He had never read a novel in his life and vowed never to begin. He thought them a trifle and a waste of time—time much better spent reading about the stock market. He was also fond of history books and had a magnificent library full of them.

"Oh, it's about a young woman who's not very pretty and becomes a governess to a wealthy English lord—"

"Wait a minute! Let me finish it." Leland grinned at his daughter. "I'll bet a thousand dollars to a hundred that she marries the lord."

"That's right, but—"

"That's the trouble with those novels. How many times in real life have you heard of a rich English lord marrying a poor, plain girl?"

Sharon knew her father was teasing her, but she enjoyed it nonetheless. He had been a doting parent, and every wish of hers within reason had been fulfilled. Despite his busy life, he had managed to spend much time with her, which Sharon had enjoyed tremendously.

She put her bookmark in the book and closed it. "How is Mother this morning?"

"She's fine. I think that baby is coming late just to annoy me. What a way to begin his life."

"Oh, Dad, you know that's not so."

"Oh, I know it, dear, but it doesn't keep me from being anxious."

"Have you settled on a name yet?"

"Yes. I admired your mother's parents so much. They were such fine people and such a help to me that we've decided to name the baby Clayton, after your mother's family."

"If it's a girl, will you name her Clayton too?"

"Nonsense. It's not a girl. It's a boy."

"You seem very sure of that. I hope you're not letting yourself in for a disappointment."

Leland laughed and shook his head as he got up. "I'm not going to the office today. I'm hanging around here until that boy decides to come. And, Sharon . . . there's . . . there's something else I came to tell you." He put his head down, hesitant to continue.

She was puzzled at his behavior, for he was usually so confident in his speech. When he looked up, she saw that his eyes were troubled. "What's wrong, Dad?"

"I talked to Alan VanHorn this morning. The poor fellow is all broken up."

"About what? Is he having business trouble?"

"No, no . . . it's worse than that, I'm afraid. Haven't you seen this morning's headlines?"

Sharon felt her heart skip for fear over news that could be this bad. "No . . . I came in here first thing. I haven't even had breakfast yet. Why?"

"It grieves me to tell you this, my dear . . . but the steamship *Lusitania* was sunk by the Germans yesterday. She was approaching the Irish coast when she was struck without warning by a German U-boat. Twelve hundred people died, including a hundred twenty-eight Americans."

At her father's silence, Sharon grew pale. "Dad, you don't mean Margaret was on that ship."

"I'm afraid she was." He pulled her into an embrace after she got up carefully from her chair. "I'm so sorry, dear."

Her eyes overflowed with tears and she gasped, "Oh,

Dad . . . she had so little happiness. She didn't have a good childhood, and then her parents made her marry that *awful* German! She hated the very thought of it, and now she's . . . she's gone."

Not wanting to give full vent to her emotions in front of her father, she pushed away from him and ran upstairs to her room. Once alone, she threw herself on her bed and sobbed.

She wept for her friend, grieving over her death but also for her wasted life. Sharon remembered so clearly Margaret's misery at her own wedding, and now there was nothing—nothing at all for her.

★   ★   ★

For two days Sharon kept to herself, despite her parents' offer to be with her. With Hannah having already sailed to Europe, she preferred to grieve alone. It was the first deep grief she had ever known, and she bore it as best she could, but she slept little and ate almost nothing.

Two days after she received the news of her friend's death, the baby arrived. It was a boy, and Sharon rejoiced at her father's joy and her mother's survival. She stood beside her father, gazing down at the tiny red-faced infant, and smiled as he declared, "This boy is going to do great things, daughter."

"I'm sure he is, Dad." Sharon reached out and traced the forehead of the baby, who blinked at her with large blue eyes, then opened his mouth and cried loudly. "I hope and pray he's everything you hope for, Dad."

"WHAT'S A HOME RUN?"

★　★　★

Leland Winslow loved breakfast. He loved it so much, in fact, that he hired a butler over the summer, Laurence Bettington, simply because his wife, May, was an incredible cook. All of May's meals were outstanding, but breakfast, in Leland's opinion, was her best work. "Well now, May, this looks scrumptious," Leland exclaimed as she brought in a tray of fresh-baked biscuits. Leaning forward and inhaling deeply, he said, "Nobody makes biscuits like you do."

"Thank you, sir," May said, bobbing a polite curtsy. She was a short woman, blond and heavyset, in contrast to her husband, who was tall, lean, and dark. "And I've got fresh strawberries fixed just the way you like them."

"Bring them on!" Leland called out exuberantly.

Sharon smiled at her father across the table. His enjoyment of food amused her, but it was also getting to be a problem. "You need to lose some weight, Dad. I'm afraid May's not helping you any in that regard."

"Yes, yes, yes . . . you're right, as always. I'll start cutting back tomorrow."

"You always say that. Why don't you begin right now?"

30

Sharon teased. "Eat just one biscuit and one slice of ham and let that be it."

"With fresh strawberries the way May fixes them? Not likely!"

May not only cooked, but she also tended a small greenhouse off the kitchen, where she grew strawberries as well as the herbs she needed for her specialties.

Leland ate his eggs Benedict, and then May brought in the strawberries. She had piled them on top of long strips of baked pie crust, letting the juices soak in, then topped that with a thick layer of whipped cream. May's eyes twinkled as she said, "Your daughter may be right, sir. Maybe you ought not to eat these."

"Not eat them! Have you lost your mind, woman? You give me those strawberries."

"I agree, Leland," Lucille added. "You do need to cut back a bit." She was holding five-month-old Clayton in her arms and eating with her free hand.

When the master of the Winslow house had had his fill, he leaned back and sipped the rich black coffee he always drank in a heavy white mug. "What are you up to today, daughter?"

Sharon had been waiting until her father was in a good mood, for she was not sure how he would take her newest venture. "With Hannah married now and off on her world travels, I've been rather bored lately. I've been thinking about trying out for a part in an operetta."

"A part in a play?"

"It's not a play, Dad. It's an operetta. It has singing like an opera but spoken lines, too, like a play. It's by Gilbert and Sullivan. You must have heard of them."

"Hmm, I suppose, but I'm not sure that's a good thing for you to do. Why would you want to get involved in show business?"

"This isn't show business, Dad." Sharon had planned her campaign well. She knew her father and mother would never let her get involved in anything that smacked of show business, but this was different. "This is the New York Civic Drama Society. They do only very tasteful things."

"It's still a stage show," her father insisted.

"But it's being sponsored by the Vanderbilts. Elizabeth Vanderbilt and Jeffrey Astor will be in it." This was Sharon's trump card, and she immediately saw a change sweep across the features of both of her parents.

"And you say Jeffrey Astor will be in it?" Lucille asked.

"Yes, it's a very exclusive troupe. They are extremely careful about who they let in." Sharon smiled at the interest her parents suddenly displayed. Anything that was exclusive and hard to get into was exactly what they wanted for her. "Of course, we may not be prominent enough for me to be accepted."

Exactly as Sharon had hoped, both parents immediately urged her to try out for it.

"After all, why have I been paying for all of these singing lessons for so long if not to hear you perform?" Leland reasoned. "You must audition for a part, and you'll get one too. You have a beautiful voice."

"All right, Dad. If you think I should."

"Of course you should," Leland insisted. "When does the play open?"

"Oh, it'll take about three months to learn it all."

Leland inquired more into the theatrical aspects of the operetta, and then after Sharon got up from the table, he turned to his wife. "Lucille, I think this would be a good thing for Sharon. With her friends gone now, she does seem a bit lonely of late, just reading her books."

"Well, if the Astors are behind it and the Vanderbilts, of course it'll be acceptable."

"I wouldn't like Sharon to get bitten by the acting bug, though."

"I don't think that's likely. She's very level-headed."

"On second thought, we don't know all who will be in this thing. She might take up with an actor."

Lucille laughed. "She wouldn't do that. She's far too wise."

"We've been afraid that she might take up with a trades-man, but an actor. . . ! That would be even worse. But, as you say, she's a good girl. She's never given us a moment's trouble."

"No, and this one won't either," Lucille said, gazing down at her infant. "You have a beautiful son, Leland."

"For which I thank you, dear." Leland got up from the table, went over and kissed his wife, then took the baby. He loved to hold him in his arms and talk to him as if the child could understand him. "You're going to be a better man than your dad. One of these days everybody in America will know about Clayton Winslow!"

★   ★   ★

When the chauffeur dropped Sharon off at the Olympic Theater, she told him, "I don't want you to wait, Franklin. This will probably take a long time."

"I'll be glad to wait if you like, miss."

"No, you can go on home now. I'll get a cab."

"As you say, miss."

Sharon looked up at the Olympic marquis. Sharon had seen several productions there, but she had never been on the stage. As she walked in, she saw that the lobby was filled with adults of all ages. Chairs were scattered around for those auditioning, and she sat down to wait her turn while watching the crowd mill about.

"Do you mind if I take this seat?"

Sharon looked up to see a handsome young man with tawny hair and blue eyes so dark they were almost black. There was a vibrancy to him, Sharon thought as she smiled at him. "Of course not. It may be a long wait."

"Have you ever tried out for one of these before?"

"No. Never."

"My name is Robert Tyson," he said with a smile.

Sharon gave him her name and asked, "Are you from New York?"

"Not the city. I'm from Buffalo."

Sharon tried to think of something complimentary to say about Buffalo, but her mind went blank. "Did you come all the way from Buffalo just to try out for *Pinafore*?"

"Oh no. I've lived here about six months. I came here to study singing."

"Really? Who is your teacher?"

"Carl Dartman."

Sharon blinked with surprise. "Why, he's my teacher too."

"You don't say! What a coincidence. He's a good teacher, isn't he?"

"Yes. He certainly is. A bit of a slave driver at times."

Robert laughed. "I'll agree with that."

"Did you do much singing in Buffalo?"

"Quite a bit. But I don't think any of that counts here." He glanced around. "If I understand correctly, we can have any parts that the Vanderbilts don't want."

"I'm afraid you're right. I've heard Elizabeth Vanderbilt will be auditioning for the female lead. I don't know why she has to go through with an audition. Everyone knows she'll get the part."

"Can she sing?"

"Actually she's a very good singer. I've heard her several times."

At that moment a large balding man waltzed in and clapped his hands. "May I have your attention, everyone!" He waited until the talking stopped and everyone turned to face him. "My name is Roger Hammond, and I am the director of the production. We are going to begin the auditions at once. They will be relatively brief, and I ask that after you have sung, please leave the stage and come back to the lobby." His eyes ran around the room as he said, "All casting decisions will be made today. If you care to stay around until everyone has been heard, you can hear the results for yourself. If you must go, then leave your name and number so we can get in touch with you. Now everyone please fill out this information sheet and wait for my stage manager, Roy Delaney, to call your name."

Sharon filled out the form quickly but hesitated at the question asking about her past singing experience. Embarrassed, she simply wrote "church solos" and left it at that. Robert was writing rapidly, and she said, "It must be nice to have some bona fide credentials. I'm afraid I don't have any."

Looking up, the young man smiled. "I don't think they pay much attention to that. What will decide it for them will be how well we sing—except for the Vanderbilts, of course."

The two continued to sit together as they waited. The assistant didn't seem to be calling them in any particular order, so there was no way of telling how long they would have to sit.

Sharon could hear the singers through the closed doors, and she felt somewhat daunted as she listened. Everyone seemed so accomplished. Singer after singer got up, both men and women, and from what she could hear, most of them were very good indeed.

Finally Mr. Delaney called loudly, "Tyson—Robert Tyson!"

"Wish me luck," Robert whispered and smiled.

"You'll do well," she whispered back. "I know you will."

Robert strode confidently into the theater, and from the lobby, Sharon and the others waiting could hear his voice clearly. He obviously had a great deal of confidence and showed no nervousness at all. Everyone in the lobby fell silent. He had a magnificent voice, reaching all the high notes without strain.

When he came back to the lobby and took his seat beside Sharon, she said, "That was wonderful! You're bound to get the lead."

"I'm not so sure about that. Your turn must be coming soon."

After three more had auditioned, Sharon heard her name called.

"Good luck. You can do it," Robert said and smiled at her encouragingly.

Sharon felt shaky as she climbed the steps to the stage and gave the music to the pianist. All of the singers had been asked to sing one of the songs from *H.M.S. Pinafore*, and she knew hers well. Her throat seemed to close up, however, and she was acutely aware of Hammond sitting in the audience with Mr. Delaney and another man.

Sharon had little to lose. She did not expect to get a large role; she would be happy with a spot in the chorus. As she began to sing, her confidence returned. The song was an easy one for her, and she had rehearsed it thoroughly. She went through it, smiling out at the nearly empty theater as if to a full house, thinking about Robert Tyson out in the lobby, knowing that she had at least one person pulling for her. When she finished, she nodded and stepped down from the stage and then walked back up the aisle to the lobby.

"That was very, very good indeed, Miss Winslow!" Robert whispered warmly.

"Thank you," Sharon replied. She felt as if a weight had been lifted from her shoulders. "Are you going to stay to hear the results?"

"Oh yes. I don't have anywhere to go." He pulled his watch out of his vest pocket and said, "Eleven o'clock. Suppose we go get a bit of lunch, then come back here. I'd like to know the results today."

She hesitated. Ordinarily she would not consider going out to lunch with a man she had just met, but the theatrical atmosphere seemed to have weakened her customary reserve. "All right," she agreed.

They left the theater together, and when they were outside, Robert said, "Do you know any place that's good?"

"Not really."

"There's a nice little Italian restaurant around the corner. Do you like Italian food?"

"Very much."

"So do I. Let's give it a try."

The restaurant was not crowded, there being only three tables occupied. The proprietor greeted Robert by name. "Ah, Mr. Tyson, it's good to see you. Welcome, miss."

"Thank you, Leo."

Leo smiled. "Come and sit down."

Sharon felt awkward, but it was an adventure for her. She asked Robert to order for her, and he said, "Spaghetti is always safe. With meatballs, Leo, and some of that fresh, hot bread—and that good salad you make."

While the meal was being prepared, the two talked about the different singers. Sharon found herself able to talk to Robert easily, and soon she said, "We may as well get on a first-name basis. If we both get a part, we'll be seeing a lot of each other."

"I'd like that very much."

The meal met all of Sharon's expectations. The crisp salad and steaming bread spread with fresh butter were enough to make up an entire meal. "The spaghetti is wonderful," she said, twirling another forkful of noodles and skewering a meatball.

"I always eat too much, but it's so good," he agreed. "Have you lived in New York City for long, Sharon?"

"Yes, all my life."

"What about your family?"

"I have a father and mother. My mother's name is Lucille and my father's name is Leland. He's in the lumber business. I was an only child until just recently. Now I have a brand-new baby brother."

"You don't say! I'm sure you're pleased about that."

Sharon spoke of the new baby and the changes he had made in their lives. "What about your family?"

"I have two brothers and three sisters. My family's in the dry cleaning business. My father started with one establishment and now owns six. He and Mother had a hard time of it in the beginning, but things are going well for them now."

An alarm went off in Sharon's head when she heard about his family. She knew her parents wouldn't approve of her having any kind of relationship with a man from such a family. Still, she was having a good time, and she put aside her concerns as the two sat there for well over an hour. As they started into their spumoni, she asked, "What do you want to do, Robert? Do you want to be a professional singer?"

"Oh yes. That's all I've ever really wanted. My parents are sympathetic, thank goodness. I couldn't make it without them. Lessons are expensive."

Sharon never had to think about the cost of anything, and it was one more indication of the vast gulf between her family and the Tysons. "You have a wonderful voice," she said. "I'm sure you'll be very successful."

"It's a very competitive field. Most of the great singers come from Italy, of course."

"You mustn't let that worry you. I'm sure you'll do fine."

"Do you like Gilbert and Sullivan?"

"Oh yes, I've always loved them."

"So do I, and I think *H.M.S. Pinafore* is my favorite."

The conversation turned to favorite operas, and he asked, "Would you like to be in an opera someday?"

"Oh, Robert, I don't have the voice for it."

He started to protest, but she interrupted him.

"No, it's good to know your own limits. I'm thankful for what God has given me, but I don't have the voice to be an opera singer."

He did not argue, and soon their talk turned to the war. "I hope it doesn't come over here," he said, a look of gloom touching his face. "If it does, I'll have to join up, of course."

"Oh, let's hope it doesn't come to that."

"Yes, let's do. I certainly hope they'll settle it over there. Well, maybe we should get back and see if they're close to announcing the cast list."

The two walked back to the theater, which was still filled with people. Several singers had not had their turn yet, so they realized it could be a long wait. "I'm staying here if it takes all night," Robert said.

"I'll stay too, if it's not too long."

As it turned out, the wait was pleasantly short. Thirty minutes after the final singer had auditioned, Mr. Hammond came back to the lobby and announced, "My colleagues and I have made our decisions. In a moment I'll read the cast list. The first rehearsal for the entire cast will be Monday evening at seven o'clock. For those of you we didn't choose, I thank you for coming and ask you not to be too disappointed. There will be other opportunities, of course." He looked at his list and began: "The male lead will be sung by Mr. Robert Tyson. Mr. Tyson, are you still here?"

"Yes, I am, Mr. Hammond." He stood and waved his hand.

"Very good."

As Hammond continued to read through the list, he said, "The role of Buttercup will be sung by Miss Sharon Winslow."

A thrill went through Sharon. This was a much larger role than she had hoped for. She would have one solo and at least two or three duets. She stood up and smiled and felt Robert take her arm and squeeze it encouragingly. "Congratulations. I'm looking forward to seeing you do a great job."

After the rest of the list was read, they left the theater together. As they stepped out into the street, Robert said, "I always feel sorry for the people who didn't get a part."

"I know. I do too." His understanding touched a chord in Sharon. It was generous of him to say this after winning. "I'll have to go home now," she said. "I enjoyed the day."

"I'll see you Monday, Sharon."

"Yes, I'm looking forward to it." She signaled a cab at the curb. She was excited and thrilled about the production, and her thoughts often returned to Robert Tyson. He was so entertaining and had such talent. *I hope he can make it in opera. He would hate to go back to the dry cleaning business*, she thought.

When she got home, she found her mother feeding Clayton. "How was it?" Lucille asked.

"I was chosen for the part of Buttercup. It's not the female lead, but I'll have some specials."

"That's wonderful, dear! Did you see Jeffrey Astor?"

"Yes, he'll be in the production too."

The answer satisfied her mother, and Sharon did not see fit to mention that Jeffrey was a very poor singer indeed. But when your name is Astor, you get whatever part you audition for with the New York Civic Drama Society.

★ ★ ★

Sharon went to rehearsal on Monday and then again on Thursday evening. She did not have much personal contact with Robert while she learned her own role and the blocking for the chorus. On Saturday, after a morning rehearsal, she encountered Robert on the way out. "You're doing so well," she said with a smile.

"Well, thank you. I hope so. And are you enjoying it?"

"Very much."

Robert squinted in the bright October sunshine and said, "What a fine day. Are you going straight home?"

"I was planning to."

"Do you have to?"

"Why . . . no, not really."

"Come with me, then. I'm going out to the Polo Grounds to see the Yankees play the Boston Red Sox."

"I've never been to a baseball game. I don't know the first thing about it."

"All the more reason to come, then. They're a lot of fun—noisy and sometimes a little rowdy. I played baseball in college. As a matter of fact, I thought about becoming a professional. I think I would have tried for that if I hadn't wanted to be a singer. Come on," he said with a smile. "If you've never seen a game, it'll be an exciting new experience."

For an instant Sharon hesitated, but then his smile won her over. "All right, but I may not be able to stay for the whole thing. How long do they last?"

"Oh, two or three hours. It'll be good to have someone to talk to."

★ ★ ★

Sharon and Robert were seated in the stands watching the game. Vendors were selling soft drinks, hot dogs, and peanuts, and Robert bought two hot dogs and two soft drinks. "You can't watch baseball without eating a hot dog," he said. "Here, I hope you like mustard. It looks like they used plenty."

Sharon was enjoying the taste of the first hot dog she had ever tried when suddenly the crowd stood up, yelling. "What's happening?" she asked, startled.

"New York just hit a home run!"

"What's a home run?"

"That's when a player hits the ball and gets around all three bases, back home, and scores."

"It's all so confusing."

"I suppose it is. I'm surprised the Babe let that one get by him."

"The who?"

"The Babe. Babe Ruth. The Red Sox pitcher—the big guy on the mound in the middle—he's a phenomenal young player! Looks like the Sox'll be the new league champions, but the Yanks have got one more shot to take them on this afternoon."

"It seems odd for grown men to play a game instead of going to work."

Robert laughed. "I suppose it does at that. But I guess having a few men who take the game seriously allows the rest of us to relax and get away from our work! That's why they call it America's favorite pastime."

After a private discussion between the umpire and Ruth on the mound, the game continued with the young pitcher still in place. The crowd was a bit subdued now as the Babe wasn't letting any other hitters on base after allowing the Yankees to get a home run. One player was tagged out at first, but he had a few choice words with the umpire over the call. Before Sharon knew what was happening, a brawl broke out with players pouring out of both dugouts onto the field, joining in the fray. "Oh my! What are they fighting about!" she exclaimed, standing up with everyone else. The crowd was screaming again now, and some were shouting, "Kill the umpire!"

Robert laughed at her concern. "It's nothing. When they disagree over something they start throwing punches. It happens pretty often."

Sharon flushed at his teasing grin and settled back down again. It was the first time she'd ever witnessed a fight of any kind, and she was embarrassed to find her heart pounding with excitement.

The fight apparently energized the teams, and before Sharon knew it, runs were being scored on both sides with New York eventually emerging the victor in a four-to-three win. The crowd went wild, even though the outcome couldn't topple the Red Sox from their place in the World Series that was scheduled to begin the next day.

Sharon was amazed at how quickly the time flew by, and before she knew it they were filing out of the Polo Grounds with the jubilant Yankees fans. Being a diehard Yankees fan himself, Robert was elated at his team's win over the powerful Boston team, and Sharon tried to follow his discussion of the game's fine points as they made their way out to the street. "You'll have to let me take you home now, Sharon. I wouldn't want you to go alone."

"All right, Robert. I'd like that."

He hailed a cab, and the two got in. On the way home Sharon found herself feeling more liberated than she had in a long time. Baseball was indeed a rowdy, rude sort of sport, and she had heard some language she didn't even understand. Still, she had found it all quite exciting, and being with Robert had made it all the more pleasant.

"You've got some mustard on your face," he said, taking out his handkerchief. "Let me get it for you."

Sharon laughed as he removed the spot from her face. "Thank you. You'd make a good maid."

They talked until they got to the Winslow mansion, and when the cab drew up in front of it, Robert gawked at the elegant façade. "This is where you live?" he asked in awe.

"Yes, it's my home."

"Whew," he whistled. "Some place! Your father must do well in the lumber business."

"Yes, he's been very successful. Thanks for bringing me home. Thanks for the hot dog and the game."

"It was my pleasure. I'll see you next week."

Sharon went inside and found her parents in the drawing room. Her father was working on some papers at his desk, and her mother was rocking Clayton.

"Well, you're getting in later today. Was the rehearsal this long?"

She did not wish to deceive her parents, so she said, "No, the young man who's starring in the operetta invited me to a baseball game."

"A baseball game! Whyever would you want to do that?" Lucille asked.

"It was rather fun, Mother. I've never seen one before."

"Who is this man?" her father wanted to know.

"His name is Robert Tyson. He's a very fine singer."

"Where is he from?"

"His family lives in Buffalo." Sharon hoped they would not ask what his family did, but of course her father asked.

"They're in the dry cleaning business," she answered. "I

think they own a number of such businesses."

Neither parent spoke, but Sharon could sense their displeasure. She went over and picked up Clayton and began to walk around the room with him, speaking quickly about the rehearsal and how excited she was to be a part of the production.

When she returned Clayton to his mother and left the room to change for dinner, Leland said, "Lucille, I don't much like this."

"I'm sure it's a harmless friendship. After all, they're just doing this operetta together. She's not serious about him."

"I certainly hope not. We didn't raise our daughter to marry a man who owns a dry cleaner."

"Don't worry about it, dear. When the play's over, I'm sure he'll go back to Buffalo and they'll never see each other again."

CHAPTER THREE

MEETING THE PRESIDENT

★ ★ ★

The months passed quickly as Sharon's life centered around *H.M.S. Pinafore*. Her first thoughts each morning were about ways in which to improve her performance. All day she lived for the moment when the curtain would go up on opening night. One frosty morning she noted the date on her calendar: January fifth. "The day before opening night," she whispered. "I so hope I'll do well."

Somehow she endured the long wait until evening, and when she arrived for the dress rehearsal, she found herself more nervous than she could ever remember. Some of the other cast members, she was gratified to notice, were also jittery. After warm-ups the dressing rooms buzzed with excitement as everybody got into costume and checked their makeup. She glanced in the mirror one last time and made a final adjustment to her ensemble before heading to the greenroom to await the opening curtain. Robert met her on the way and smiled. "Tomorrow's the big night."

"I'm scared to death, Robert."

"No need to be," he said. "You've been doing fine in

rehearsals. Just think of tomorrow's show as one more rehearsal."

Robert's encouragement calmed her nerves, and she began to relax as she talked and laughed with several members of the chorus. Suddenly an arm went around her waist, and she felt herself being hugged. Startled, she turned to look into the face of Jeffrey Astor. His eyes were red, and she could not miss the odor of whiskey when he spoke. "Hello, lovely," he said. "How have I missed you all these weeks?"

Sharon was shocked that he had publicly put his arm around her. She knew it was the first time he had noticed her, except once to speak when passing. Now she drew away from him as best she could and spoke politely. "I'm a bit nervous, Mr. Astor."

"You can call me Jeff," he said. "I'll tell you what. After rehearsal, let's you and me go out and celebrate."

"Celebrate what?" Sharon asked. As she looked at the pouches under his eyes and listened to his slurred speech, she thought of her mother's admonition: *"Be sure to make the acquaintance of Jeffrey Astor. He's quite an eligible young man."*

Jeffrey squeezed her arm as he leaned forward and shoved his face close to hers. "You and me'll do the town tonight, sweetheart."

"I'm sorry," Sharon said, drawing back, "but I have other plans."

Astor stared at her in amazement and snarled, "Oh, so you're too good for me! Is that it?"

Sharon freed herself from his grasp and walked quickly away, moving to the other side of the room. When she glanced back in his direction, she saw him coming on to another young woman. A voice behind her said, "I'd stay away from him if I were you."

Sharon turned to see a girl who sang in the chorus. "Why's that, Alice?"

"He's chased half the girls in the chorus," Alice said with a shrug, shaking her blond curls. "He's a lecher. I know he's got lots of money, but he's out to get all he can from a girl."

There was no time for more talk as the stage manager called "Places!" and the orchestra began the overture. Sharon put Astor out of her mind and threw herself into the production, singing just as heartily when in the chorus as she did for her special numbers. As the play unfolded, her nervousness melted away and she enjoyed herself. She was, as always, impressed by Robert's performance. He was quite a bit more talented than the singers in the chorus. More than once while they were on stage together, he would turn his back to the audience, wink at her broadly, and give her a conspiratorial smile.

He's such a fine singer and so much fun, Sharon thought. *I'm going to miss all of this when it's over.*

★   ★   ★

The next night Sharon's parents arrived early and made their way to their excellent seats a third of the way back from the stage. Lucille entertained herself by looking around and pointing out the social and financial giants who were arriving. Finally she settled into her seat as the music began and the curtain opened.

"Look, there she is! Isn't she beautiful?" Lucille whispered, her eyes following her daughter as the chorus swept around the stage dancing and singing.

"By george, she is pretty!" Leland exclaimed. "I'm sure glad she got your looks instead of mine."

Time passed quickly as the Winslows were caught up in the entertaining performance. As the cast took their bows, they applauded until their hands ached throughout the numerous curtain calls. A roar of approval went up for Robert as he sprinted out from the wings for his bow. "He seems like a fine young man," Leland remarked, and then he said, "Look, he's taking Sharon's hand."

Robert had indeed grabbed Sharon's hand as he was

taking his bows, and now they smiled at each other. She curtsied, and he took a deep bow. For the Winslows, this was the crowning moment of the evening.

"Let's go backstage," Leland said as the house lights came up.

"Oh yes, I would like that very much!" Lucille took his arm, and the two wove their way through the throng. There were crowds of people backstage, including several of the Astors. Lucille beamed proudly when Agnes Astor said to her, "My dear, it's so good to see you. Your daughter has a simply magnificent voice!"

"Yes, and I thought your son Jeffrey did very well too." Lucille tried to sound sincere, but in truth she was just being polite, for Jeffrey was not the great singer he imagined himself to be.

Sharon spotted her parents and pushed her way through the people milling about. "Did you like it?" she cried, her eyes sparkling as she took their kisses and hugs.

"It was excellent, my dear!" Leland said. "I was so proud of you, I could practically burst."

"You were wonderful! Just wonderful!" Lucille beamed.

"Oh, I want you to meet the star." She turned and grabbed Robert's arm as he made his way past. "Robert, come meet my parents."

Robert smiled warmly and shook hands with her father as she introduced them. "I'm very happy to meet you," Leland said sincerely. "I'm no authority, but I thought you sang magnificently."

"Very nice of you to say so, Mr. Winslow."

"Oh, you were so good!" Lucille agreed. "Are you a professional singer?"

"Not yet, but I plan to be one day. Right now I'm still studying."

"He's going to be a great singer!" Sharon exclaimed.

"I spoke with Jeffrey's mother," Lucille said. "We'd like to say hello to him too."

"I saw him right over there," Sharon said. She gave Robert a slight grimace, then turned and led her parents over to meet Jeffrey Astor. He was in better condition than he had been the previous day and took their congratulations with a smug air.

"Your daughter has a beautiful voice," he said. "I wanted us to do one of the duets, but it didn't work out that way."

"Oh, I'm sure something could be done in future productions," Lucille said quickly.

"I'll look forward to that."

As they moved away, Lucille said, "Of course he doesn't sing as well as some of the others, but he's quite presentable, don't you think?"

At Sharon's hesitation to answer, Lucille gave her daughter a strong look, almost critical. "I'm thinking of inviting them over—Jeffrey and his parents."

Sharon found no pleasure in this, and she changed the subject at once. It had been a triumphant evening, and she didn't want to spoil it with thoughts of her mother's incessant matchmaking. She was so excited over the performance she knew she would hardly sleep a wink that night. But there was another performance tomorrow and two more after that, which gave her cheer as she made her way into the dressing room.

★ ★ ★

"Why don't we go out and get something to eat, just you and I?"

Sharon looked up with surprise. She had changed out of her costume and exited from the ladies' dressing room to find Robert waiting for her. Members of the cast were gathering to go out for a snack, but she had planned to go directly home. Now Robert was smiling at her, and she found she wanted very much to go with him.

"I couldn't stay long," she said.

"Just long enough to get something to eat, and we can

tell each other how wonderful we were tonight. Come along."

"I'll see if Franklin can give us a ride and then wait for me."

"Franklin? Who's that?"

"He works for our family. He's waiting to take me home."

"Okay, let's check with him, then." They went out to the street, and Franklin approached.

"I came in to watch tonight, Miss Sharon," he told her. "I enjoyed your performance."

"Did you, Franklin? I'm glad you liked it." Quickly she said, "Mr. Tyson and I are going to have a bite to eat. Would you give us a ride please?"

"Surely, Miss Sharon."

"That's some car," Robert said. "Could you take us over to Gambino's?"

"That I could, sir. Get right in."

Gambino's was a small Italian restaurant six blocks from the theater. Sharon had never been there, but Robert had. "You must know every Italian place in town," she said, remembering the first time they had eaten together on the day of the auditions.

"I know most of them. I love Italian food. I'll probably swell up like a balloon if I don't stop eating so much of it. Shall I order for you again?"

The time passed pleasantly. Robert was quite witty and could easily make Sharon laugh. After the meal was over, he said, "I hate for the night to end."

"So do I," she said. "But there's always tomorrow. We've still got three more performances."

"What will you do after all this is over?" he asked.

"I think I'll die. It's been so much fun, and now I have to go back to the same old routine."

Robert reached over and took her hand. "No, you mustn't do that. I'll see to it that you're not bored. We can arrange to have our singing lessons on the same day. That way you can listen to me, and I can listen to you, and we can critique each other."

"That would be nice," she said, very aware of his hand on hers. When he released her hand and stood up, she waited while he picked up her fur coat and put it over her shoulders.

"This is quite a coat," he said. "Just think how many little animals had to die to keep you warm."

"Oh, that makes me feel bad!"

He put his hands on her shoulders and squeezed them lightly. "It was for a worthy cause," he said. "They probably knew they were going to hold a beautiful girl in their embrace."

"You're so silly!" Sharon said but could not help laughing.

"You make me that way, I'm afraid." He walked her back to the car, where Franklin was waiting, and when she got in, he said, "I'll see you tomorrow. Maybe we can do this again. Next time I'll let you pick the place."

"All right, Robert."

★   ★   ★

For the next two nights the two ate at a different place after the show each night. They were the most pleasant dates Sharon had ever had. She had never been out unchaperoned before, and the freedom of being alone with Robert gave her a delicious feeling. She did not tell her parents about their dates, and when one of them mentioned that she was coming home late, she told them a half truth. "The members of the cast like to go out and get a snack after the performance. It's really very nice."

Roger Hammond surprised them all before the final performance. When they gathered before warm-ups, he told them, "I have some good news for you. We have been invited to put on our operetta in Washington, D.C., for three days, and the proceeds will go for the starving people of Belgium."

Sharon turned to Robert and whispered, "My parents will never let me go."

"We'll have to convince them, then. Where there's a will, there's a way."

Hammond waited until the excited talk died down and then said, "Some of you are, perhaps, wondering if you can go. But I urge you to make arrangements if possible. The President of the United States will attend, and there will be chaperones for all the girls, so everything will be perfectly proper."

"You see?" Robert laughed. "It's going to be fine. The president will love us, I'm sure."

Sharon tried to join in with his enthusiasm, but she was still troubled about what her parents would say.

★ ★ ★

Sharon's fears had been unwarranted, for her parents were easily enough convinced when they learned the circumstances. Her father was especially proud. "Singing for the president! I wish my dad could have been here to see that. He would have been so proud of you, daughter, just as I am."

"When will you leave?" Lucille asked.

"In three days. We'll be taking the train."

"And there'll be chaperones?"

"Yes indeed. Mr. Hammond was very clear about that. It'll be quite proper."

"Maybe you'll be able to spend some time with Jeffrey," Lucille said. "He's such a pleasant gentleman."

"Perhaps," Sharon murmured.

★ ★ ★

The trip to Washington was the most exciting thing Sharon Winslow had ever done. The train had an elegant dining car, which the troupe easily filled by themselves. She and Robert shared a table with two of the other cast members, all of them remarking over the snow-white tablecloths, crystal glasses, china, and sparkling silverware—not to mention the delicious cuisine.

Wanting the best for his daughter, Leland had helped to foot the bill to put the entire group up at one of Washington's most posh hotels, reserving an entire suite for Sharon. She invited several members of the cast to her suite that evening, including Robert, of course, and the rooms were filled with laughter as they enjoyed a specially delivered meal together.

The next day they rehearsed to get the feel of the theater, and that evening they gave their first performance. The president was not there that night or the next, but the production was well received. Every seat was filled, and each night there were celebrities in the audience. On the third and final night, the president arrived moments before the overture was to start. Sharon, peeking out between the curtains, saw him. "Robert," she said, "there he is—the president!"

Robert came over and put his arm around her to steady her as the two peered out the curtain. "By george, he looks just like his pictures. A fine-looking man, isn't he?"

"He looks pale to me."

"No wonder," Robert said, straightening up and shaking his head. "This war business is bound to be a tremendous burden on him."

"He wants nothing but peace."

"That may be what he wants, but that's not what he's going to get," Robert said, his face sober. "Sooner or later we're going to be pulled into that war over in Europe. The rumor is that Germany is going to declare total submarine warfare. If they do that, we'll be at war in thirty days."

His statement sobered Sharon too. She looked at Robert,

thinking, *He'll be one who will have to fight.* The thought depressed her, but she had no time to dwell on it, for Roy Delaney was calling for everyone to take his position for the opening scene.

The operetta went off magnificently, with everyone doing their very best for the president. After the curtain calls, they all went backstage to greet the many visitors. Suddenly Sharon looked up and nearly dropped her jaw. There was President Wilson coming straight toward her! He stopped to shake hands with several people, and then when he came to her, he extended his hand. As Sharon grasped it, he said, "Your singing was exquisite, young lady. I enjoyed it more than I can tell you."

"Thank you, Mr. President."

President Wilson then turned to Robert, who was at his usual place beside Sharon. "And you, sir—I have never heard a better voice. You're going to put Enrico Caruso to shame."

Robert flushed with pleasure as he shook the president's hand. "I hardly think anyone will do that, Mr. President. It's such an honor to have you here."

"It was a welcome respite from rather heavy days."

"I want you to know, sir, that my family and I pray for you every day. I can only imagine the tremendous burden that is on your shoulders, and our hearts are with you."

President Wilson grew still, examining Robert carefully. "That is very kind of you, young man, and I will not forget it. Give my best regards to your family."

"Yes, sir, of course."

As they watched the president move through the crowd, greeting others along the way, Sharon whispered into Robert's ear, "Imagine, the president shaking hands with us. And you did so well, Robert. I could tell he was moved."

"I meant it. My family and I do pray for him every day, and I hope you do too."

"I . . . I haven't been, but I will from now on."

* * *

The trip back to New York was much more subdued than the trip down. The excitement was over now, and the troupe was experiencing the natural letdown after a job well done. Sharon found herself somewhat sad that it was all over, even though meeting the president had been the high point of her life.

"You look a little downhearted, Sharon."

Sharon turned to Robert, who was sitting beside her in the dining car. The meal was over, but they sat drinking coffee listening to the *clickety-clack* of the wheels and staring out the window. A fresh snowfall covered the landscape, making a beautiful wintry scene as it flashed by.

"I am a little sad. It's going to be hard to go back to things as they were."

"Well, we can't be involved in a play all the time unless we become professionals. Have you ever thought of trying that?"

"Oh, I'm not good enough for that, Robert, but you are."

"Nonsense. You don't know until you try."

Sharon, however, knew her own limitations. "I have a good voice, but you have a marvelous voice. That's the difference. One day you'll be singing at the Metropolitan, maybe in *Carmen*, and I'll be sitting out in the audience applauding wildly."

Robert smiled and shook his head. "That's a long way off, but it's what I hope for." He suddenly changed the subject. "Sharon, could we see each other after we get home?"

She had wondered what she would say if he asked her out once the show was over. She knew her parents would disapprove, and now she could not hide her dismay.

"Don't you like me at all, Sharon?"

"Like you? Why, of course I like you!"

"Then why not see me?"

"It's my parents. They are very careful about my social

56

contacts and would have to approve."

"Well, I want to put myself forward as a candidate to come courting. Would you ask me to call so I can meet them? They seem like very good people indeed."

"Oh, they are," she said. "It's just that—"

Robert suddenly got the picture. "I think I see. If my family name were Astor there wouldn't be any problem, would there?"

"They . . . want me to marry well."

"By 'well' they mean wealthy, I suppose."

"Yes, that's part of it." Sharon found it hard to formulate her parents' attitude. Now that he had asked to come call on her, however, she hoped she could persuade them to accept Robert. "Yes, come next Tuesday," she said. "We'll be glad to have you."

★ ★ ★

Robert's visit at the Winslow home did not meet with the success Sharon had hoped for. As they said good-night on the front steps, he held her hand and said, "I'm sorry I was a disappointment to your parents."

"Oh, don't say that!"

"It's pretty obvious they would not be happy with me as a suitor. I'm sorry about that, but I can't change what I am."

Sharon could not think of a good response. "I enjoyed the evening, but I enjoyed our meals out together much better."

"Will I see you at Mr. Dartman's day after tomorrow?"

"Yes. Good night, Robert."

When she went back in, she found her parents still in the drawing room. They both looked at her, and a moment of silence passed among the three of them. "A very nice gentleman," Lucille said.

"Oh, very personable," Leland added quickly. "You say his parents are in the dry cleaning business in Buffalo?"

"Yes, Dad. I'm sure they're very nice people, although I haven't met them."

"It was nice to have him visit. Of course, now that the play is over you won't be seeing him anymore."

Sharon almost said, *Yes, I'll be seeing him at my singing lessons*, but something prompted her to keep that back.

Leland lit a cigar, and the silence in the room seemed thick. Sharon wanted to defend her right to see Robert, but she felt she was outnumbered.

Leland blew a stream of smoke toward the ceiling. "I think it might be best if you not make friends among this theatrical group. Some of them are very nice, I'm sure, but your mother and I envisioned a more apt group of friends for you." He got up, came over, and put his arm around Sharon. "I was so proud of your performance in the play, but you ought to concentrate now on other things."

Sharon was crushed. She could not argue and only said, "I'm quite tired. I think I'll go to bed. Good night."

After she had left the room, Leland looked at Lucille. "I wish she hadn't asked that young man here."

"I'm afraid she likes him a little too much for my inclinations."

"You don't think she's serious about him, do you, Lucille?"

Lucille had seen her daughter's expression as she had watched Robert that evening. "She might get serious. We'll have to see to it that she has other things to occupy her mind."

"You know, one of the disadvantages of having money is that there's always a danger that some fellow will be after our daughter for what she has and not for who she is."

"You think this one's like that?"

"I'm not saying that," Leland said quickly. "But it's always a possibility. In any case, he wouldn't be a suitable match for our family."

"No, he wouldn't. But now the play's over and the relationship is over. We can schedule some parties here. I can invite all the suitable young men."

"That's the idea," he said. "You're good at that, Lucille. I'll put it in your hands."

★ ★ ★

Sharon arrived at Carl Dartman's apartment for her singing lesson almost an hour early. Robert was having his lesson, and the two men greeted her, Dartman somewhat surprised. "Have I got my times mixed up? I thought you were scheduled for eleven, Sharon."

"I am, but if you don't mind, I'll just wait." She smiled. "I love to hear Robert sing."

"Doesn't bother me if it doesn't bother him."

Sharon sat quietly throughout the rest of Robert's lesson. When Robert was done, he said, "Mr. Dartman, I think I'll pay Sharon the compliment of listening to her as well, if you don't mind."

Dartman looked from one to the other, and a smile turned the corners of his mouth upward. "Fine with me. Always good to have an audience."

After Sharon's lesson, she and Robert left together and made their way down to the front entry. "I'm glad to see you, Sharon," Robert said as they walked along the sidewalk. "How have you been?" The weather was bitter cold, and the city was swathed in white. A strong wind churned up icy crystals that bit at their faces, and the snow crunched beneath their feet.

Shivering, he suggested, "Let's have coffee or something to eat to warm us up."

Sharon smiled. "You're always thinking of food."

"Not always. Sometimes I think of other things."

She saw his teasing smile and laughed at him.

They ducked into a nearby restaurant and found a quiet corner to sit and drink cup after cup of steaming coffee. Robert had a piece of pie and shared it with Sharon, who found it so good she ordered a slice of her own.

"Look, Sharon," Robert said finally, "I'm not much at hiding my feelings. I hope you know that I've come to care for you—"

Her face flushed and she nodded. "I can see that, Robert, but it's . . . difficult."

"Because of your parents. Well, I'm sorry they don't approve, but I still want to see you all I can."

Suddenly Sharon, who had never had much difficulty obeying her parents, felt a sense of rebellion. Here was the one man she had found whom she truly felt she could be serious about, and her parents didn't approve. She loved her parents dearly, but she disagreed with them on their deeply held beliefs about marriage.

"We'll see each other as often as I can. I hate to deceive my parents, but I . . . I do so enjoy being with you."

Robert leaned over, took her hand, and raised it to his lips. He kissed it, then held it firmly between his hands. Her lips were trembling, and she was close to tears. "Don't cry," he whispered. "We'll find some way to convince them. God will help us!"

CHAPTER FOUR

A Clandestine Romance

★ ★ ★

Robert and Sharon continued to see each other without her parents' knowledge for a year. Every week they shared their lesson times together with Mr. Dartman, and Robert starred in another Gilbert and Sullivan production, this time *The Pirates of Penzance*. Sharon did not audition for that one because her parents continued to disapprove of any socializing with "those theatrical people." She went through the motions of graciously entertaining suitable suitors, all the while seeing Robert on the side and falling deeply in love with him. She did not know how she would ever tell her parents of her deception. For all she knew, they might be so dismayed they would turn their backs on her and make her leave home.

On top of enduring the stress of her clandestine romance, which caused her no small measure of anxiety at home, Sharon lived with the daily fear of watching the war in Europe grow to monstrous proportions. She, along with her fellow Americans, knew that if the conflict did not end soon, the United States would not be able to stay out of it. And for Sharon that would mean saying good-bye to her beloved Robert, as he would undoubtedly be called to the war.

On the last day of January 1917, Germany began unlimited submarine warfare, warning that all neutral ships in the North Atlantic were to be attacked. President Wilson responded with an angry blast, and a wave of fury swept the country. The United States severed diplomatic relations with Germany. During the month of February, German submarines sank the United States liner *Housatonic* off the coast of Sicily, the British steamer *California* off the coast of Ireland, and the American schooner *Lyman M. Law.*

President Woodrow Wilson had been the staunch leader against declaring war, but even he could not overlook what was happening at sea. Too many Americans were losing their lives. On the twenty-sixth day of February he asked Congress for power to arm merchant ships. This unprecedented act brought the war hawks to a high fever, and the national discussion changed from "Will America go to war?" to "*When* will America go to war?"

Sharon read the stories in the newspapers and knew that her country was on the precipice of entering a conflict that had already slaughtered millions of French and Russian soldiers. While she was disheartened about all of this, her spirits were always raised by seeing her dear Robert every week at her voice lesson, and as many other times during the week as she could find some reasonable excuse to leave the house. She and Robert escaped the war stories by listening to popular music and singing the romantic war songs floating over from England. One of her favorites was a soldier's plea to family to "Keep the Home Fires Burning." Robert loved the happy-go-lucky marching song "Pack Up Your Troubles in Your Old Kit Bag and Smile, Smile, Smile."

Sharon loved the times when she and Robert would get together at their favorite music store and sing the new songs together from the sheet music while the store owner played the piano. They always gathered quite a crowd, and the owner was delighted to have two such fine singers freely advertising the store's merchandise.

One evening they went to a dance hall, where they learned to dance the tango, a craze that was sweeping the country, as well as the lively fox trot. Neither Robert nor Sharon were first-rate dancers, and they teased and laughed their way through their awkward attempts. They left the dance hall hand in hand and started down the street. He pulled her to a stop in front of the famous Flatiron Building, the towering pie-shaped skyscraper that had already become a New York City icon.

Robert turned to her and said, "I wish we were in a more romantic place."

"Why do you wish that?"

"Because I'm going to say something that should be said on a beach in Tahiti at sunset, or perhaps sung to guitar accompaniment in a canoe on the Swanee River with massive trees dangling moss over us."

For a moment she thought he was just playing around, but there was a seriousness in his eyes as he said, "Come on. Let's find a better place than this."

Sharon went along, protesting halfheartedly that she should be getting home. He led her to Madison Square Park, where there were people out walking their dogs, and lovers also. They walked in silence until they reached a quiet place, and then he turned and said, "I know you can guess what I'm going to ask."

His words brought a sudden rush of emotion to Sharon. She began to tremble and started to say, "Oh, Robert—"

"No, I'm going to say it. I love you, Sharon, as much as a man ever loved a woman, and I want to marry you." She let him draw her closer. She was flattered that this man, who was so talented and of such good character, would desire her. She lifted her arms to his shoulders and tipped her face up. When their lips touched, she clung to him, giving herself to him freely until he finally lifted his head. "You must love me, Sharon," he said simply. "God wouldn't give me this love for you unless he had put something in your own heart for me."

Her response was so soft he had to lean forward. "Oh, Robert, I do love you!"

Robert felt that this was the best moment of his entire life, and as the fragrance of her hair touched his senses and her head rested quietly on his shoulder, he whispered, "You're the only one for me, sweetheart."

Sharon wished that the moment would never end, but she knew it must. She had, however, made a decision while he held her. "My parents will have to agree, and that won't be easy, Robert."

"We'll find a way."

She reached up and put her hand on his cheek. "Yes," she said. "We will find a way."

★ ★ ★

Sharon stood straight in the Winslow parlor, her hands clasped tightly in front of her. She saw by the expression on her parents' faces that her announcement was most unwelcome. She had called them together as soon as she had gotten home and declared, "Robert and I love each other, and we want to get married."

Her parents were shocked. They had not even known she was still seeing him and could hardly believe their obedient daughter had been carrying on a clandestine romance for a whole year! Both Leland and Lucille were beside themselves with grief to think that Sharon had so betrayed their wishes. But they could also see the love in her eyes that she held for him, and their hearts were torn.

Leland stood by his resolve to make light of it and shook his head. "This is just an infatuation, daughter. He is a good-looking young man who has turned your head, and you have momentarily lost your senses. You cannot be serious about him."

Lucille echoed his sentiments but with a measure of understanding over her daughter's dilemma. She was young enough to remember the power that romantic desire could have over a girl. But outwardly she remained in agreement with her husband and their need to maintain their family's social reputation. "He's not the sort of man we've hoped you would find, dear."

This was the most difficult discussion Sharon had ever had with her parents, but it was also the first time she had ever willfully opposed their wishes on anything important. She listened to all that her father said but never once did she retreat. Her parents were shaken to the core at her resistance, for she had always been an obedient child and easily persuaded. But both Lucille and Leland now witnessed a streak of steel in her they had never seen before. She stood firmly, her shoulders back, her head high, and no matter what they said, she simply replied, "I'm sorry you are not sympathetic, but Robert is the man I love. He's the man I want to spend the rest of my life with."

"Sharon, you know this is not what your father and I want," her mother said, "but I'm going to ask you one thing."

"Don't ask me to give him up, Mother. I won't do it."

"Will you do this, then? Will you wait for a time until his future is a little more secure? You're both still young, and you have plenty of time."

When Sharon hesitated, Leland jumped in. "Yes, that's all we ask, dear. Just wait."

Sharon could not say no to this request. It was reasonable enough, and since they had not given a specific length of time she was to wait, she stepped forward and extended a hand to each of them. "Yes, of course," she said with tears in her eyes. "You don't know how it hurts me to stand against you, but Robert is my life."

Sharon embraced her parents, both of whom stood awkwardly, then left the room.

At once Leland turned and said, "Lucille, we cannot let

her go through with this wedding."

"I know, but we must be wise and very cautious. You saw how determined she's become."

"I've never seen her like this before."

"Neither have I, but she is a lot like you, Leland."

"Like me? What do you mean?"

"She's firm, and perhaps even a little stubborn, like you are. You always were a masterful man, and you gave some of that to her."

Leland did not know how to take this and shook his head, his brow furrowed. "Let's just hope and pray that this infatuation will pass."

★   ★   ★

One thing Sharon had settled with her parents was that she could now see Robert under normal circumstances. Having confessed to their secret meetings, she had asked their pardon for her deception, and they had reluctantly granted her that. Then she had pleaded, "But we need to be together, and I want him to come visit here often so you can get to know him."

Leland and Lucille both agreed to this, and over the next few weeks, Robert came to have dinner with them three times. After these visits, Leland admitted to his wife, "You know, if Robert only came from a different background, I couldn't think of a better match."

"I know. He is everything a young man should be, but he's not quite top drawer socially."

Now that everything was out in the open, the tensions in the Winslow home eased somewhat, but on the international front, the war news was growing worse, and they all felt the increasing angst of the country. On the fifteenth of March, Czar Nicholas II abdicated, leaving a gnawing uncertainty over the fate of Russia. The Russian offense on the German front had resulted in two million casualties, and now no one could tell which way that enormous country would go.

Despite the pressures at home and the specter of war, Sharon awoke each morning smiling and singing. Her maid, Lorraine, fussed at her constantly, saying she had become like a peasant, never taking time to dress properly. Sharon usually merely laughed and hugged her, saying, "Robert doesn't love me because of the clothes I wear."

Toward the end of March, Robert appeared at the mansion unannounced. The butler, Laurence, met him at the door.

"I've got to see Miss Sharon at once."

"Why, yes, sir. Please come in. I hope nothing's wrong."

"No, everything is right, Laurence!" Robert said as he shrugged out of his coat.

"I think she's in her room, but if you'll care to go to the drawing room, I'll let her know you're here."

"Fine! Fine, Laurence!"

Laurence went upstairs and knocked on Sharon's door. When it opened, he said, "Mr. Tyson is downstairs. He's very anxious to see you."

"Is something wrong?"

"No, he seems very excited. Happiest I've ever seen him."

Sharon headed straight to the drawing room, where Robert threw his arms around her and picked her up off the floor. He swung her around in a wild circle, ignoring her protests.

When he set her down, he said, "I have wonderful news!"

"I can see you have." Sharon smiled breathlessly. "What in the world is it?"

"I have been selected to play the lead in *Carmen* in Boston! Think of that!"

"Oh, Robert, that's wonderful! When did this happen?"

"My agent has been working on it for a long time. I went to audition a week ago, but I didn't tell you because I didn't think I had a chance in the world. I got a telegram today. It's all set. I'll be singing the lead role!"

"Oh, Robert, I'm so happy for you!" She threw her arms around him, and they talked rapidly, interrupting each other and laughing with joy at the good news.

"We must tell Mother and Dad," she said. "Come along." Seizing his hand, she towed Robert out of the drawing room and went down the hall, crying, "Mother—Dad, where are you?"

"I believe they're in the small parlor, Miss Sharon," Laurence said. "It must be good news."

"Yes, it is. Very good."

She pulled Robert into the parlor, where her parents were sitting by the fire listening to gramophone records. They stood up at once. "What in the world is it?" Lucille cried. "What's wrong?"

"Nothing's wrong, Mother. Robert has an announcement."

Robert shook his head. "It's the best thing that's ever happened to me, sir, ma'am. I've been selected to sing the lead in an opera in Boston."

"Well, congratulations, my boy," Leland said. He was genuinely pleased and came over to shake Robert's hand. "You'll be moving to Boston, then?"

"No, I'll just stay there for three weeks of rehearsals and then the opera's month-long run, which begins the last week of April."

Lucille asked, "I know nothing about such things, Robert. Do they pay well?"

"Yes, this will pay very well. In fact it'll be more money than I've ever made. Of course, as good as that is, the great thing is it will perhaps open the door for me to the Metropolitan right here in New York."

Sharon listened as her parents questioned Robert, and they seemed genuinely pleased for him. When she was finally able to break into the conversation, she said, "Now I'm going to ask you to let us get married right away. We could have a simple private ceremony here at home and then I could go to Boston with Robert."

As shock washed across the faces of the older Winslows, Robert said quickly, "I love your daughter very much, and my agent says this is just the beginning. He promises me I have a lucrative future in opera. Now I'll be able to care for your daughter properly."

Both Leland and Lucille were taken off balance, but they saw they could not prevent the couple from marrying, with or without their approval.

"I think it would be more proper to wait at least six months before the nuptials."

After some debate and much give-and-take, Sharon reluctantly agreed to wait till June. That way she and her mother would have time while Robert was in Boston to plan an elegant wedding. "The first Saturday in June," she said. "I'll be a June bride, and that's what you've always wanted for me, Mother."

CHAPTER FIVE

THE BEST-LAID PLANS

★ ★ ★

A few days later Robert came early one evening to take Sharon out to a performance at the Metropolitan Opera, but as soon as they were sitting in the backseat of the Winslow limousine, he reached into his inner pocket and pulled out a small velvet-covered box and handed it to her. He put his arm around her and urged, "Go ahead. Open it."

Sharon looked up, her eyes dancing. "What is it, Robert?"

"You're a smarter girl than that. Open it."

Opening it gently, she took one look and exclaimed, "An engagement ring! Oh, Robert, it's beautiful!" She took it out and held it up close to examine it. It was a gold love knot with a sparkling diamond set in the middle. "I've never seen anything so lovely."

"I know you've seen larger diamonds, but I hope you like it."

Sharon slipped the ring onto her finger and turned her face up for his kiss, feeling secure as his arm went around her. "It's so unusual."

"I like the love knot—it has no beginning and no end.

That's what our love is going to be like, sweetheart—without any end."

Franklin had been sitting quietly throughout this exchange, but now he cleared his throat and spoke up. "Shall we get started for the opera?"

"Oh yes, drive on, Franklin," she said, but her attention was on the ring. She had never felt happier in her life as her head spun with plans for her upcoming nuptials and the marital bliss that was to follow.

While the car moved along, Sharon reached into her reticule and pulled out a small box of her own, mischief dancing in her eyes. "And here is something for you," she said. Opening the box, she took out a ring. "I hope you like it."

"Why, I didn't expect this!" Robert exclaimed. He held the ring up to the light and said, "There's something inscribed, but I can't read it in this light."

"It's got the date of our engagement and our initials. Here, let me put it on." He held out his left hand, and she put it on the third finger. "A perfect fit."

"How did you know what size I wore?"

"Women know things like that," Sharon said mysteriously. "How did you know what size I wore?"

"That's easy. I just asked your mother to get me one of your rings, and I took it with me to the jeweler's."

"You are a sly one!"

Robert sat back with a smile, his arm around Sharon, listening as she rattled on. She was so excited she could not seem to speak fast enough, and he was amused by it all.

When they reached the opera house and made their way inside, quietly taking their seats, Sharon was still whispering, "And I've got to have a trousseau."

"You mean a wedding dress?"

"Of course I'll need a wedding dress, but a trousseau is different. I'll need a wardrobe of new gowns, at least a year's supply of—" she hesitated—"delicate undergarments all trimmed with tucks and laces and embroidery, and an assortment of household linens."

The performance began, and Robert put aside thoughts of the wedding that lay ahead, but Sharon found it hard to concentrate. She could not suppress the well of joy that was rising in her, and she felt certain that her feelings were much stronger than what most brides experienced.

As they left the opera and got back into the car, Sharon said, "I think you can sing much better than that tenor."

"You wouldn't get many people to agree with you. He's considered one of the best."

"You're better," she said firmly. "And one of these days you'll be singing at the Met."

Robert laughed and shook his head. "It's great that you have such a good opinion of me. I hope you convert all the other music lovers in the world." He turned to look at her and said, "I've got another surprise for you."

"Another ring?"

"No, not until we stand before the minister and change your name to mine. My parents are coming to New York City."

"Oh, how nice! When will they be here?"

"Day after tomorrow. Dad says he's thinking about opening up some new dry cleaning establishments here. But that's just a pretense. I think they're really coming just because they want to meet you."

"Do you think they'll like me?"

"Like you! I'm positive they'll love you! Who could help that?"

★ ★ ★

Sharon made arrangements with her mother to invite Robert's parents over as soon as they arrived in New York City. They sent Franklin to pick them up at their hotel and bring them to the Winslow mansion for tea on Sunday afternoon followed by dinner that evening.

Maurice and Clara Tyson were attractive people in their

early forties. Maurice was a tall, well-built man with blond hair and a neat mustache. Clara was a small woman with a wealth of brown hair and warm brown eyes, and she was more stylishly dressed than any of the Winslows had expected.

As they sat drinking their tea, they did not seem at all overwhelmed by the splendor of the Winslow mansion. Leland and Lucille were a bit surprised, for while their home was not as elaborate as the Vanderbilt mansions, it was ornate enough to cause most visitors to be somewhat awed.

"Lovely home you have here, Mr. Winslow," Maurice said, perusing the parlor. "Did you build it yourself?"

"Oh no. It's a much older place. But my wife decorated it."

"You did all of this!" Clara exclaimed as she also admired the room. It was a magnificent parlor—large and airy, filled with the late-afternoon sunlight from the four windows extending down to the floor along the two outside walls. Curtains of gold satin were held back with dark blue braided cord, and the walls were covered in a dark blue paper with gold outlines of birds and leaves scattered throughout. Paintings in gilded wooden frames filled the walls, and the furniture was upholstered with blue-and-gold-striped damask. A grand piano filled one corner, and two red high-back chairs flanked the stone fireplace. The carpet was a deep burgundy outlined in dark blue, and the mahogany tables and buffets were filled with fine porcelain and china figurines.

"I could never do such a beautiful decorating job."

"You're very generous to say that. It did take a long time," Lucille said.

Lucille had put herself out to make the Tysons' visit as pleasant as possible for Sharon's sake. And, in truth, she was pleased to discover that the Tysons were very pleasant people. They were both well-dressed in the latest fashions, and they were able to hold up their end of an intelligent conversation.

Both sets of parents insisted that Robert and Sharon sing for them, so they spent the rest of the afternoon listening to a private concert, with Robert accompanying on the piano.

After tea Leland and Lucille took the group on a walking tour of the grounds while it was still light out. Maurice and Clara were gracious guests, exclaiming over the beautiful grounds and asking questions about the young plants that were emerging from the ground. Robert and Sharon hung back from their parents when they could politely do so, exchanging happy glances and whispers of love.

The Winslows' cook, May Bettington, exceeded all their expectations with the evening meal. The first course was lobster bisque, followed by garlic-roasted squab, twice-baked potatoes, baby peas with pearl onions, fresh-baked croissants, spinach salad with hot bacon dressing, and for dessert, a strawberry cake with fluffy white frosting. Neither Robert nor Sharon said much during dinner while Leland and Maurice discussed the nation's economic problems and the war in Europe.

"It can't go on like this!" Leland exclaimed as he shook his head over the increasing attacks on allied ships by the German U-boats. "Wilson has kept us out of the war for a long time, but he's not going to be able to do so much longer." He took a sip of his coffee. "They said when the war began that it would be a quick one, but now the troops are settled down to trench warfare. They lose fifty thousand men just to gain twenty yards of ground and then lose it back the next day. Not like any war that's ever been fought."

Lucille jumped in to change the subject to more pleasant topics—namely the wedding plans—and the spirits of the group rose as they all thought of happier times in the future. When it was time for the Tysons to leave, Maurice and Clara made a point of saying, "We're very happy about the wedding, and now that we've met you, Sharon, we're more excited than ever."

Sharon beamed at this but noticed that her own parents made no complimentary remark about Robert, and this gave her pain. *They'll get over their old-fashioned attitudes,* she thought. *When we're married, they'll see what a fine man he is.*

After the Tysons had left, Sharon asked her parents, "What did you think of them?" She waited hopefully for a good response, but when her mother spoke, it was not with much enthusiasm.

"They're very nice, dear."

"Yes, they are," Leland agreed. "And Mr. Tyson seems to be a level-headed fellow. I'm a bit surprised, though, that he's so enthusiastic about Robert going into this opera business."

"That surprised me too," Lucille said. "He did say that he had planned for Robert to go into the dry cleaning business with him, but his older brother is doing so instead."

"Well, one good thing about it. If this singing thing doesn't work out, he can always go back into business with his father. He'll be young enough to learn how the real world is."

Sharon felt a twinge of disappointment over her parents' reaction, yet it was not unexpected. Anyone less than an Astor or a Vanderbilt or a Morgan would not have found favor with her parents. She was grieved that her choice of a husband was not to their liking, but there was nothing to be done about it. She excused herself early that evening and wrote in her journal just before retiring:

> I liked Robert's parents so very much. They're kind people and far nicer than so many I have met. I think about Hannah's in-laws—horrible people that make life miserable for her. I just know the Tysons will always be supportive. Mrs. Tyson didn't intrude at all about the details of the wedding, and I know we'll be good friends after Robert and I are married.

Thoughts of Robert brought her such joy that even her parents' disapproval could not dampen her spirits for long. She climbed into bed and fell peacefully asleep, believing that she was indeed the happiest woman in the world.

* * *

Robert left for Boston shortly after his parents' visit to begin rehearsals for *Carmen*. Sharon could hardly bear the thought of not seeing him again until their wedding day on June 2. She and her mother were sitting in the parlor the following Friday afternoon working on wedding plans when Leland entered the room, his face lined with concern.

"What is it, dear?" Lucille asked.

"President Wilson has declared war on Germany."

"Oh, dear, that is terrible!" Lucille cried. "I can't believe this is happening."

"I guess we've all known it was coming for some time, and here it is. I just heard the radio broadcast of his speech. It received a tremendous ovation, and it was reported shortly afterward that one of the president's close friends heard him say, 'My message was one of death for young men. How odd it seems to applaud that.' And then he said the president put his head in his hands and wept."

Sharon had tried not to dwell on the thought that Robert might have to go fight in the war in Europe, but now that possibility was suddenly very real. She listened in fear as her father spoke of the actions of Congress now that a state of war existed. "Everything is going forward full speed. Everyone seems to think they'll choose General John Pershing as commander of the American troops."

Sharon could not keep from expressing what was on her heart. "I pray that Robert won't have to go."

Leland turned to look at her, his eyes troubled. "I expect mothers and wives and sweethearts are praying that all over this country, but many will have to go. Has Robert said anything about volunteering?"

"No, not a word. He's been so busy with the opera."

"A great many lives are going to be interrupted." Leland shook his head sadly. "I'm afraid this may not be an entirely volunteer army."

"What do you mean, dear?" Lucille asked.

"I think there'll be a conscription act passed."

"What will that mean?"

"It means men who haven't volunteered will have to serve. It happened in the Civil War. Both the North and the South had to conscript men when volunteers weren't enough."

"This will change your plans, I'm afraid, Sharon," Lucille said. "About the wedding, I mean."

"Not at all!" Sharon shot back. "We'll go right ahead with them." She saw a flicker in her father's eyes and knew that he was doubtful, but he said nothing.

★ ★ ★

An uneasy month passed as Sharon continued making her wedding plans while listening anxiously each day to the war news. She and Robert talked often by phone. The opera was going well, and the Boston critics were hailing Robert as a rising young star in the opera world.

On May 18 the president signed into law a bill requiring all American men between the ages of twenty-one and thirty-one to register for possible service in the United States armed forces. The Selective Draft Act was designed to mobilize an army of five hundred thousand men for service in the war against Germany. Some people estimated that approximately ten million men would be subject to registration. Their names were placed in jury wheels from which five hundred thousand recruits would be drawn.

In their phone conversation that day, Robert said very little to Sharon about the war except to mention that he had decided not to volunteer. He added, "Of course, when they draw the names, mine might be one of them."

"Surely not," she said. "It couldn't happen now. Not when your career is just taking off so wonderfully."

"I don't think that has anything to do with it," Robert

said ruefully. "We can't win the war in Germany by singing in an opera."

When Sharon remained silent on the line, he asked, "Would you like to postpone the wedding indefinitely until this thing is settled?"

"No," she said firmly. "We can't do that."

"It'll be your choice, of course, Sharon. If I did have to go, you'd be the one who would have to remain alone."

But Sharon had made up her mind. Her mother and father had given broad hints that it might be wise to postpone the June wedding, but she steadfastly refused.

★ ★ ★

The next two weeks sped by for Sharon. The wedding dress had been made, and the arrangements were all complete. They would be married at Calvary Baptist Church on West Fifty-Seventh at ten o'clock on Saturday, June 2, 1917.

Sharon was just finishing reviewing her schedule for the busy activities that would precede the wedding when Lorraine came in to say, "Mr. Robert is here."

"Oh," she cried, "I'll be right down, Lorraine. Thank you."

She raced down the stairs and found Robert waiting in the foyer. She threw herself into his arms and cried, "Oh, darling, I didn't expect you so soon!"

They kissed and he held her close, breathing in the fresh scent of her hair and perfume. "I took an early train to get here as soon as I could. We have to talk, Sharon."

Something in his voice and manner troubled Sharon, and her heart raced as she peered into his eyes. "Come into the parlor," she said. "There's nobody there." As soon as they had entered the room and shut the door, she asked breathlessly, "What is it?"

"I've got bad news, I'm afraid. I'm being conscripted."

Sharon stood perfectly still. The fear she had been dreading flooded over her, black and terrible. She reached out her hand, and Robert took it. "Oh no, it can't be!"

"Yes, I'm afraid it is."

Sharon melted into his arms and began to cry.

"There's no easy way to tell you a thing like this," he said, gently wiping away her tears.

She rested her head on his chest, everything in her rebelling against the news. She found herself wanting to scream or strike someone, but who was there to strike? She straightened up and said with dry lips, "When . . . when do you have to go?"

"I have to leave in two weeks."

"That gives us so little time."

"Sharon, I think you know how much I love you, but I'm troubled by all this. I want you to make the decision."

She looked into his face, unable to understand his words or his expression. His features were tense, but there was a tenderness about his mouth as he spoke . . . as though he were trying to shield her from something.

"What do you mean, Robert?"

"I mean it might be best if we called off the wedding."

"Call off the wedding! Surely you can't mean that!"

"I think you need to pray about this and think it through and talk to your parents."

Instinctively Sharon knew what her parents would say, but she could not believe that Robert agreed with them. "But we love each other."

"Of course we do, but we'll have so little time together. And then I may be away for years, and . . ." He hesitated to say what was on his mind. "Sharon, we may as well face the truth. I might come back maimed . . . or I might not come back at all."

"No, don't talk like that!" she cried.

"It's the reality of war, my darling."

"Do *you* want to call off the wedding?" she whimpered.

"I would marry you this day, but it's different for me. If we become man and wife, you might have a child. And if I left after just a few days, you might have to raise that child alone. I would not want that for you. I know these are hard things to face, but this is a difficult world we're living in."

Sharon felt as if she were going to faint. She looked up at him and said, "I do want to marry you, Robert."

"This is a big decision, Sharon. Maybe the biggest you'll ever have to make, but you're the one who has to make it. I know how your parents will feel, and in this case they might be right. Talk to them first and then make your decision."

★   ★   ★

She went to her parents as soon as Robert left and told them what had happened. Both of them expressed shock and sadness, and her mother said gently, "I'm so sorry, Sharon. I know how hard this is for you and for Robert, but this means, of course, that the wedding will have to be postponed."

"But, Mother—"

"I know this isn't what you want," Leland said. He came over and put his arm around her. "It's just the right thing to do. I'm sure Robert has talked to you about how imprudent it would be to marry now."

"He said the decision would be up to me."

"I think that's very proper and kind of him, but you must not marry now."

"It wouldn't be fair to either of you," Lucille said. "The first six months of a marriage is such an important period. A man and a woman get to know each other, and that wouldn't be possible under these circumstances. You'd have only a few days, and then Robert could be gone for years. People change, and when he comes back, you can't know how either of you will have changed."

"I'll never change. I'll always love Robert."

Sharon put up the best argument she could for going on with the wedding, and finally she decided to consult with their minister. Franklin drove her to the church, and Reverend Smith pretty much echoed the words of Robert and her parents. After Franklin drove her back home, Sharon went to her room, where she stayed the rest of the day. She knew that the decision had to be made quickly. If the wedding were to be postponed, everyone invited or involved would have to be informed without delay.

She found herself praying for an answer from God, but God had not played a large part in her life, and she wasn't sure how to be certain that God was speaking to her. She had been a faithful church attendant, but she had no certainty of a relationship with her Creator. She considered her life to be as morally upright as any young woman's might be, but that did not bring her any peace.

She slept little that night, and the next morning she felt she had to talk to Robert. Franklin drove her to his apartment, and he let her in at once, not at all surprised to see her. He shut the door and held her in his arms.

"I know this is so hard on you, dear."

"Robert, this is so terrible. I wish—"

"I know. We all wish it hadn't happened. What have you decided about the wedding?"

Sharon hesitated. She could not bear to let him go, but she had reached her decision. "I . . . I think, perhaps, we ought to wait until after you come home."

Robert saw the tears in her eyes and took out his handkerchief. "Don't cry, dear. Maybe it won't be very long."

"I'll wait for you no matter how long the war lasts. You know that, don't you?"

"That means a great deal to me. This is painful for both of us, but perhaps this is best."

In the last year and a half, Sharon had come to know Robert very well, and although there was nothing in his voice or in his expression that told her so, she sensed his disappointment. The impulse came to reverse her decision, to cry, *Yes, we will get married even if we only have a few days.* But she knew she had made the right decision, and she let the moment pass. "We'll have to spend every spare moment together until you leave," she said instead.

"Yes, of course we will. We'll make it a two-week celebration."

★   ★   ★

The hubbub in New York's Grand Central Station was deafening as young men and women gathered to say their tearful good-byes. Sharon had accompanied Robert to the platform where the train would take him to his training camp, and now he put his bag down and turned to her. "I hate good-byes," he said.

"So do I. Oh, Robert, I don't know how I'm going to bear it!" Suddenly she blurted out the words that had been on her heart for the past two weeks. "I wish I had been stronger. We should have married. At least we would have had these days."

He put his arms around her and held her tightly. He whispered in her ear, "We'll pray that I will come back and that you will still be here for me."

"I will be! Oh, I will!"

He kissed her, and she clung to him as the conductors cried out, "All aboard!" When he lifted his head, he said, "I want to say one thing before I leave."

"What is it, Robert?"

"If I . . . don't come back, go on with your life, Sharon. Find a companion and have a family."

Sharon began to weep. He kissed her one last time, then turned and picked up his suitcase and left. She stood watching him through her tears until he joined the line of men boarding the train and started up the steps. He turned and waved, and she saw his lips form the words, *I love you.*

She stood there as a shrill whistle rent the air, and the train inched away from the platform. After watching until the last car had disappeared, she turned away with a grief in her heart she could hardly bear. "I should have married him! I was a coward," she whispered as she pushed her way through the crowd.

CHAPTER SIX

A BIT OF METAL

★ ★ ★

The gray sky was dotted with sullen white clouds as the long line of American troops and supply vehicles moved forward. They were advancing into St. Mihiel in northeastern France, and the troops stirred with anticipation as they moved toward the front. The late summer of 1918 had proved to be good for the Allies. Winston Churchill said, "Before the war it seemed incredible that such terrors and slaughters could last more than a few months. After the first two years it was difficult to believe they would ever end."

But now the end was in sight. General Ludendorf's German army continued to fight, but the German cause had deteriorated. Starvation and the threat of revolution back home had plagued them and created a manpower shortage on the front lines. By contrast the Allies had gained strength and pushed steadily forward in separate battles that were merging even now into the victory drive.

Robert and his comrades stopped as dark fell, and the units gathered around to draw their cold rations. They had reached the trenches and knew that morning would bring a new offense.

The night passed, and as dawn came, Lieutenant Robert Tyson walked among his men, gauging their strength and finding it sufficient. He spoke to his men individually by name, and they responded. He was a popular officer, never holding back out of concern for his own safety, but always in the front when it was time to go out to meet the enemy fire. He moved back to one of the sheltered areas, sat down on a box, and began to write on a single sheet of paper. He had written Sharon a week earlier, but now before heading into the furnace of battle, he felt the need to write again. He wrote slowly, pausing to think, for he had only a single sheet and one stub of pencil.

He was almost through when his captain, Jesse Stanton, came busting by. "All right, men, get ready!" Stanton stopped and gave Robert a friendly slap on the shoulder. "You writing a novel to that girl of yours?"

Robert grinned as he folded the letter and put it in his inside pocket. "Do me a favor, Captain."

"What is it?"

"If I go down, see that this letter gets to Sharon, will you?"

"You're not going down. This thing is almost over. We'll be home in a month."

"Sure. But just in case."

"All right. Now see what you can do about your habit of running forward ahead of your men."

"You can't lead from behind," Robert said with a shrug.

Stanton had a firm affection for this young man. He was a career officer himself and had had little confidence in some of the recruits, but Robert had proved to be a gem. It was Stanton whose recommendation had led to the medal Robert had won.

"There's the air cover," Stanton said.

Both men rose and went to their positions. Robert watched as the fragile-looking biplanes flew over the German lines, their machine guns flickering and making a deadly rattle as they strafed the German trenches.

Robert turned to the person behind him, a small man named Willie Greer, who came from Georgia. "All right, Greer, let's get at it. You all right?"

"Sure, Lieutenant." Greer displayed his gap-toothed grin that showed no sign of fear. "We'll get 'em all this time." Then the captain's voice sounded, and gripping his forty-five, Robert Tyson yelled at the top of his lungs, "All right, lads, over the top! Let's show 'em what the Yanks can do. . . ."

★ ★ ★

"No, Clayton, you can't eat dirt."

Sharon stooped down to remove the fistful of dirt that her three-and-a-half-year-old brother held firmly.

"I like dirt!" Clayton cried, resisting Sharon's efforts.

His face was smeared with dirt, and his cornflower blue eyes were flashing as he struggled to get away.

"No, dirt is not good to eat. Come on, now. We'll go see the horses."

"Yes, see the horses!"

The two were in the rear of the house on a warm and sunny late September day. Ever since Robert had left for Europe, Sharon had devoted much time to her little brother. Now as she walked along, adjusting her pace to Clayton, who forged ahead steadily on his sturdy legs toward the stable, she thought about how slowly time had crawled by.

As she often did, she relived the moment of Robert's departure when he had told her she mustn't mourn for him forever if he were lost in battle. The memory of his smile as he stood on the train steps lifting his hand, his lips forming the words *I love you*, came to her often. She usually could not keep back the tears, and even now she struggled against them.

The year and a half Robert had been gone seemed like an eternity. She knew from his letters that he had been rushed through his training in the States and was soon put aboard a troop ship bound for France to join the Eighty-fourth Infantry Brigade commanded by Brigadier General Douglas MacArthur.

The months had been grim, and nothing seemed normal anymore. America's efforts to liberate France from the German invaders had resulted in a million of her own young men dying in the trenches, yet the war only grew more terrible. Sharon followed the war news carefully, and anxiously searched through the mail each day for a letter from Robert. The German armies had fought the Russians to a standstill. After the Russian Revolution of October 1917, there was no longer an eastern front. The Russians eventually signed a peace treaty with the Central Powers and occupied themselves with their own civil war.

In April 1918 Manfred von Richthofen, the famous Red Baron, who had become the idol of Germany, was killed in battle after having destroyed eighty Allied aircraft in less than two years of fighting. In May the American troops won their first battle at Cantigny, where the First Division took a heavily fortified town and captured two hundred German soldiers. A small victory, to be sure, but the first American offense of the war.

In June the Americans joined in a huge battle at Belleau Wood. The American marines proved to be tough soldiers, convincing the European Allies that they were to be counted on.

Sharon had tried to keep her faith during the long, dreary months, but it had proven difficult. She suffered a deep sense of guilt and regret over her decision not to marry Robert before he left. Even though everyone agreed she had done the right thing, her spirit kept uttering, *I should have married him.*

When Sharon and Clayton entered the stable, the two sleek bays the family kept for rides in Central Park stuck their heads over the stall for their expected treat. Reaching into her pants pocket, Sharon pulled out some apple pieces and said to Clayton, "Here, you hold a piece in your palm and let the horse eat it."

Clayton held his hand out flat, as Sharon had taught him, and giggled with delight when Lucky Lady leaned over and lipped the apple off of the little boy's hand.

"Well, what's going on here?"

Sharon turned to see her father coming from the house. He was smiling, and when he reached them, he stooped over and picked up Clayton. "What are you doing, young man?"

"Feeding the horses!" Clayton cried. "Throw me, Daddy!"

In response to the request, Leland tossed the boy high into the air and caught him as he came down. Clayton squealed with pleasure and begged for more.

"That's so dangerous, Dad," Sharon admonished. "You're going to drop him."

"Not a chance. I wouldn't drop you, would I, son?"

"More!" Clayton demanded, and after a few more tosses, Leland turned to Sharon, holding the boy tightly. "He's getting bigger every day."

"Yes, he is, and his sentences are getting longer too."

Leland studied his daughter as the two spoke of Clayton's accomplishments. She did not look unwell, yet something had gone out of her during the past anxious months. There was a shadow in her eyes, and a curtain of reserve seemed drawn across her features, hiding her deepest emotions. "Are you going to the ball tomorrow?"

"I don't think so, Dad."

"Oh, come on. Your mother and I are going. Come along with us. It'll be fun."

Sharon paused, then shrugged. "All right. If you wish."

She had no desire for balls or parties, knowing that Robert was shivering alone in some muddy foxhole in France. Parties seemed so frivolous with men dying by the millions.

Knowing her thoughts, Leland said quietly, "It can't last

much longer. The Germans are collapsing on every front. He'll be home soon."

She tried to smile. "I hope so, Dad. It seems to have gone on forever."

"I know it has, but we can't let the war rule our lives. What say we all go to the ball and take our minds off the war for a little while."

★ ★ ★

Sharon turned on the light in her bedroom and removed a box from the top drawer of her dresser. Putting it on her dressing table, she lifted the lid and picked up the letter that lay on the top. She had kept all of Robert's letters, reading them over and over again until they were memorized. Now she picked up the one that had arrived only a week ago. It was stained and crumpled as if he had carried it in his pocket, but the writing was clear and firm. It was a cheerful letter in which he spoke of his fellow soldiers and the weather. He never described the horrors of war. Sharon had to learn that from other sources. She knew he deliberately kept these things from her, and she loved him all the more for trying to protect her in that way. She read through the letter slowly and then reread the last section:

> I've received a citation. Just a bit of metal, but I'll bring it with me when I come home. Maybe our children will be proud of their dad when they see it. We've got a spot of action coming up soon. We're going to give those Huns a push. Things are winding down over here. I think it'll be over soon.

Robert had never been this optimistic before. He had always written as though his stay in France would be endless. "'I think it'll be over soon,'" she read aloud as she gripped the paper tightly. He ended the letter by saying:

I wish we could go to that little Italian café we went to so often while we were doing Pinafore. *Do you remember those days? I think of them over and over. It is what has kept me going—the times we had together and my love for you. That never changes. I love you, and I always will. I still wear your ring, and I treasure it more each day. God has been very good to me, and the best gift of all, aside from giving me a Savior, was to give you to me. Your loving Robert.*

Sharon sat for a long time perusing the letter. Then she put it carefully back in the box, closed the lid, and took out some blank paper. She began to write, feeling a swell of pride when she addressed it to Lieutenant Robert Tyson. He had risen through the ranks from private to lieutenant as a result of his courage under fire. She knew it had to be that.

She wrote several pages, filling the sheets with her activities, stories about Clayton, and her visits to the opera (and how he could have sung the lead better).

Her fingers began to ache, and she closed the letter by saying, *I love you with all my heart, and I live for the day when you will be home again and I will be your wife. With all my love, Sharon.*

Several times she had almost included the thought she lived with daily, that she should have married him, but she knew it could serve no purpose now. She would tell him when he got home.

She sealed the letter and leaned back, looking up at the picture on the wall of Robert in his new officer's uniform. He'd had the photo taken while he was on leave in Paris, and he looked so handsome and brave smiling at her. She stared at the picture for a long time, then whispered, "It can't be long now. You'll be home soon."

She jumped at a knock on the door. "Yes, what is it?"

Her maid, Lorraine, opened the door and announced, "A gentleman to see you, Miss Sharon."

"Who is it?"

"His name is Tyson."

For one wild moment Sharon experienced a blinding

hope. *It's Robert! He's come home!* But then she knew that could not be true. "Thank you, Lorraine." She moved past the maid and ran down to the foyer, where she found Maurice Tyson standing there.

"Mr. Tyson!" she said breathlessly. She moved toward him, but the look on his face stopped her. She could not take another step, and she stood paralyzed.

Tyson moved forward and said, "I'm afraid I have very bad news."

There was a roaring in Sharon's ears, and she felt as if she were falling. "It's Robert? He's wounded?"

Maurice Tyson's face was marred with sorrow, and when he shook his head, she knew everything.

"He's dead, isn't he?"

"I'm afraid so, my dear. We got the telegram just yesterday. I didn't want to tell you the news over the phone, so I took the first train available."

Sharon could not move. Her mind refused to function, and she could not accept the truth. *He can't be dead—he can't be dead!* The thought went through her head over and over, and she tried to speak but found she could not.

Maurice moved forward and put his arms around the young woman. "He loved you very much. He talked about you constantly in his letters."

"But he won't come home now. He can never come home...." Sharon tried to think, but all she could hear in her mind was the pounding of the old refrain: *I should have married him, I should have married him....*

★ ★ ★

Sharon was walking along the sidewalk in front of the house on a blustery November day when a cab pulled into the drive. The weeks that had passed since she'd received the news of Robert's death had been a blur to her. She and her parents had traveled to Buffalo to attend the funeral, though Robert's body remained buried in France, a simple white cross marking his grave among thousands of others. The only way she could endure the pain was to follow a daily routine, which she did mechanically, trying not to think and not to feel. When she got up each morning, Lorraine dressed her almost as if she were a child. She ate without tasting her food and tried to smile from time to time, but she was like a ghost, and her parents were worried sick about her.

She had been walking now for over an hour, up and down the street, when the cab pulled up in front of the house and a tall man in an officer's uniform got out. He said something to the driver, then, leaning heavily on a cane, moved slowly toward the house.

Sharon knew this had something to do with Robert. When she stepped toward him, he saw her and paused.

"May I help you? I'm Sharon Winslow."

"My name is Jesse Stanton."

"Captain Stanton. Come inside. Robert wrote about you often."

Sharon adjusted her pace to his slow gait. It took some effort for him to climb the steps, and when they reached the parlor, he sat down with relief. "I'm still a bit unsteady on my pins."

"When were you wounded?"

"In September at St. Mihiel."

Sharon knew this was where Robert had lost his life. She sat down and studied the face of the soldier. It looked strong, full of character, with direct gray eyes and a determined chin. He looked like the sort of man that other men would follow. "Robert wrote of you so often, Captain. He had such respect and admiration for you."

"The feeling was mutual," Stanton said. "He was the finest young officer I ever met. I can't tell you what his loss meant to me."

"You were in the action where he . . . was lost?" She could not bring herself to say the word *killed*.

"Yes, I was. I came because we were such good friends, and I wanted to tell you about him."

Sharon listened as Stanton told her about his friendship with Robert. He went into detail about what a fine soldier he had become, how he always put the safety of his men over his own. He spoke of how the men admired him and trusted him, and he could not say enough about his courage.

"He was not foolhardy, but he was very, very courageous. Just before the attack he was writing a letter," he said as he reached into his pocket. "I asked him who it was for, and he said it was for you. So I came to bring it."

He handed an envelope to her, and with trembling hands she opened it. It contained a letter, crumpled and stained, and a small oblong box. She would save the letter for later, when she was alone. She opened the box and saw it contained a medal.

"That's the Croix de Guerre, the highest honor that the French can designate."

"What did he do, Captain?"

"He crawled out under fire and pulled back three wounded men, one after another. The air was full of sniper fire, and shells were bursting everywhere. I don't see how he survived it, but he came through without a scratch. A French general was in our lines, and he saw it. The award ceremony was quite a scene, with the French all lined up and saluting Robert as he went forward. The general pinned the medal on his uniform and then kissed him on both cheeks." Stanton smiled. "Robert told me he didn't care much for the kissing part. That he'd rather have one from you than the medal itself."

Stanton stayed for over an hour and then finally got to his feet. "Thank you so much for coming, Captain Stanton. It means so very much to me."

Stanton said heavily, "This is what makes war so bad. Your fiancé had a fine career. He always entertained the men by singing popular songs. Not opera so much. They loved him for it. I'll miss him and so will the world. Good-bye, my dear Miss Winslow."

Sharon waited until he had left; then she went to her room and sat down on her bed with the letter. It was very brief, speaking not of the danger that lay ahead but of his love for her.

Some men go all their lives and never find the right woman. I am so fortunate to have found the one woman who is in my sight a jewel of great price. You remember what I said at the station. If something should happen to me, my dear, do not grieve any more than you can help. I wouldn't want you to miss out on life. Think of me sometimes, but let God bless you with a good life.

The letter broke off there abruptly, and she had the feeling it was unfinished.

Sitting there holding the wrinkled letter, Sharon knew she would never find another man like Robert. A flood of emotion overwhelmed her, a grinding bitterness at what the war had done. She had been so happy until she had been struck down mercilessly by the hateful gods of war.

She rose and went over to the window, staring out blindly. For a time she stood perfectly still; then she slumped to the floor, crying out, "I should have married him! I loved him so, and I should have married him!"

PART TWO

February 1922–October 1928

★ ★ ★

CHAPTER SEVEN

THE RELUCTANT DOCTOR

★ ★ ★

Dr. Franz Steiner wore a troubled expression as he looked across the desk at Leland. "I'm afraid, Mr. Winslow," he said with his thick German accent, "that we have a very troubled young woman on our hands." Leaning back in his chair, he clasped his hands together, apparently finished with his diagnosis. The tall, stooped man wore a Vandyke beard and gold-rimmed glasses, which he fingered nervously from time to time. His austere attire—a white lab coat and black trousers—matched his office. The bare room was furnished with one desk, empty save for a pen and note pad on top, and two wooden chairs. The walls, however, were much busier, covered with floor-to-ceiling bookshelves packed with books, papers, and periodicals stuffed wherever possible in between volumes. One window provided the only break from the cluttered walls.

Dr. Steiner took his glasses off, exhaled on them, and polished them slowly with a handkerchief from his lab-coat pocket. "Yes," he said slowly, "a *very* troubled young woman."

Leland was somewhat intimidated by the office and by

the tall man who sat in front of him. He was accustomed to being in control of situations, but there was no way he could control this one. Steiner was not the first doctor he had come to see on Sharon's behalf. There had been others with whom he felt he could be direct, demanding to know the root of his daughter's problem. As months, and then years, had passed with no diagnosis and no improvement, he had grown less secure in his hope of finding a solution to Sharon's problems. She had grown progressively more withdrawn and silent. In the business world he was master of every situation, but sitting across from Steiner he felt weak and ineffectual, and his voice had an abnormally uncertain tone to it.

"Dr. Steiner, my daughter's been in trouble for over three years. At first we thought it was just the result of her fiancé going to war and then, of course, his death—and perhaps it is. But other women lost their men in the war and have managed to come out of it. Sharon has just been getting steadily worse."

Steiner nodded. "Yes, I understand. It is unusual, perhaps, but not at all unique."

"She simply doesn't care about anything!" Winslow complained, his voice growing intense. "Sometimes she just sits for hours and stares out the window, or she goes on long walks. She doesn't seem to hear what people are saying. Look," he said, a shade of his authority returning to his voice, "you've been seeing Sharon for weeks now, and her mother and I can't see any difference. We need to know something, Doctor."

"Some cases are more difficult than others," Steiner said gently. He was accustomed to dealing with shocked relatives and had learned to build up an emotional wall so he did not become personally involved with their predicament. It was the patient who mattered, not her family, and Sharon Winslow was the patient.

"What's wrong with her, Doctor? Can't you tell us anything?"

"Her trouble is not physical, of course. She's troubled in her mind."

"Yes, we *know* that!" Frustrated, Winslow rose and walked to the window and stared out at a sparrow defending his crumbs from several other more aggressive sparrows. As Leland watched the miniature warfare, he began to feel like that one sparrow battling against an unbeatable force. Sharon's problem had defeated him, and he was beside himself with anxiety. He turned back to the doctor, his face creased with worry lines. "We expected you could help her, Dr. Steiner."

"And I wish I could, but I've obviously had no success so far. And you're right. Her trouble has its roots in the loss of her fiancé."

"Why is it so hard for her? One of my business associates had a niece who lost her fiancé in the war. She grieved for six months, but she slowly came back. Why is Sharon so different? Why has she just tuned out the whole world?"

"That's what we're trying to find out, Mr. Winslow."

"We're . . . we're afraid she's going to lose her mind."

Dr. Steiner was familiar with Leland Winslow's dark fear. Many parents and relatives of his patients experienced the same misgivings.

"It's a possibility we must consider."

Winslow slammed his large fist into his palm and exclaimed, "We've got to *do* something! You're supposed to be the best psychiatrist in New York City! Maybe we should take her to Europe. Those fellows over there are supposed to know something about this sort of problem."

Steiner nodded slowly. "I have thought of that, and I can recommend some fine physicians. But . . ."

Winslow caught the hesitation in Steiner's voice and saw the doubt in his eyes. "But what?"

"But I am not sure that any of my colleagues over there would be of any more help than I. Without being immodest, I might say that I use the same methods as they do, and I've had as much success as any one I know of. Of course, I can recommend some fine men over there."

A silence fell over the room, and Leland's frustration plainly showed. The corners of his mouth drooped, and he ground his teeth together. "I've never experienced anything like this, Doctor. I had a hard time growing up as a young man, but fighting the world of business is one thing. Hard as that was, it's nothing like this."

"I know. This is the most difficult thing any parent ever has to face." Steiner spread his hands apart in an unexpectedly eloquent gesture and shook his head vehemently. "I have been troubled about your daughter. Sharon is . . . she is in danger." He hesitated before continuing. "I had thought once that—"

He broke off. "You thought what, Doctor? You've got something on your mind you're not telling me."

"I'm not certain I *should* tell you."

"Go ahead. Let's have it with the bark on it. Lucille and I are desperate, Dr. Steiner. We've got to do something."

"Well, there *is* a doctor in Canada who has had considerable success with patients where others like myself have failed."

Quickly Leland asked, "What's his name?"

"Dr. Philip Chardoney. I have not mentioned him before this because I was confident that my methods would work. And I hesitate to mention him now."

"What's wrong with him?" Winslow demanded bluntly. "Is he a quack or what?"

"Indeed, I'm afraid some of my colleagues might say so."

"But you don't."

"I have been following his work, but I have recommended him only rarely."

"Why?"

"His methods are . . . unusual, to say the least."

"Unusual how?"

"Well," Steiner went on reluctantly, "he feels that patients should be taken away from all their normal surroundings, so he has established what he simply calls 'the

Camp' in Canada. It's about fifty miles northeast of Montreal. He will treat only those who agree to stay there until they are either healed or he feels he cannot help them any longer."

"That doesn't sound so bad to me. It might be exactly what she needs."

"Yes, it might, but he has other strange ways. All the patients there must work—I mean do physical labor. They hire very few people at the camp. The patients all wash dishes, cook, cut firewood, mop the floors. Everything that must be done."

"How is that supposed to help a person who has mental problems?"

"That I cannot say, but it's part of his program. He has other methods. I understand that he does not counsel patients in an office, as is customary. He doesn't even have a couch like many of my colleagues use."

"How and where does he talk to them, then?"

"He goes to them wherever they are. Sometimes when they're reading a book outside or perhaps just sitting in their room listening to a gramophone record. He just drops by. Very, very informal."

Steiner went on for some time explaining Chardoney's unusual methods, and finally he said, "Although I can't say I condone this man's approach, as I said, he has met with some success where others haven't. Several years ago a patient of mine, a young man, was in terrible condition, on the brink of insanity. I had failed with him completely—absolutely. I was embarrassed by my failure. His father heard of Chardoney and sent him away to this camp. A decision, I might add, that I completely disagreed with."

Steiner hesitated and ran his eyes over the books lining the wall. He seemed to have forgotten what he was saying, so Leland prompted, "What happened?"

"This young patient of mine came back six months later. The change in him was indescribable. He was a different person. His eyes were bright. He was filled with hope. He had all the signs of normalcy—he was totally functional. It was a miracle to me. I can put no other name on it."

Leland was accustomed to making quick decisions in the world of business, and now he had heard all he needed to hear. "Let me have his phone number."

"Please, Mr. Winslow, I urge you to think this over. It's a very serious matter." Steiner now apparently regretted that he had mentioned the man's name. "You may do your daughter harm. While this man certainly has his successes, it doesn't always turn out that way."

"Do you have any other recommendations?" Winslow demanded.

"Well, no, except you may choose to send your daughter to Europe as you suggested."

"But you don't believe that's hopeful."

"No, I do not."

"Then give me the number."

Steiner opened the top drawer of his desk and took out a small book. He riffled through the pages, then took out a blank card and slowly wrote out a name and number. He handed the card to Leland with a final warning. "You need to understand that I do not recommend this."

"Would you do it if she were your daughter and everything else had failed?"

"Yes, Mr. Winslow," he said slowly, "that is exactly what I would do."

★　★　★

Lucille twined her fingers together nervously as Leland reported on his interview with Dr. Steiner. She waited until he hesitated and then said, "What is it, Leland? You're not telling me something." Fear swept over her, and with tightly pressed lips she whispered, "He didn't say it was hopeless, did he?"

"No, dear, he didn't say that. As a matter of fact, he recommended a doctor who has had rather spectacular results in cases like this."

Hope leaped into Lucille's eyes, and she impulsively grasped Leland's hand. "Who is he? We must go to him at once."

"His name is Philip Chardoney, but, well, there's a slight problem. This doctor is in Canada. He has a clinic in Quebec that he calls the Camp. One of the conditions he insists on is that his patients must come and live there. Quite different from other psychiatrists."

"Did Dr. Steiner feel this man would be able to help?"

"Yes. Steiner told me about one instance of a cure that was nothing short of miraculous."

Lucille asked question after question, and Leland concealed his own doubts about Chardoney's methods. He was worried about Lucille, for she was with Sharon constantly and was much more exposed to the behavior that brought such distress to both of them.

"I believe this is the right thing to do," he said cheerfully. "I think we should get her there immediately."

"Have you talked to the doctor?"

"Yes, I called Dr. Chardoney the minute I got home, and he has agreed to take her as a patient. I think I'll go up right now and tell Sharon about this."

Rising from the couch, Leland went straight upstairs and knocked on Sharon's door. As usual, she was sitting in a chair staring vacantly out the window at the frigid February scene. She turned and said tonelessly, "Good morning, Dad."

"Good morning, Sharon."

As he moved across the room to stand over her, Leland saw a pile of letters on Sharon's lap and knew they were the ones Robert had written her. He saw grief on her face and the trace of tears on her cheeks.

I wish she wouldn't read those letters over and over. I think maybe Chardoney has the right idea. Get the patients away from home and keep their hands and their minds occupied. Aloud he said, "I've come to tell you about a new doctor I think is going to be a great deal of help to you, Sharon."

Leland spoke quickly, not going into great detail, making Chardoney sound as attractive as possible.

" . . . he has this place he calls the Camp, and you must go and stay with him for a time. I think it will be good for you to get away," he said as cheerfully as he could. "I've made all the arrangements."

"If you say so, Dad."

She's lost her will entirely. She'd do anything I told her to. Leaning over, Leland kissed her on the cheek and gave her a quick hug. "I'll take you there myself, daughter. We'll go tomorrow. Have Lorraine help you pack."

"All right, Dad."

Returning to the parlor, he found Lucille anxiously waiting for him. "How did she take it?"

"Like she takes everything. It seems she doesn't care. She's lost her will to do anything."

"When will you leave?"

"In the morning. We'll have to go by train. Too much snow for an automobile." He reached out and enfolded Lucille in his arms. "Don't worry, darling. I feel this is the right thing to do."

The two clung to each other for support, and after a moment, Leland said, "I'll go make sure Lorraine knows what to pack." He kissed her on the cheek and made himself smile. "I have a good feeling about this, dear. I believe this Dr. Chardoney is just the man we've been looking for."

CHAPTER EIGHT

THE CAMP

★ ★ ★

Leland stepped out of the ancient Oldsmobile that belonged to the camp and moved around to open the door for Sharon. When she got out, the driver said, "Go right into the big house there, Mr. Winslow, Miss Winslow. I'll see that your bags are brought in. Dr. Chardoney said he'd be waiting for you."

"Thank you."

Leland took Sharon's arm, and the two of them made their way toward the large house at the end of the long walkway. They had made the trip from New York City in two days and arrived in a small town in Quebec at two o'clock in the afternoon, where a driver had been waiting for them. Sharon had said nothing on the trip from the station, but then she had said practically nothing during the train trip either. Leland had put a great deal of effort into trying to keep a thread of conversation going.

Now as they moved toward the sprawling three-story Gothic-style house, Winslow noted the turrets and gables. The structure was covered with stone, and smoke spiraled upward from four chimneys. The place looked solid, yet welcoming.

The large house was surrounded with small cedar-sided cabins that had smoke rising from their chimneys as well. A narrow river, a snowy streak hardly discernable from the surrounding countryside, was to their left. Overhead the sky was an iron gray, and the sun was so pale it appeared to be stricken with the cold.

"It looks like a nice place—very old, I would think," Leland said. He looked to Sharon, but she did not answer. A long porch extended across the front of the house with Adirondack chairs spaced along the length of it. *In the summertime it must be nice to sit out here,* Leland thought as they climbed the front steps. He turned to admire the snow-covered hills surrounding the camp on all sides, making a peaceful and inviting scene. When they stepped inside, they were met by a young woman.

"My name is Greta," she said with a warm smile. "If you'd like, you can hang your coats here," she said, indicating the many hooks in the entryway. "Dr. Chardoney said for me to bring you right to his office."

The pair hung their coats and followed Greta up a beautiful winding staircase made of gleaming walnut. From the second-floor landing, they could look down on a spacious and inviting living room, pleasantly decorated with light green wallpaper and furnished with antiques in excellent shape. There was a dignity and warmth to the room, highlighted by a crackling fire in the huge fireplace, around which several people were gathered, some talking quietly and others reading. It was an encouraging sign to Leland, who had pictured a dreary work camp with stark furnishings. At the top of the stairs a broad corridor ran down to a huge window, which admitted the pale sunlight. Greta stopped at the last door and said, "This is Dr. Chardoney's office. You can go right in."

"Thank you," Leland said. He nodded to the girl, opened the door, and stepped aside to let Sharon go in first.

The room was nothing like other doctors' offices he had seen. It was furnished more like a drawing room. A large couch with a restful light blue weave dominated one wall. The room was decorated with prints of paintings, some by the Old Masters, others more contemporary. It was obviously designed to be inviting, not intimidating. His eyes went to the small man with thinning gray hair who was coming toward them, hand extended.

"I am Philip Chardoney, Mr. Winslow, and this must be Sharon."

"Yes, indeed. Good to meet you, Doctor."

Chardoney wore gray slacks and a maroon sweater over a white shirt. He appeared to be in his forties. Leland felt a momentary disappointment, for he had expected someone more impressive. Chardoney would have been ordinary in any circumstances. As he welcomed them, Leland noted that his voice was the only exceptional thing about him— rich, smooth, and warm. Leland had the impression that if the man wished, he could lift it to operatic heights.

"I see you're tired, Sharon," Chardoney said. "Let's go look at your room, and you can rest before dinner." He turned to Leland and said, "I assume you'll be taking the early train tomorrow, Mr. Winslow."

Actually Leland had planned to stay for at least another day, but he recognized the firmness with which he was being ushered out. He ordinarily would have resisted such pressure, but he had agreed to commit his daughter into the hands of this man and knew he must give him free rein.

"Yes, I am."

"Fine. After we show Sharon her room, you and I will take a turn about the grounds. Then we'll have dinner together tonight."

During all this time Sharon had said nothing at all, nor did she speak as Chardoney opened the door and motioned for her to step out. The three walked down the hall until they came to another broad stairway leading to the third story. "Your room is my favorite in the whole place. It's like living in the tower of a castle. A little like Rumpelstiltskin. Do you know that story, Sharon?"

"It's a fairy tale, isn't it?"

"Yes. About a young lady with long hair who lived in a tower. Well, that's almost what you'll be doing."

When they reached the third floor, they turned down a hallway, and then Chardoney opened a door. "Cozy, isn't it? And look at the view you have."

Indeed, it was a cozy room with high ceilings and walls papered in pale yellow paper, decorated with pictures of serene country settings in plain wooden frames. An antique mahogany armoire sat along one wall, and a four-poster bed with a yellow-and-white comforter was along another. A small desk and comfortable chair had been placed next to the large window, which was framed with sheer white floor-length curtains. The highly polished dark wood floor had a large area rug of light blue, yellow, and green wool. A small stone fireplace was along the far wall, in front of which was a small couch with soft pillows.

"The view is wonderful," Leland said, gazing out the enormous window. From this height he could see the river as it wound away and a valley with cows pawing at the snow for the grass underneath. "This is very nice, isn't it, Sharon?"

Sharon looked around and nodded. "Yes, Dad, it's very nice."

"I'm sure you'll like it," Dr. Chardoney said. "I'll have your bags brought up. Why don't you lie down and rest awhile, Sharon. Then come down at six o'clock and have dinner with your father and me."

"I'm not very hungry," Sharon said.

"You won't see your father for some time," Chardoney said firmly, "so I'd like you to make this effort for him—and for me, of course."

Sharon hesitated, then said, "Very well, Doctor."

"Good. Come along, Mr. Winslow."

For the next hour Chardoney gave Leland the grand tour,

starting with the house. "This house once belonged to a rather eccentric millionaire," he explained. "I think he had been reading too many Gothic novels, so the place looks like a castle but it's comfortable. I had to do a lot of renovation, and of course it takes a lot of work to keep up."

As they moved through the house, Leland's sharp eyes took in the occupants. It was hard to tell the hired servants from the patients. Once he asked, "Is that man over there a patient?" He indicated a large man with a blunt face who was mechanically peeling potatoes.

"Oh yes, that's Ralph. He's one of our newer residents. Came last week."

Leland was encouraged that nearly everyone spoke to the doctor in a familiar fashion, and he never failed to call them by name, usually adding some personal remark such as, "Have you written your mother this week, Charles?" Or "You did a good job on the dining room floor, Cecilia. I'm proud of you."

Chardoney led Leland outside, explaining that the camp was virtually self-sufficient. "We raise our own beef, our own pigs, and our own chickens for eggs. And in the summer we grow most of our own vegetables."

"I must say I'm impressed," Leland said. "Where did you get the idea of taking this approach?"

"I think the Lord gave it to me."

Winslow was startled at the doctor's calm answer. "You think *God* told you to do this?"

"Yes, I do," he said as they went down the porch steps and headed toward the river. "When I started out, I had a practice like everyone else. An office where people came in for an hour, then went back home. I didn't seem to be helping too many people, so I took three months off and I prayed and asked God to show me a way I could be of more help. This is what came to me. Of course, most people would not think it was of God, but I have no doubt of it."

Leland liked the way Chardoney spoke so easily of God,

although he was not sure that others would take so well to this approach.

The two turned onto a cleared path along the river. "The patients spend a lot of time in the summer walking along here. Some of them like to fish in it. I've caught some fine trout myself."

Winslow stopped and looked at the smaller man. "Do you really think you can help my daughter?" He found himself held by the warmth of his eyes.

"I pray that I can. Some I can't help. I don't know why. We try equally hard with all our patients, but I feel I must tell you that sometimes the approach fails."

"I appreciate your honesty, Doctor. I can't tell you how much this means to me."

"I think I can sense that. Really, I think the cure for mental illness is the same as that for physical illness. Doctors can do some things very well, but it's always God who does the healing, whether it's a broken bone or a troubled mind. Faith in God is the key."

Winslow was fascinated by Chardoney and spent the rest of the afternoon learning all he could of his treatment methods and how he operated the Camp. When they returned to the house, Chardoney showed Winslow to his room on the second floor. They paused at the door and Winslow said, "Dr. Chardoney, I hope you understand that no expense is to be spared for Sharon."

"None will be, I assure you. Sharon will have the very best that I can give her, just as she would have if she had no money at all. I'll let you freshen up now and I'll see you at dinner."

★ ★ ★

The dinner was excellent that evening and Leland ate heartily.

"We have a fine chef here who was trained at the Culinary Arts Institute in Montreal," the doctor explained. "Some of the patients are learning from him."

Sharon sat beside her father, across from Dr. Chardoney, at one of several small tables in the dining room that held four to six people. Sharon was terrified that the doctor would ask her to talk, but he did not, other than to ask her if she liked her room.

When dinner was over Dr. Chardoney said, "Every night after dinner we entertain one another in the concert room— at least, that's what we call it. If nobody else is inclined to participate, I do the entertaining, which must test everyone's patience. I play the piano very poorly and sing worse, but they don't seem to mind."

The concert room turned out to be the largest room of the house. A fire was blazing in another stone hearth as about thirty people wandered in and took seats on scattered chairs and couches. Sharon studied them, wondering what sort of people she would be living with, but she mostly kept her eyes down as Dr. Chardoney introduced her.

"All right, we have a treat tonight. Loretta's going to sing for us."

A petite woman with a frightened expression came to stand beside Chardoney at the piano. She had a thin, almost feeble, voice as she sang "When You Wore a Tulip."

Everyone applauded, and Leland leaned over and said, "If you sing, you're going to be the star of this show. Would you like to give it a whirl, Sharon?"

"Oh no, Dad, I can't!"

Dr. Chardoney had caught the little interplay and did not insist that she sing. The rest of the entertainment was of equally limited talent, but one fellow named Tony had a fairly good tenor voice and sang a song that Leland recognized. "I know that song but I can't think of the title. What is it, Sharon?"

"It's 'When I Was a Lad' from *H.M.S. Pinafore*."

Leland anxiously glanced at her, remembering how she had performed with Robert in this very play. He said nothing but saw that she was sadder than usual.

After a couple more songs, the group broke up, with some leaving and others remaining to talk.

Leland walked Sharon up to her room on the third floor, and at the door he turned her around to face him. "I'll be leaving early in the morning before you get up, dear, so we'll say good-bye now."

She looked frightened, and Leland took her hand and said, "Anytime you want to leave, I'll come get you. You don't have to stay here."

"All right, Daddy." Sharon unconsciously used the word *Daddy*, which she had not used since she was a child, but Leland could see that she felt very small and helpless.

"You're going to get better soon, dear," he said. "And then you'll come back and be with us." He put out his arms, and she clung to him; then he kissed her and said, "Your mother and I will write often, and you must write to us."

"All right, Dad." She tried to smile. "I'll do my best to get better."

"You *will* get better. I know you will."

As Leland descended the stairs to the second floor, a heaviness came over him. He was afraid he was doing the wrong thing by leaving her here alone, but then he thought, *This is the only hope we've got. God, you've got to help Sharon get better. Guide this man Chardoney and make our daughter whole again.*

★ ★ ★

Sharon slept fitfully, drifting off from time to time only to awaken in fear as she found herself in the unfamiliar room, lit by the small oil lamp she had left burning. She was lonely and wished she were home again. As she lay in her bed before dawn she heard stirrings throughout the house. The room was cold, for the fire had died down. The covers were warm and comforting, however, and she kept her head underneath, hiding from the outer world.

Eventually she heard a knock and a voice at her door. "Sharon, time to get up!"

She resisted the impulse to remain in her warm cocoon and climbed out of bed at once, shivering in the cold as she quickly dressed. When she opened the door and stepped outside, she found Greta coming down the hall.

"Good morning, Sharon. Are you hungry?"

"A bit." Sharon had not been able to figure out the girl's position and asked, "Do you work here, Greta?"

"Oh no, I'm a patient just like you."

Sharon stared at Greta, who was plainly attired in a blue wool jumper, a white blouse, white stockings, and a blue sweater. Her hair was done in a neat twist at the back of her head, and there was a cheerful expression in her eyes. She seemed so well balanced. "You don't seem crazy like I am."

Greta laughed. "You're not crazy, and I'm not either. We just have some problems. Come on. We don't want to miss breakfast."

They got in line at the pass-through that separated the kitchen from the dining room, where Tony was serving bacon, eggs, and buttered toast with jam. Sharon recognized him as the same person who had sung the song from *Pinafore* the night before. Sharon and Greta sat down at an empty table, and a few minutes later Tony joined them.

"Now I'll have to eat fast to catch up with you girls," he said.

Greta smiled at the eager way he dug into his breakfast. "Tony's leaving next week," she told Sharon. "What are you going to do, Tony?"

"I'm going to find a job, and I'm going to make my parents proud of me."

"Have you been here long?" Sharon asked rather timidly.

"Almost a year. I was in pretty bad shape when I got here."

"I wasn't here then," Greta said, "but I've heard that you wanted to fight everybody."

116

Tony smiled brightly. "I guess you could say I was a bit aggressive, but Dr. Chardoney helped me get over that."

"How did he do that?" Sharon asked.

"Well, one of the first things I did when I got here was I tried to hit him, and he flipped me flat on my back. I think he used to be a wrestler before he became a doctor. So that settled that."

"But what about everybody else? Did you try to fight the others?" Greta asked with a smile.

Tony stabbed a piece of bacon, shoved it into his mouth, and chewed with evident pleasure. "It took a while, but I finally learned that the world wasn't against me. You know," he added thoughtfully, "Dr. Chardoney's a pretty crafty fellow. He kind of sneaks up on you with his ideas. I was all prepared not to listen to a thing he had to say. To laugh at him, to poke fun at him for being a crazy man's doctor. But he was just . . ." Tony shook his head as he tried to think of a good description. "I don't know how he did it. He came out to the woods once when I was splitting logs. We started talking about hockey, which I love, and before I knew it we were talking about God, whom I didn't love. So that was the beginning."

Sharon listened as the young man spoke enthusiastically of his stay at the Camp and more enthusiastically about his leaving. After a while he turned to Sharon and said, "I expect you're a little scared of being here with all these new people, but take it from me—this place can help you."

Sharon nodded and said without much enthusiasm, "I hope so."

"Do you skate?" Greta asked.

"Do you mean ice-skate? Yes, a little."

"Good. We play a lot of pickup hockey out on the river here. Tony's the coach."

"I've never played hockey. I don't think I could do that."

"I didn't know how to play when I got here either," Greta said, "but it's great fun. I hope you'll join us. Now if you're finished eating, Dr. Chardoney said he would like to see you."

Instantly Sharon froze up. Both of her companions noticed it, but Tony said, "Tell the doctor to come join the hockey game this afternoon. It's the only chance I get to rough him up."

Sharon made her way to the second floor, where she found Chardoney in his quarters. "I didn't get to come down for breakfast," he said, "so I had a little brought up. You don't mind if I finish, do you?"

"Of course not."

Chardoney had a plate heaped with eggs, bacon, and toast, and he ate with obvious enjoyment. Sharon was as stiff as a poker as she waited for him to finish. She had never felt very comfortable visiting Dr. Steiner. He had frightened her, even though he had always been gentle, because he insisted she discuss things that caused her much pain, and she usually refused.

"Your father has told me about your background," the doctor began. "Is there anything you'd like to talk about?"

"No," Sharon said quickly. "Not really."

"Well, if you do decide you'd like to talk about anything, just let me know. Now, let's figure out what kind of work you're going to do."

Sharon's father had told her that part of the treatment was physical labor, and she told him, "I'm afraid I'm not very good at anything. I can't even cook."

"I'm sure we can find something you'll be good at. I believe in work, Sharon. I've done enough manual labor myself to know that it can't hurt you. I'd like you to take the rest of this morning to walk around the camp, meeting some of the other residents and seeing the types of jobs that need to be done around here. Along with having a job to do here, I hope you'll make friends as well. I think that's very important too. I know you've come here because you need help to get your life back on track," he said slowly and then smiled, "but it's possible you might be able to help someone else."

"How can I do that?"

"Just by being a friend to them. Open yourself up to them. That's what friends are, people who open themselves up."

Sharon had doubts about this. She had deliberately shut herself off from others, and now this man was asking her to let people into her life! "I'm not sure I can do that."

"I think you can, and I think you should make the effort. And one other thing. I want you to allow God into your life too."

Sharon did not answer. Her father had told her that part of the treatment was learning to have faith in God, but she had been extremely doubtful. To Sharon, going to church and praying were rituals people followed to make themselves acceptable to God. She could not understand how such things could change anyone's life.

"So you see there are four components that will play a part in your treatment here: hard work, letting other people into your life, letting God into your life, and talking to me when you feel like it."

"It doesn't sound like much."

Chardoney leaned forward and said intently, "Sharon, believe this if you can. Every patient who has done these things has been healed."

CHAPTER NINE

THE WOODCHOPPER

★　★　★

A cold blast of air struck Sharon's face, and she pulled her coat more tightly about her. She had brought her winter clothes, but it seemed much colder here than in New York City, which was four hundred miles farther south. The sky was blue today, and the sun hung over the pristine white landscape like a rosy red wafer. The newly fallen snow crunched under her feet and was so bright it hurt her eyes. As she walked on, she smelled the acrid odor of wood burning, and from almost every cabin tendrils of gray smoke spiraled upward.

She was pleased that Dr. Chardoney had told her to spend her first morning simply getting acquainted with her surroundings and with the people. So far she had managed to avoid most of the people except for Greta and Tony, but she had been refreshed by the snap in the air, which reddened her face and numbed her fingers, even inside the wool mittens she wore.

She made her way down to the frozen river and started tracing its serpentine winding, following tracks in the snow that she expected were deer. Being pulled out of her old life into this one was a shock, but she could already tell that being out in the open with the snow-laden trees and seeing the hills rising in the distance with the same wintry cloak was good for her. The cold bit at her nose as she inhaled, and when she exhaled she watched her breath rise like incense toward the sky.

The sound of barking startled her, and she turned to see a large dog bounding toward her. For a moment she froze with fear, but the dog stopped five feet away, sat down with his red tongue lolling, and regarded her curiously.

She loved animals but was wise enough to be cautious with unfamiliar ones. "Hello, dog."

The dog, which she recognized as a husky from pictures she had seen, took this as an invitation. He barked sharply once, then scampered to stand in front of her, tail wagging. She put her hand out so he could sniff it, and he barked again as if in approval.

"You're a handsome fellow," Sharon said, smiling. She had had a dog when she was a child, but it was a small spaniel, nothing like this one, whose muscles moved like steel springs beneath the smooth, thick coat. He had intelligent-looking brown eyes, and when she knelt down, he lifted his right paw and placed it on her knee. *Woof!*

"*Woof* yourself," Sharon said, taking off her mitten to stroke his fur. He sat very still while she petted him and scratched behind his ears. She finally rose. "Did you come out for a walk?" Once again she got a *woof* for a reply, so she smiled and said, "Come on. You can walk with me."

The dog wandered along beside her as she walked along the river. When her nose got too cold, she turned and headed back, but still he followed her. "I wonder who you belong to. You're not a stray. You're too healthy for that."

When she got back behind the main house, she saw a man splitting wood and asked, "Whose dog is this?"

"He's the doctor's dog. His name is Rooney."

The speaker was a burly blond man wearing a red mackinaw coat. His hands and wrists looked strong, and he handled the ax as if the weight of it were nothing. Rooney followed her to the front of the house, and when she got to the stairs, she saw Dr. Chardoney step outside.

"Oh, I see you've made a friend." He came down the steps. "I was just going out to walk with him, but it looks like you've already done that."

"He's a beautiful dog."

"Yes, he is. Do you like animals?"

"I do, but I don't get many opportunities to be around them."

"I'm a bit surprised to see Rooney following you. He doesn't take up with everyone. You can always trust a woman that a dog likes," he said with a grin.

"I doubt that."

"Why don't you go on inside and get warm. Lunch is nearly ready. I think it's stew today. I hope you like that."

"I'm sure I will."

"After lunch you and I will get together and decide on some things."

Sharon wanted to ask, *What things?* but she only nodded. She paused at the door and looked back to see Rooney bounding along beside the doctor, who was running through the snow and laughing.

She went inside and hung her coat on one of the hooks and left her boots on the large entry rug. She went into the dining room and found Tony serving the stew. She didn't see Greta, but a middle-aged man named Frank and Helen, a woman in her late fifties or so, invited her to eat with them. As she enjoyed her stew, Frank talked about world events. He was evidently a student of current events, for he seemed to know everything, and he didn't seem to mind that the women weren't contributing much to the conversation.

During the meal Sharon worried about her conference with Dr. Chardoney. When she had finished her stew and Frank was between stories, Sharon excused herself and approached Dr. Chardoney, who was eating alone on the other side of the dining room. "Would you like me to wait in your office?"

"No, sit down. We can talk here. Why don't you get some coffee? It's good and strong today—would float a horseshoe nail, I think."

"No thank you. I don't drink coffee."

As Sharon took her seat, Dr. Chardoney asked her, "Have you given any thought to the type of job you'd like to do? Tony's leaving, so you could be a server."

Sharon did not mind the work itself, but she had noticed that the servers, including Tony, talked a great deal. She was not ready for this kind of exposure. "Is there anything else?"

"You could help the cook."

"I'm afraid not," Sharon smiled slightly, the first smile Chardoney had seen on her face. "I'm a terrible cook. I've never learned."

"That's all right. I'm a terrible cook myself. Let's see. There's always dishwashing, house cleaning, or laundry. That's pretty tough work. That'd be my last choice."

Sharon immediately thought of how much she had enjoyed being outside. She would not be obliged to make conversation there. "I saw a man out back chopping wood. Could I help with that?"

Chardoney laughed and shook his head. "That's pretty rough work. I like it myself, but the men usually take care of that."

"Please, I'd like very much to try it. I know I won't be good at it at first, but I'll learn."

"There's nothing to learn, Sharon. Chopping wood doesn't require much intellectual activity—just muscles. But if you'd like to give it a try, that's fine."

"Thank you, Doctor."

"You'll have to have sturdy gloves and some warmer clothes, and you'll have to let me know if it gets too hard so I can find you something else."

"Thank you, Doctor. I think I can do it."

★   ★   ★

Sharon had never had to work in her life. She was fairly fit physically, but chopping wood was another world. Nelson Kane, the woodchopper she had spoken to on her first day, was a big, strong man in his thirties. He simply stared at her when Dr. Chardoney told him she was to be his new partner. "You show her the ropes, Nelson, and watch out for her. We'll have her start by working three hours a day and see how she adjusts to the physical labor."

Nelson hardly said ten words the first day. He showed her how to split wood with a maul, and it looked so easy that she was deceived into thinking she could do it. When she tried, she could barely lift the maul, much less hit anything. She laughed ruefully and said, "I think it's going to take me a while to work up to this." Later in the morning he let her help him run a two-man saw, but she knew he was doing ninety percent of the work.

"I'll cut the wood. You can load it," Nelson said, which was a long speech for him. He sawed the wood off in standard lengths and split it, and she loaded it onto the trailer that was attached to a tractor. When the trailer was loaded and Nelson left to deliver it to the cabins, she insisted on staying alone and waiting for him to return.

Actually she was not alone, for Rooney had assigned himself as a permanent companion, it seemed. He watched her carefully, and whenever she grew still he would come nudge her leg with his nose until she petted him and spoke to him.

While Nelson was delivering the wood, she ran through the woods with Rooney and discovered he was as playful as a puppy. The two wrestled until Rooney bowled her over and then she got up and they did it all over again.

After her first day she was so stiff she thought she'd never be able to sleep, but exhaustion quickly overtook her. The next day every muscle was sore. The work was hard, but she liked it. Chardoney was worried about her, she knew, but she told him firmly, "I like it, Doctor. Let me keep at it."

By the fourth day she found herself able to work for longer periods. Chardoney was afraid she was overdoing it, but Sharon found herself staying outdoors even when her work was done.

One day Chardoney met them at the edge of the woods as they were coming in, Sharon seated on the load of wood while Nelson did the driving. Rooney was following alongside, and when she got down, he came over and sat down on her feet. She laughed and said, "Get off my feet, you big lug! You weigh a ton."

"He's always liked to do that," Chardoney said, patting the big dog and shaking his head. "I think he's adopted you."

"He's such a beautiful animal and so sweet."

"Not always. He can get pretty fierce at times."

"Really?"

"He doesn't like to see anyone mistreated. Once I saw him go after a man who was roughing up a boy. I think Rooney would have killed him if I hadn't pulled him off."

"That's amazing. Where did you get him?"

"Well, there's a little story behind that. Rooney was hit by a car when he was about a year old. The owner was afraid his injuries were too extensive and wanted to put him down, but I knew the dog, and I didn't want to see him die so needlessly. So I took him in. I sewed him up and set his broken bones. He nearly died. I had to feed him like a baby for a time and sometimes even force-feed him. It took a long time, but you made it, didn't you, Rooney?"

Rooney agreed with a *woof!* and came over to sit down on Chardoney's feet.

Sharon was fascinated. "Why did you save him? Most people would have just let him die."

"I never like to see a good dog wasted," Chardoney said. He looked at her strangely, Sharon thought, and then added,

"Or a good young woman either."

Sharon straightened up. "Is it time for my treatment out here with Rooney sitting on your feet?"

"I take my patients where I find them."

Sharon rather liked the approach, but she was wary. "I'll tell you one thing, Doctor—you're not going to make me love God no matter how hard you try."

"Is that right?"

"No! Why should I love Him after what happened to me?"

"What did happen?"

"You know what happened." Sharon turned and walked away, and Rooney followed her. She soon found Chardoney walking beside her, and they continued on in silence. She finally turned to the doctor with tears glistening in her eyes. "I was going to get married. Robert and I loved each other. He had a tremendous talent, Doctor. I think he could have been one of the great opera stars of our time, and he was snuffed out. God took him from me."

"I think the Germans had a little something to do with that."

Anger flared in Sharon, and she snapped bitterly, "You don't understand what it's like to lose someone like that!"

Chardoney's voice did not change. Without a hint of anger, he said calmly, "My wife and two children were burned to death in a fire."

Sharon stiffened. She waited for him to say more, but he stood silently.

"We'll talk about God when you're ready," he said after a few moments, his voice still calm. "I'm not going to preach to you. But I want you to find something more creative to do than chopping wood."

"But I like chopping wood, and I'm getting better at it every day."

"Everybody needs two kinds of work, Sharon. You need hard physical work, and yours, apparently, is chopping wood. No one here thought you would last at this. Me, least of all—but you have. I like that. It shows you're tough, despite that rather beautiful outside."

Sharon found herself blushing at his compliment. "But what else do you want me to do?"

"You need a hobby. Something that will challenge you creatively. Do you want to continue your singing?"

"No!"

Chardoney seemed to understand the sharpness of her reply. "All right, I won't insist, but you're going to have to find some creative outlet to fill up your time. I'm the doctor, and I insist."

"I won't do it!" Sharon exclaimed. "I'll go home first."

"Go ahead. The train leaves in the morning at seven o'clock."

Sharon had not expected this. She stared at Chardoney, who simply stood there. His face was peaceful, as always, but he obviously meant what he said. "All right, I will," Sharon said. "I don't have to stay here."

"No, you don't, and I don't want you here unless you choose to stay."

"I'll leave on the train in the morning."

"The driver will be ready at six-fifteen to take you to the station."

Sharon whirled away, anger burning in her. She had not expected him to take her up on her threat, and now as she stomped off she thought belligerently, *He can't make me do anything! I'll go home!*

She went straight to her room and began to pack her things, which didn't take long, and then there was nothing else to do. She paced the floor and began thinking of what it would be like to go home. Somehow the thought of returning to her old routine was not very exciting. The days here had at least been different, and she found herself wanting to stay. She unpacked her bag and went to Dr. Chardoney's office. When he opened the door after her knock, she said abruptly, "What kind of hobby?"

Chardoney did not gloat. "Come inside. We'll talk about it."

As they discussed possible ideas for a hobby, Chardoney saw that Sharon had a keen appreciation for art, but she had never had much opportunity to try it except for a little painting at her finishing school.

"Were you any good at it?" he asked.

She shrugged. "Not great, I guess, but I didn't try it for long."

Chardoney had an idea. "I see you enjoy working with your hands, Sharon. Have you ever tried working with clay?"

"You mean sculpture? No. I've seen some of the great works in museums, though. But I don't think I could ever do anything like that."

"You never know until you try," Chardoney said. "I had a patient who left about a year and a half ago. He was big on this. He had all kinds of equipment, and he left it all here. Come on. I'll show you."

He led her to a room that was used mostly for storage. "Never mind the clutter. We can get rid of that. This could be your studio. Those windows let in plenty of light." Chardoney went to a cabinet and opened it. "Here's where I put all the things he left, including his books on sculpture. I don't know much about it, but I do know that he made his clay by mixing this powder with water, and this other powder is what he used for plaster of Paris. Look, he left one of his pieces with us."

Sharon moved forward, intensely interested. She looked at the bust that Chardoney held up and exclaimed, "Why, that's you!"

"I'm much better looking than that," he said with a grin. "It is pretty good, though, isn't it? He was going to make a bronze out of it, but we didn't have that kind of equipment here, so he just let me keep it as is."

Sharon said with discouragement, "I don't know a thing about all this."

"You didn't know anything about opera either, but you learned to sing. Why don't you try it?"

"All right, but what will I make a statue of?"

"How about Rooney?"

She laughed. "He'll probably look like a dinosaur."

"So he'd be a dinosaur dog, then. Like I say, you won't know until you try. And if you do well, we'll get you a kiln."

Sharon was amused by the doctor. "I know what you're trying to do."

"What?"

"You're trying to cure me."

"Of course. Or trying to help you cure yourself."

"You think I'll find God by messing around with clay and plaster of Paris, Doctor?"

"Maybe. You'll never know until you try."

★ ★ ★

As Sharon and Nelson Kane spent more time together chopping wood, they actually became friends, although neither one was inclined to engage in lengthy conversations. When he had expressed some interest in her sculpting work, he'd said, "Maybe I'll come and watch someday."

"Of course," she had agreed. "Anytime."

It was late afternoon now, and Sharon had worked all morning cutting wood, but she now looked forward to her afternoons, when she would come to her studio to work with clay. She had been so engrossed in what she was doing that she did not hear Nelson come in, and his voice startled her. "That's very good, Sharon."

She jumped and turned to him, smiling. "You scared me."

"That's very good," he repeated.

Sharon turned back and examined the bust herself. She had been astonished at how much pleasure she had found in working with the clay. She had tried only very simple things at first, making more bowls than anything, but spent her evenings now reading books about more complex sculpting. "I think I'm ready to try something a bit more complicated."

"Why don't you make a statue of Rooney? Of his head anyway. The legs might be hard."

"Okay, I'll try it. And if it's good, I'll give it to you, Nelson."

★ ★ ★

Dr. Chardoney stood back, his eyes intent as he studied the work that Sharon had finished. "I can't believe it. It looks just like Rooney."

"As you can see, I was afraid to try the whole body. I'm not sure I could make good legs."

"I think you need to build those up with wire first to give them the needed support. At least that's what Ramsey did."

"Oh yes, there was a chapter in one of the books about how to make that kind of a framework, but I wanted to try just the head first."

"Well, you've captured him. I've seen him look just like that a thousand times."

Sharon had worked for several days on the bust of Rooney. She had given up twice and destroyed her work, but this time she was pleased with what she had caught. Chardoney continued to praise her work, and then he said, "Would you like to try a bronze?"

"I understand that's very complicated, Dr. Chardoney!"

"I guess it is, but there's a friend of mine who does bronzes. He doesn't live too far from here. Not more than a two-hour drive. If you'd like, we could make a trip over to see him."

"Oh, I wouldn't want to take up his time."

"Nonsense. He's a fine fellow. He'd be interested in what

you're doing. He likes to encourage young talent."

"I guess I would like to learn," Sharon said, realizing how true that had become.

"All right. I'll call him. His name is Giles Frenoit. I'll see when it would be convenient for us to see him."

Sharon felt a warm glow. Somehow her sculpting work had released a new interest in life. She turned and said very quietly, "I'd like to talk to you—about myself, Doctor."

Chardoney smiled. "That's fine. Would you like to do it now?"

"I think I would."

"Come on. Let's go for a walk."

Sharon left with the doctor, and as they reached the woods, she found herself talking as she had not been able to for more than three years. She told the doctor how she had met Robert, about performing with him in *H.M.S. Pinafore,* and about struggling to decide whether or not they should marry before he went overseas. She hadn't spoken to anybody in this way since his death. And as she told him more and more, she suddenly knew that something was taking place inside her that she needed desperately.

★ ★ ★

Spring was now in full bloom in Canada, so Sharon's woodcutting work took much less time. She had, however, thrown herself fully into her sculpting work. It had come as a surprise to her when Chardoney had suggested she move out of the big house into one of the cabins, but she had been willing. She had a roommate, Lillian Brough, with whom she had learned to get along quite well.

Sharon had mastered the fundamentals of bronze casting, and her prize was the statue of Rooney. She had worked on it for over a month, and Giles Frenoit, the sculptor who had taught her the art, had helped her with the final bronzing.

Early one Thursday afternoon in June, Dr. Chardoney came by to watch her. He had followed her progress, and he was curious about the new piece she was working on. After he watched for a time, he broke the silence by saying, "I think it's time for you to go home and pick up your life now, Sharon."

Chardoney's words came as a shock to Sharon. She turned quickly and stared at him. She was wearing a white cotton smock, and her hands were stained from the clay. "Go home? But I'm not ready."

"I think you are. You've done what you came for." Chardoney hesitated, then said, "God wants more of you than you're willing to give Him right now, but as you get stronger and become more comfortable in your faith, that will come. You've learned to live with your loss, Sharon. You've learned how to be at ease around people again, and you're listening to God. That's all I can do for you. Your life is just beginning afresh. Go home, draw near to God, and enjoy being with people."

Sharon found herself shaken by his words and could say little in response. But all afternoon she thought about what he had said, and when she went down to supper that night, she found herself seated with a new patient who had just arrived. Her name was Patricia. She was obviously frightened, and Sharon, along with Greta and Lillian, tried to encourage her. "You're going to love it here, Patricia," Sharon said. "I know it feels strange right now, but you'll make friends, and Dr. Chardoney can help you."

Patricia said nothing, but obviously she had serious problems.

"You'll have to watch out for her, Greta," Sharon said.

"We both will," Greta said quickly.

"No, Dr. Chardoney told me this afternoon that it's time for me to leave."

Greta shook her head sadly. "I knew you wouldn't be here much longer. Dr. Chardoney doesn't let people hang around when he feels they're ready for the real world."

"What about you, then?"

Greta chewed her lip. "I'm getting better, but I still have some problems I need help with."

After dinner the group gathered in the concert room, and the woman who had been planning to sing, a large woman named Tilly, said, "My throat's sore, Doctor. I can't sing tonight."

"Well," he said, "I guess I'll have to sing, then." He looked around from the piano stool, and his eyes met Sharon's. "Unless someone else will."

Sharon understood his message, and in a moment of boldness stood up and said, "I'd like to sing."

"Fine! Come along. I'm afraid I'm not pianist enough to accompany on most things unless it's 'Three Blind Mice.'"

"That's okay," Sharon said. "I can play a little."

Chardoney took another seat, and Sharon sat down at the piano. She put her hands on the keys, hesitant for a moment, but then she looked up and saw the doctor watching her intently. He nodded and smiled, and she began to play. A murmur went over the group as she played for a time; then she lifted her voice and sang. She had no more started the song than she saw the shocked amazement of the crowd.

When she finished the song, the group applauded and cheered, and Greta yelled, "Hey, you've been holding out on us. Shame on you!"

She sang five numbers, the last one a tune she had sung with Robert many times. When she finished there were tears in her eyes, and she stood up. Chardoney came to her and did something he had never done. He put his arm around her and squeezed her. "You are ready to go home," he said proudly.

"All right, Doctor. I think you're right."

"God wants more of you than you've been giving, but I think He's going to find it soon enough. I think you're equipped for whatever comes your way."

"I'll miss you, Doctor, and I'll miss all my friends here."

"That's as it should be. I'll be expecting to hear from you."

Chardoney then turned and announced, "It's time for Sharon to leave us. So in the morning we'll have a special good-bye breakfast."

After that announcement, many in the group came to talk to Sharon, and she found herself sad to have to leave them—something she had never expected. After the group thinned out, she saw Patricia, the new patient, sitting alone. Sharon went over to her and said, "I'm leaving, but you'll be in good hands. You'll find friends here." The woman nodded silently.

Sharon went to bed that night feeling strange about leaving a place that had become a haven for her. She picked up her Bible and read the Twenty-third Psalm aloud, as had recently become her practice.

Finally she climbed into bed and, before falling asleep, said, "God, thank you for bringing me to this place. Now please go before me, wherever it is you want me to go. . . ."

CHAPTER TEN

"GRANDFATHER WAS A POOR IMMIGRANT"

★ ★ ★

During the four months that Sharon was in Canada, Leland and Lucille had made the decision to sell their home in New York City and move to a lovely location in a secluded area north of the city. They thought it would help them all to get away from the memories the old house held and give the family a fresh start in a new environment. Clayton was an energetic and growing boy and needed room to run and play and ride his beloved Lucky Lady. And Sharon had made a new life for herself, with the help of Dr. Chardoney, and needed a place where she could enjoy the fresh air and peaceful surroundings, as well as have a spacious and well-lit studio to devote to her sculpting work.

The family servants had all decided to stay in the city, and Leland helped them find other positions in prestigious homes. Then he hired some new young servants for their country home. Now a year had passed since Sharon had returned, and life at the Winslows' country estate was a pleasant place for servants and visitors alike.

The young chauffeur, Mike Jones, was sitting in the kitchen, reared back on a chair, helping himself to the cookies that Mabel had made. She promptly reached over and slapped his hand. "You're gonna be fat as a pig if you don't stop eatin' those cookies!"

"That's all right. There'll be that much more of me for you to love." Whenever Jones wasn't driving the Winslow family around, he was in the kitchen romancing the cook at every possible opportunity.

Mabel giggled and went back to the counter, where she began mixing the dough for a new batch. "It's amazin' how well Miss Sharon does with those sculptures of hers, ain't it, now?"

"Yeah, she sure is a good artist. I hear she had a lot of troubles after her fella was killed in the war, but it seems like she's over that now, doesn't it?" Jones said. He got up silently and crept up behind Mabel, throwing his arms around her and kissing her on the neck noisily. "How long would you grieve for me if I went up the plume, Mabel?"

Mabel squirmed but not very hard. "Not long, I'm sure. I'd be up dancin' again 'fore you knew it. Now, you go sit yourself down."

Jones went back to his seat, pausing to fill his coffee cup. He bit off half a cookie and said, "That Miss Sharon stays busy all the time. I haul her around day and night, it seems like."

"Yes, I know. But she works so hard in that studio of hers, it does her good to get out and about. Did I show you that statue she made of my head?"

"Not half pretty enough to do you justice, sweetheart."

"Never mind that blarney."

"Only the truth. But I will admit she does good with animals. I was always partial to dogs. So is she, it seems."

"You know I think she could make a livin' at it if she really wanted to."

"Make a living at it! With all her money? Why would she want to?"

"I suppose you're right. She doesn't need any more money, does she?" Mabel shrugged. "I guess you're driving her to that big party in the city at the Vanderbilts' tonight. My, I'd like to go to one of those parties."

"I don't suppose we can go to the Vanderbilts, but there's a new Doug Fairbanks movie on at the Royal. Maybe we could take that in after I drop Miss Sharon off at the party. Then afterwards we can park and study the moon."

Mabel giggled. "None of that, now. You'd better be on your way before Mrs. Winslow catches you loafin' around here."

* * *

Sharon had been working diligently in her studio all day, and it was now almost three o'clock. The sculpture in front of her was the most challenging piece she had ever tried, and she intended to cast it in bronze. Having mastered the technique now, she had equipped her new studio in the old carriage house with a complete foundry. The studio no longer resembled the original building after all her renovations. A crew had taken out the second-story floor and inner walls to create a large, airy work space, and they had added skylights in the roof.

She stepped back now and looked at the piece she had been working on for over a month. It was a full-sized statue of an officer with a pistol in his left hand and his right hand waving forward. He was turning back as if urging his men forward into battle.

Sharon quietly studied the face. It was Robert, of course. She did not talk about him even now, but somehow she had conceived the idea of creating a sculpture that would commemorate his life. It saddened her that one day no one would remember Robert, but if people could see this statue, they would at least understand a little of what he was like. She had thought at times that this was the purpose of art—

to keep things we wish to remember frozen in time. As her favorite poet, John Keats, had expressed in his poem "Ode on a Grecian Urn"—art is better than life because everything in life we lose, but art lasts forever and never changes.

The thought gave her an inner satisfaction, a sense of purpose to her life. As she continued to work she remembered warmly how Dr. Chardoney had led her into sculpture. She had found a passion for it she had never had for anything—even singing—and she was better at it too. The fulfillment it brought her was both calming and exciting. She mulled over memories of the last year since she had returned from the Camp—how she had been welcomed back with joy by her parents and had the opportunity to begin a new life in a new home. For the first six months she had stayed away from the city and had attended no parties while she had immersed herself in building her studio and setting it up. For the last six months she had gone out occasionally and found that she was able to cope with society even at its worst.

"Miss Sharon, please come! It's time to get ready for the party."

"Just a few minutes, Ruth."

"No, come *now*!"

Ruth was Sharon's new maid. Lorraine had left for another position when Sharon had gone to Canada and had since gotten married. Sharon missed Lorraine a great deal, but young Ruth had a fresh and bubbly personality and had proven to be a good helper and companion for her.

"Come now," Ruth said again. "I want you to look very beautiful tonight."

"That's going to be difficult, but we'll do the best we can," Sharon said with a smile. She put down her tools and took off her smock, and as she left the studio, she felt a twinge of regret. *I much prefer doing this to going to any party*, she thought, but Ruth was insistent, so she went without protest.

* * *

The party was a large, ornate affair, with the usual lavishness that seemed so wrong now to Sharon. She had always felt that the ostentation of the very rich was somehow crude and gaudy, but now she felt even more strongly about it. Her parents obviously did not agree, so Sharon kept her opinion mostly to herself. Even though they had moved out of the city, her mother was still anxious to maintain the important social connections that could lead to a suitable marriage partner for Sharon.

She had danced with several such potential partners and found herself putting these men under a microscope of scrutiny. The chances of her caring for any of them were slim, especially after what had happened to her friend Hannah Astor, now Hannah Astor Fulton. Sharon had been hopeful that Hannah's marriage would be happy, but from the start it was miserable. The last time she had seen Hannah, Sharon had learned that her husband had been unfaithful to her. Hannah occupied her life with her two children, rarely speaking of her marriage. It was obvious to Sharon that Charles had married her solely for her money.

This tragedy had alerted Sharon to the dangers of men being attracted to her for her money. She was not so young anymore, but she was reasonably attractive, and there were plenty of men who wanted a wealthy wife, no matter how old she was.

Now as she danced and talked with Ralph Windom, she categorized him in one of her mental boxes, this one labeled "acceptable but a crashing bore." She found herself amused as Ralph spoke of his one passion—polo. He apparently knew the name of every player and every horse and the breeding of each, and had not a single other thought in his head.

Sharon listened as he babbled on about his most recent match and tried to follow but found his words blending into meaningless gibberish.

She smiled politely until the dance ended, and Ralph took her over to where her parents were standing. Her mother was smiling, and Sharon thought, *She thinks Ralph would be a perfect husband for me, but it would drive me insane to have to listen to stories of horses and polo matches for the next forty years.*

"Did you enjoy the dance, dear?" Lucille asked.

"It was wonderful. Ralph was telling me the most fascinating story about his last polo match. He simply must tell you about it."

"Oh yes, I would so love to hear it!"

Sharon excused herself and heard Ralph repeating exactly the same story in exactly the same words as he had told her.

Later on during the evening, her mother confirmed what Sharon was afraid she would think. "Ralph is such a fine man, dear, and he comes from such a good family!"

"Yes, that's true, I'm sure. But, Mother, he does nothing but play polo."

"Well, he's young yet. He hasn't found a more interesting use of his time."

"He's thirty years old, Mother, and he's done nothing but play polo for twenty-five years, I suppose. He apparently intends to do nothing else for the next fifty. As long as he's able to climb onto a horse."

"Come, now. You're too critical, dear."

"I suppose I am."

"Oh, Lucille, Sharon, I'm so glad to see you both." Mrs. Windom approached them, smiling broadly. "I saw you and Ralph dancing, Sharon. You dance so well together."

"Thank you, Mrs. Windom."

Mrs. Windom was every bit as society conscious as Mrs. Astor. As Lucille hurried to catch up with a friend she spotted nearby, Mrs. Windom launched into a monologue about the importance of retaining a good bloodline. Sharon understood that she was being interviewed as a prospect for Ralph's hand, but she let none of this show in her face.

"... and so you see, dear," Mrs. Windom rattled on, "we're determined to keep the family pure. The bloodline is so important."

"Yes, I'm sure you're right," Sharon said politely. While Ralph was playing with horses for the next half century, Mrs. Windom would spend her life tracing the bloodlines of suitable members of society.

"And what about your family, Sharon? Where did they originate?"

With a perverse grin, Sharon said, "Oh, my great-great— oh, I guess I don't know how many 'greats'—grandfather was a poor immigrant. Came over on a boat, you know."

Mrs. Windom's face froze. "Oh, indeed—an immigrant, you say!"

"Oh yes. He had nothing at all when he got off the ship."

Mrs. Windom was clearly already tuning Sharon out. "And what ship was that, my dear?" she said absently, her eyes already searching the room for a more fit candidate for her son.

"The *Mayflower*."

Mrs. Windom's head swiveled. "The *Mayflower*! Your people were first-comers?"

"Yes. My grandfather was Gilbert Winslow, and his brother, Edward, was the first Governor of Plymouth Plantation. Well, it was so nice talking to you, Mrs. Windom."

As Sharon nodded politely, Mrs. Windom started to sputter, and Sharon saw that she was back in the running for Ralphie, but she'd had enough talk of horses and bloodlines. "I think I'll go home early. It was nice talking with you, Mrs. Windom." As she took her leave, she muttered under her breath, "I hope you find a good brood mare for Ralphie with bloodlines that go all the way back to Methuselah."

Turning back to her mother, she said, "I'm tired. I think I'll go home."

"But Ralph was looking for you."

"I'm sorry, Mother, but he's impossible."

"But, dear—"

"I know you want me to marry, but I think it's unlikely. It's not that I'm bitter. I've gotten over that. But I don't think that married life is for me. I'll have to make my own life."

"But that's not . . . not natural."

Sharon squeezed her mother's arm. "Then I guess you simply have an unnatural daughter. I'll get Mike to take me home. I've had about all of this high-society evening I can stand."

CHAPTER ELEVEN

A LORD FROM ENGLAND

★ ★ ★

The large art gallery was crowded as people moved around the samples of Sharon's work. She stood smiling, noticing that her mother was nervously speaking with one of the Astors. She had not planned to ever have a show, but for the past five years she had worked diligently, and her father had insisted she should let the public have a chance to purchase her work. Her father was tremendously proud of the skill she had developed, despite his disappointment that she had not married. As she looked across the room, she saw him talking with a tall, distinguished-looking gentleman, whose picture she knew hung on the wall of his office. *Say, that's Andrew Mellon,* she realized, pleased that he would come from Washington, D.C., to visit her show. Her father was very proud of his association with this giant of the financial world. Leland had originally met him through their mutual association in the lumber industry, but Andrew Mellon had gone on to become an internationally renowned industrialist and the president of the Mellon National Bank. Now he was the U.S. Secretary of the Treasury. Sharon also was aware that he was an avid art collector, and she was greatly honored and humbled by his presence here today.

Mellon was not the only famous person present. The gallery was like a *Who's Who* of high-society arts patrons, all eager to be the first to purchase an impressive new work by this greatly gifted member of the Winslow family.

Sharon was not particularly interested in the opinions of these high-society members, but she was pleased to see several New York art critics there. She had not yet spoken to any of them; she merely watched as they went thoughtfully from piece to piece.

A slender man with a stoop and a pair of thick glasses approached her. She thought he looked vaguely familiar.

"You do not remember me, do you? I'm Dr. Steiner."

"Oh, Dr. Steiner, of course! Forgive me. I didn't expect to see you here."

"You were so kind to write me after your recovery, and I have been keeping up with you secretly." He swept his hand around the room. "You have done marvelously well. Your pieces are wonderful."

"Thank you, Doctor."

"And you are completely recovered?"

"I have a few scars inside, of course, but Dr. Chardoney was a great help to me."

"I have recommended him to several others. Do you ever see him?"

"As a matter of fact, I have gone back twice to visit. He's a wonderful man."

"My colleagues are still suspicious of his methods, but when they voice their concerns, I simply say, 'You go talk to Sharon Winslow. There is the proof of Chardoney's skills.' Let's see. It's been five years, hasn't it?"

"Just about."

"I am so glad to see that you are recovered, my dear. I know there's always a little pain. That scar, perhaps, will always be there." He hesitated, then said, "You haven't married. I thought, perhaps, you might."

"I am no longer a romantic young girl, Doctor. I'm thirty-two now."

"Why, you don't look a day over twenty."

"Now, Dr. Steiner, be careful with that flattery." Sharon enjoyed the doctor's kind words but added, "I have a career, and besides it's . . . it's not easy for a woman in my position to marry."

"I should imagine not." Steiner grew serious. "It must be very difficult. People who are rich or famous or both never know if people of the opposite sex are attracted to them simply because of what they own or have achieved in life, rather than for who they are."

Sharon nodded. The doctor had summed up her position exactly. They spoke for a time, and after he left, she noticed a couple standing over to one side, watching her covertly as if afraid to approach. Smiling, she went to them. "It's so good to see you again." She had seen Robert's parents only once since his funeral. At their invitation, she had traveled to Buffalo for a weekend visit. Several years had passed since then and she impulsively hugged them both.

"We don't want to bother you, my dear," Mr. Tyson said.

"Bother! How could you bother me? Let me walk around with you."

"We thought we might buy one of your pieces."

"Nonsense. You pick out what you like. It'll be my gift."

She showed the Tysons around the room, and when they had selected a small bronze bust, she said, "I hope you enjoy it."

"You know, my dear," Mrs. Tyson said, "I think of Robert every day."

Sharon hesitated, then replied in a gentle tone, "So do I. Every single day."

Clayton had been allowed to come to the show. He was twelve now and tall for his age. Sharon spoiled her little brother dreadfully, as did her parents, and now he claimed her attention. "How much will you get for all these statues, Sharon? I don't see any prices on them."

"I don't know what the total will be, Clayton."

"I hope you charge a lot for them," he said.

"My agent over there handles each one on an individual basis," she said, nodding toward a portly man in his late twenties.

"How much does *he* get?"

"That's between him and me, Clayton. Why are you so interested in money?"

"I just want to make sure you're being careful. You ought to know that some men take advantage of women. When I'm grown up, I'll handle all your money."

Sharon laughed. "You'd be capable of it, I'm sure."

Clayton stayed close by Sharon's side until Leland approached and informed him that it was time for him to go home. Clayton said loudly enough for several to hear, "Jimmy Adkins asked me when you were going to get married, and I told him I'd ask you."

"You just tell him I haven't made up my mind yet."

"You'd better hurry up," Clayton said seriously. "And you'd better marry the right fellow."

"If some man proposes to me, I'll send him to you first. I'm sure you'll be able to judge if he's suitable for me."

Clayton grinned at her. "You bet I will. See you later, Sharon."

★   ★   ★

By late afternoon the guests had thinned out and Sharon gathered her things to leave. She was about to tell her agent she was going home when Hannah Fulton came flying across the room, crying, "I'm so glad we caught you, Sharon! We thought you might be gone."

Sharon took Hannah's kiss, thinking sadly how worn out she appeared. After embracing her, Sharon said, "I was just leaving, but I'm glad I got to see you."

Turning to the man who had accompanied her, Hannah

said, "Colin, I'd like you to meet my very dearest friend, Miss Sharon Winslow. Sharon, this is my friend Sir Colin Hardie."

"I am very pleased indeed to meet you, Miss Winslow. Hannah has told me so much about you." The speaker's erect bearing gave an impression of height, though he was not tall. He had fair hair, very light blue eyes, and patrician features.

"I'm happy to know you, Sir Colin."

"Oh, please, I don't think we need to use titles here," he said with a smile. He had a pleasant voice and an educated English accent, the kind that appealed to Sharon. When she was a child her family had spent two summers in southern England, and she had loved it there.

Hannah said, "I'll leave you two to get acquainted. Sharon, maybe we can get together later this week."

"That'll be fine, Hannah. I'll look forward to it." Sharon turned back to her guest and asked, "Did you arrive from England recently?"

"As a matter of fact, yes," Sir Colin said. "I have always been fascinated by America and have treasured my visits here."

"I feel the same way about England. Will you be staying long?"

"For some time, I think. I am an aspiring novelist." Sir Colin smiled and shook his head with a diffident air. "I suppose you might say I'm a late bloomer. Here I am in my midthirties and haven't published anything yet. But I wasted most of my life before I decided I wanted to become a writer."

"I'm sure you'll do well. What sort of a novel are you working on?"

"This may interest you. The hero of my novel is a sculptor."

"Really! That *is* interesting. I came to sculpting rather late in life myself."

"So Hannah told me." Sir Colin looked around the room,

and his voice was shaded with admiration. "You are a marvelous artist, Miss Winslow. I wish I could—" He broke off and shook his head as if embarrassed.

"You wish you could what, Sir Colin?"

"Please, just Colin, if you will. I was going to say the hardest part of this novel for me is trying to understand the heart of your art. I know several sculptors in Europe and the States, some of them rather famous, but they don't care to talk about their craft. At least not to an unproved novelist. I was going to ask if, perhaps, if you could spare a little time to tell me how you feel about sculpture."

Ordinarily Sharon would have refused such an offer, but Sir Colin seemed pleasant enough, and she decided she could spare the time. "I'd be glad to have you come out to my studio, Sir . . . er, Colin. And please call me Sharon."

"Thank you ever so much, Sharon. I say, that's ripping!"

"Now that my show is over, I'll be free anytime after today."

"Would tomorrow be too soon? I hate to be pushy, but I am anxious to get on with my book."

"That would be fine. Shall we say one o'clock?"

"I will certainly be there."

"You say you know of some famous sculptors. May I ask who?"

"Well, Henri Matisse is a good friend of mine. I stay with him quite often at his home on the Mediterranean. I've met the American sculptor Paul Manship and the young British sculptor Barbara Hepworth. I can't quite figure out Miss Hepworth's work, however. Her sculptures don't make sense to me."

Sharon hesitated. She had seen some of Hepworth's sculptures, and many of them consisted of pieces of wood glued together into rather formal patterns. It was not the sort of work she admired, but Barbara Hepworth was becoming an international name. "I suppose it takes all kinds, and it depends on one's tastes. I could never sculpt like Miss Hepworth, but I do like and admire Mr. Manship's work."

"He's not the most cordial man in the world. I think he's so caught up with what he does that he doesn't really care about anyone around him. Lives in his own world of art, you know?"

"Yes, I understand. I'm a little that way myself, I suppose."

"Well, Sharon, I am delighted to have met you, but I know you're tired and need to get home. I'll take my leave and look forward to our meeting tomorrow."

"Fine. I'll be expecting you."

★ ★ ★

"Mother, Dad, I'd like for you to meet our guest, Sir Colin Hardie. Sir Colin, I'd like you to meet my parents."

"So pleased to meet you, Mr. and Mrs. Winslow. Your daughter was so kind to invite me. I know she is overwhelmed by those who would take her time. I promise to be brief."

"Oh no, indeed!" Lucille cried eagerly. "We've prepared a small lunch. We'd be most happy for you to join us, Sir Colin."

"Most kind, but I wouldn't want to be any trouble."

"How could you be that?" Leland beamed. "Come along and tell us about this book you're working on."

During the luncheon Sharon sat back and let her parents carry the conversation. She could tell they were impressed with Sir Colin, especially knowing that he was of royal blood. He was certainly an accomplished man in his own right with excellent manners, yet he displayed none of the snobbishness one might expect of the British aristocracy. He was articulate, a good listener, and fine looking.

"Did you leave your family behind in England, Sir Colin?" Lucille asked.

"My parents? Yes, as a matter of fact I did."

"I mean your wife."

"Oh, I'm sorry to say that I lost my wife less than a year ago."

"Oh, I'm so sorry," Lucille expressed.

"It's been very hard, but I'm trying to go on with my life. Losing a loved one is not unlike losing a leg in an accident. You will always limp, but you learn to survive."

Sharon exclaimed, "That's exactly the way I've always felt, Colin!"

Sir Colin nodded. "She was a wonderful woman, and I had my best years with her." He shook his head. "But about this daughter of yours," he said to her parents, "I don't want to impose on her, but it's most helpful to talk to a true artist who is willing to share what it's like to create such beautiful sculptures."

After the meal Colin bowed to Lucille, taking her hand and kissing it. "You are very gracious, Mrs. Winslow." Turning to Leland, he said, "And thank you, sir, for opening up your home."

"We have Sharon to thank for that. This luncheon was her idea. And, I might add, she rarely invites anyone to her studio."

"Then I feel honored indeed!"

"Come along, Colin," Sharon said. "I'll take you to my studio. I won't work today, but we can talk."

She led the way out of the house and through the gardens to the studio, where she showed him all her pieces she had not taken to the gallery, explaining each one in detail. "These are some of my earliest pieces. You can plainly see my awkward first attempts." Sharon humbly and openly shared with him that she began her work at a special camp for mental health patients.

"Hannah did tell me about that," Colin said quietly, with sympathy in his eyes. "But you've made a marvelous recovery."

"Yes, and I believe it was all God's doing. He put me in

that place at that time to give me just the help I needed."

As they moved around looking at various pieces, Sir Colin stopped in front of the full-size statue of Robert, studying it silently while Sharon stood back and watched. He shook his head. "I've never seen such a work. Is it one of your earlier pieces?"

"I started it when I came home from the Camp and worked on it for a year. It gave me a great deal of satisfaction."

"The details are amazingly accurate. I was in the war, you know."

"Really?"

"Yes, the First Fusiliers. Lucky to get out of it alive. I met many Yanks over there. Did you use a model for this one?"

Sharon hesitated, not wanting to reveal that it was of the man she had loved. "In a way," she started slowly, "but I wanted it to stand for all of the men who risked their lives in combat to keep our freedom. I simply call it 'The Soldier.'"

Sir Colin turned to her. "It's a marvelous work." His voice was quiet, his eyes warm with admiration. "God has certainly put a special gift in your hands."

"That's very kind of you to say. Why don't we go back to the house and have some tea, and you can tell me about your book."

Sir Colin stayed much longer than the hour he had asked for, and when he left, Lucille came to Sharon, beaming. "Such a fine man! I do hope he succeeds with his book."

"I know very little about such things. I understand publishing is difficult to break into."

"I'm sure you'll help him all you can."

Sharon nodded and smiled slightly. "Yes, I believe I will. He was a soldier, you know, and I can't do enough for those fellows."

★ ★ ★

Mabel, the cook, was gossiping in the kitchen with the house maid, Ruth, a diminutive girl with enormous blue eyes. ". . . and Miss Sharon has been out with Sir Colin a dozen times," she gushed. "Since I've known her, she's never been out with anyone. Not after her fiancé died, so I hear."

Ruth sighed. "He's such a handsome man, and so obliging. He always says the nicest things, even to me."

"Yes, he does. I'm sure Sharon is in love with him."

"Do you think she'll marry him?"

"Of course! There's no doubt!"

"Oh, Mabel. When she goes home with him to live in his castle, maybe she'll take me with her as her maid. Just think of that. Me in a castle in England."

"Do you think Mr. and Mrs. Winslow would agree to that?"

"I don't know, but I'm sure they would agree to her marrying him. They are both so very fond of him! It's taken her a long time to get over Mr. Robert, but she appears to have done it at last."

★ ★ ★

Sharon was laughing as she got out of the car one afternoon and took Colin's arm to go into the house. He was telling her a story of his polo days, and as usual, made himself the brunt of the story.

"I fell off that ignoramus of a horse right in front of the queen. And my trousers, I'm afraid to say, ripped in the back from the belt all the way down."

Sharon giggled and said, "What did you do?"

"There wasn't much I could do. I looked at the queen, and I saw that she was laughing, so it was all right, you see."

They entered the house, and Sharon said, "I'm starved! Let me fix us something to eat."

"That sounds good. Can you cook?"

"I can make tea and sandwiches. Come along."

Sharon led him to the kitchen, and although Mabel was there, Sharon insisted on making the tea and sandwiches herself.

"Don't eat too much, Miss Sharon," Mabel said. "It's nearly dinnertime. Will you be staying for dinner, Sir Colin?"

"Probably so. I've become such a beggar, but your cooking is so good I can barely face restaurant food anymore."

"Of course you're invited," Sharon spoke up. "Now, you sit down."

Busying herself in the kitchen, Sharon listened as Colin told another story, keeping both her and Mabel in fits of laughter. *How very easy it is to be with him,* she thought, not meaning to compare him with Robert but realizing that he was the most amiable and pleasant man she had met since her first love.

When the tea and sandwiches were ready, Sharon filled a tray and suggested they go out to the gazebo in the garden, where they could enjoy their refreshment in private. Colin took the tray from her and they left Mabel to her dinner preparations as they made their way through the garden. "Polo is such a ridiculous game," he said, picking up their earlier conversation. "I've always hated the game myself. My father insisted I take up the sport, so I did, but I hated every minute of it. Why do you suppose we do things like that simply because we're expected to?"

"I'm sure I don't know," Sharon said as they entered the gazebo. She set the tray on a small table they moved within reach of the bench running around the edge of the structure.

"I think we're simply slaves to custom, Sharon. Don't you agree?"

"I expect so."

"Well, I for one am not going to do it anymore!"

"You're not going to play polo anymore?"

Colin took a bite of his sandwich as she filled his teacup, then said with an excited light in his eyes, "I'm not going to live according to social custom anymore. I'm tired of the social whirl. Had it all my life, and I don't need any more of it."

"What will you do, then?"

He sighed. "I've been thinking about this for some time. I have a small house on the Shetland Islands. Right on the coast. Oh, the house isn't all that much. Nothing like the place in England, of course, but it's ever so cozy. Like something out of a Dickens novel. And the sea is so beautiful there. It gets wild sometimes. There's nothing I like better than walking along the rocky coast and letting the wind whip me about the face. Sometimes I just shout I'm so exalted by it."

Sharon listened with interest, for he had never spoken of this before. "What's it like in the summer?"

"Oh, it's so lovely. The grass is so green it hurts your eyes. The flowers grow like weeds, only more beautiful, of course. And you know what I like? Every day in the summer I can spend the entire day walking through the woods or sitting there watching the ocean. Sometimes I go in for a swim."

"It sounds lovely."

Colin grew meditative. "I grow so lonely for it. There're no cars, no radio. Just the sea, a small village, and very real, warm people."

Sharon was fascinated. "I envy you, Colin. That sounds like heaven on earth to me."

He did not speak for a time, just looked down at his hands, which he had folded in his lap. She wondered if something were wrong or if she had offended him in some way. He lifted his eyes and cleared his throat. "I don't know how to say this, Sharon. It's very difficult for me."

"What is it?" Sharon was mystified by this uncharacteristic uncertainty. He had always seemed so sure of himself.

"I have been working up the courage to ask you if . . . if you'd like to go with me."

The silence that followed filled her inner being. His eyes

were locked on hers with an intensity she had not seen before. When she did not speak, he said quickly, "I know we haven't known each other very long, but I love everything about you, Sharon. I love the way you look, but even more than that I love the way you are. How everything you do is right and good. I've seen so little true kindness in my world, but I see it in you."

She was still unable to speak. In all truth she had wondered lately what it would be like to be married to Sir Colin Hardie. She would then be Lady Sharon. This did not impress her, however, as much as did the sincerity of his words.

When she remained silent, Colin reached over and took her hand, and he smiled and shrugged his shoulders in a now-familiar gesture. "I know that many men have pursued you—and some of them for the wrong reasons. I'm not as wealthy a man as you might expect—not in the sense that your family is. My family is old and respected, but we don't live on the scale that you do. I'm afraid your parents would not look on such a union with favor."

"You're right about one thing, Colin. Men have shown attention to me, but I've learned to recognize those who want me for reasons other than for myself. And I truly don't think you're one of those men."

Colin rose and drew her to her feet. He leaned forward and, for the first time, kissed her on the lips. It was a strange kiss, restrained and yet with a hint of passion, and Sharon felt herself responding. She was surprised when he drew back and shook his head. "I don't want to press you, because the advantages would all be on my side."

"Why would you say that?"

"Because you're successful, and I'm just beginning a career. I may never make it as a writer."

"I think you will, Colin. From what you've shown me, I think you have great talent."

He smiled then, and his face grew animated. "Do you really think so? That's so encouraging."

She touched his cheek. "I am honored that you have thought of me in this way, Colin."

"I'm glad you feel that way about it. As I say, I won't press you, but I implore you to try to think of me as a man you might marry. I think it best if I take my leave now and allow you to think about this, Sharon." He lifted her hand, kissed it, and smiled. "I won't sleep a wink tonight, thinking of what we've said. Good evening, my dear."

After Colin left, Sharon took a walk around the gardens, pondering his proposal. He had shown signs of deep affection before, but even so the conversation had caught her off guard, for they had not known each other all that long.

When she went back in the house, she met her mother and told her at once, "Colin has asked me to marry him."

Lucille blinked with surprise and exclaimed, "Has he really! Did you say yes?"

"I didn't give him an answer yet. You must understand something, Mother. He's told me that his people are not as rich as you might think."

"Oh, I'm sure he's just being modest, dear. Judging by the way he conducts himself, he must have a wonderful family—and so well respected. Just think, you'd be Lady Sharon! I can only imagine Agnes Astor's face on learning that news."

CHAPTER TWELVE

WHEN THE SUN GOES OUT

★ ★ ★

Clayton sat in Sharon's studio, chattering as she worked on a new piece. "You know, Sharon, Dad has told me I can have a car when I'm sixteen. I want a Stutz Bearcat."

"That's a pretty racy car. Think you can handle it?"

"I sure can." He jumped off his stool and pulled at her smock. "Hey, let's go out in your car. You can start teachin' me to drive."

Sharon turned to him and laughed. She had only just learned to drive recently herself. Now that the family no longer lived in the city, Sharon decided it was more practical to drive herself around rather than constantly relying on the chauffeur. Without her parents' knowing at first, she had begged their young chauffeur, Mike Jones, to teach her to drive. Now she thoroughly enjoyed her private jaunts around the county to visit antique shops and small art galleries. It was the first time in her life she had experienced such freedom. Now she looked with pride at her handsome young brother and found it hard to refuse such a request. "I'll have to think about that. Dad isn't all that happy yet with my own driving. He'd skin me alive if he caught us."

"No he wouldn't. We know how to handle Mom and Dad."

"You're pretty sure of that, aren't you?"

Suddenly switching subjects, Clayton asked, "Are you going to marry Colin?"

Sharon had not yet given Colin a final answer, but she had certainly given him encouragement. Her parents seemed to feel she had found an ideal partner, but she still was not able to take the final plunge. "I'm not sure, Clayton."

"Why not? Don't you want to have kids?"

"Yes, I'd like to."

"You need a husband for that." Clayton studied her and then said with a positive nod, "I hope you do marry him. You'd be Lady Sharon Hardie then, wouldn't you?"

"I would. Do you think that's important?"

"Sure it's important. We could all go to England and meet the king and queen."

Sharon listened to his patter, troubled that Clayton had absorbed so much of his parents' preoccupation with high society. She reached out and ruffled his auburn hair. "I think you're a lot more important to me than any king or queen. Come on. Let's take a ride, and if you're good, maybe I'll let you steer a little."

★   ★   ★

Sir Colin came later that day and sat quietly in the studio, watching Sharon work. She had never been able to tolerate anyone other than her little brother doing this, and it amazed her that she didn't mind. But he was so quiet, never saying a word unless she spoke to him. It was comforting just to have him nearby. Of course, she enjoyed his company when she wasn't working as well. He had received a fine education in England and knew far more about literature than she did and certainly more about current events. Sometimes he laughed at her for not knowing basic facts that any British schoolchild would be expected to know.

At one point, while she was taking a break, he came over to her and, without warning, put his arms around her, drawing her close. Sharon saw that he was intensely serious.

"I've said all along that I didn't want to press you, but now I'm going to do exactly that. I love you, Sharon. I always will. I'd like to have your answer if you can give it."

Sharon almost gave him the answer he so ardently longed for, but she was not ready to make the final decision. "Give me one more month, Colin," she said, "and then I'll give you your answer. I promise."

"It'll be a long month for me, but I can wait." He kissed her then, and as she returned his kiss, she felt a strong desire for a lifelong companion. She had not realized how lonely she was, but now in the comfort of his arms she knew what her answer was going to be.

★   ★   ★

The month passed quickly while Sharon thought about and prayed over her decision to marry Colin. She did not feel completely at peace about it, but she also realized she was not getting any younger and this could well be her last chance to marry a respectable man who clearly loved her. August brought hot, sultry weather, but neither she nor Colin seemed to notice as they walked about the grounds of the Winslow estate. As they stood beside the lily pond tossing bread crumbs to the ducks, she turned to him and said, "Colin, I've decided I will marry you."

His eyes lit up with joy. "I'm so happy, my dear, and I promise I will make you a happy woman."

As he kissed her, Sharon felt a sense of release. *At least now the decision is made,* she thought. *I just hope it's the right one.*

They went inside to tell her parents and celebrate together over the evening meal. Later that night after Colin had left, she wrote to Hannah Fulton, who was summering with her family in Sussex, England. After sharing her news, she wrote,

> *I know that Colin's family lives in Sussex. It would be so nice if you could meet them and give me a report about them. I'm sure they must be wonderful people, but I would love to get your opinion of them. I hope this news makes you happy. I know you've wanted me to marry for a long time, and now I finally will. So wish me well.*
>
> > *Your dear friend,*
> > *Sharon*

The days that followed were exciting ones for Sharon. She wrote letters to Dr. Steiner and Dr. Chardoney and to many of her other friends, inviting them to the wedding and telling them how happy she was. The announcement of her engagement was published in the newspaper, and wedding plans were made for the first Saturday of November, 1928.

"I wish it could be sooner," Colin told her one night as they walked in the garden, "but I suppose I'm simply impatient. You've made me the happiest man in the world, and I know we're going to have a wonderful life together."

Sharon smiled. "I know we're going to be happy. You're going to become a wildly successful novelist—putting Charles Dickens to shame."

Colin laughed, his white teeth gleaming in the moonlight. "I would settle for far less than that."

"When do you think you'll finish your book?"

"I'll have to interrupt it for our honeymoon, of course, but once we settle in at our home in the Shetlands, I'll have time. I won't have anything to do but concentrate on my book—and you, sweetheart."

★　★　★

October arrived, and with it Sharon's anxiety about the wedding increased. *Perhaps if I were younger,* she reasoned, *I wouldn't be feeling all these doubts. I will simply have to put them away.*

On the third day of the month she got a letter from Hannah that puzzled her. Hannah wrote about what she and her children were doing but did not address the subject of Sharon's coming marriage until the end of the letter:

> *I'll be coming home shortly, Sharon. There's something I must tell you about Colin that I wouldn't care to put in a letter. I know it's awful to mention something and then say, "I'm not going to tell you," but I'd really rather talk to you about it face-to-face. And in fact, it may come to nothing.*

When Sharon mentioned to Colin that Hannah had visited his family and would be home soon, Colin said, "That will be nice for you. I know you've been missing your friend." He was looking out the window when he turned impulsively and came over to her. "There's something you should know about me, Sharon. I probably should have told you before."

"What is it? It can't be all that bad."

"I'm afraid you'll think so." He grimaced and said, "I hate weddings."

"What?"

"I do. I hate weddings. I never go unless I absolutely have to. Well, it's not that I hate weddings so much," he admitted with a shrug. "It's the big, fancy weddings I can't stand. There's nothing I'd like better than to go to a small chapel and see a man and woman stand up with a few close friends and family members. All this expense and fuss about dresses and bridesmaids . . . frankly, it drives me up a wall." He took her hands in his and looked into her eyes. "Let's do something daring, Sharon."

She stared at him with consternation. "Daring! Like what?"

"Let's just elope," Colin said. He slipped his arms around

her and kissed her warmly. "Let's just get married and go to our place in the Shetlands."

"Why, Colin, I couldn't do that to my parents. It wouldn't be right. The wedding's only a month away. I know what you're feeling. I get tired of the preparations too, but it means so much to my parents. Especially to Mother. We just have to go through with it."

Colin seemed inclined to argue, but he no doubt could tell that her mind was made up on this. "All right. But it's all so unnecessary."

★ ★ ★

A week after this conversation Sharon was being fitted for her wedding dress. She had marked in her journal that morning, *October 10, 1928, a day I never thought I'd see—I'm actually getting fitted for a wedding dress.*

Now she stood still as the tailor did his work on the shimmering white gown, her mother fluttering about in a state of almost frantic excitement. Sharon felt a sudden intense nervousness that had been growing in her. She thought of her first fiancé, and, not for the first time, she wondered: *Am I failing Robert? I told him I'd always love him, but he told me that if he didn't come back from France, I should go on with my life. And that's what I'm doing.*

That evening after dinner Sharon was in her room talking with Ruth about the matter of the trousseau when a knock at the open door interrupted her. The butler stuck his head inside and said, "Two ladies to see you, Miss Sharon."

"Ladies? Who are they?"

"One of them is Miss Fulton. I don't know who the other one is."

"All right. I'll come right down. Ruth, we'll continue our discussion later this evening."

Sharon left her room and went downstairs into the drawing room. She was excited to see Hannah again. Next to her was another lady Sharon did not know. Hannah came forward and put her arms around Sharon, but Sharon's happiness at seeing her friend again was overshadowed by her tense look and pinched features.

Sharon hugged her friend in return, but on seeing her face said, "Is something wrong, Hannah?" A sense of foreboding came over her. She glanced at the other woman cautiously, a rather attractive blond woman in her late twenties, she would guess.

"This is Miss Mona Pierce," Hannah said. "She's from England. I brought her with me because—" Hannah broke off, unable to find the right words, and finally said hurriedly—"I want you to listen to her story. I'll wait outside."

"Why . . . of course." Sharon waited until Hannah had left the room, then turned and said, "What is it, Miss Pierce?"

Mona Pierce was dressed in the latest fashions, but there was a troubled air about her. "I'm afraid I have some news for you, Miss Winslow, that will not be welcome. Mrs. Fulton found me and told me about your engagement to Colin. We had several long talks, and she finally persuaded me to come to America with her. She felt you needed to hear this from me."

"Hear what, Miss Pierce?" Fear filled Sharon's heart over what this woman might have traveled all this way to tell her about Colin. She stood rigidly still as she listened to the woman speak.

"I fell in love with Colin when he was eighteen years old," Mona began, "and I must tell you we were lovers. He was going to marry me, but he had no money. An older woman with a great deal of money fell in love with Colin, and he married her instead."

Sharon felt that the world was stopping. She knew Mona Pierce had not finished her story, but Sharon had already heard enough to know she could not possibly marry Colin now.

"We kept up our relationship all through the years they

were married. During this time I got pregnant and bore him a son. Colin is an impulsive gambler, and he ran through his wife's money rapidly. She died about a year ago, and by then there was little money left."

"But how could he marry another woman if he loved you?" Sharon whispered.

"You'll have to understand Colin. His family had a great deal of money at one time, and he grew accustomed to it. But they lost most of it, largely through Colin's extravagances. They still have their home in England and a reputable family name but hardly any money at all. Colin's only solution was to find a rich woman to marry, but as I said, he lost most of his wife's money too."

The room was deathly quiet except for the ticking of the grandfather clock. It tolled out the seconds as if with an air of doom as the woman continued to speak. "After his wife died I thought we would marry, but Colin said it was impossible. That he would have to marry a wealthy woman. He told me he was coming to America to find an heiress."

Sharon felt that the sun had gone out of her. She could not speak for a long time and knew she was trembling. She had to say something to this woman and finally asked, "How did Mrs. Fulton find you?"

"She found and met the Hardie family, and she heard rumors. I think she hired a private detective to investigate them. It wouldn't have been hard to find me because our relationship is no secret to anyone. She came to me and asked about Colin, and I simply told her what I've just told you." The woman lifted her head then and said, "Colin is weak, but I love him—even though I don't think he will ever marry me."

Sharon sat still through all of this, her face frozen. She desperately wanted to weep, to lash out, but she kept an iron grip on herself. "I appreciate your coming to tell me this, Miss Pierce. I know you haven't done so out of a vindictive spirit."

"No, indeed. Mrs. Fulton convinced me that you were a

good woman and that you didn't know Colin's background."

"I would be glad to reimburse you for any expense—"

"Oh no," Mona said. "Mrs. Fulton is taking care of all of
that. I just . . . I just didn't want another woman to be hurt
by him. It wouldn't have worked out happily for you."

Sharon got up and walked to the door. Opening it, she
said quietly, "Come in, Hannah."

When Hannah came in, Sharon saw there were tears in
her eyes. "I didn't want to hurt you, Sharon, but my own
marriage has been so unhappy. I made a mistake in marrying the wrong man. I couldn't let you do the same thing.
You can't marry him now."

"No, of course not."

Sharon turned to thank Mona for coming but stopped
midsentence when Ruth came in and said, "Sir Colin is here,
Miss Sharon."

Sharon's eyes met Mona's, and taking a deep breath, she
said, "Ask him to come in, Ruth."

"Yes, ma'am."

Sir Colin Hardie entered the door and stopped as
abruptly as if he had run into a stone wall. The room was
silent, and his face went absolutely pale. Sharon saw that he
was stricken, and despite the hurt she felt, she found she
could not lash out at him as she had already planned to.

"Hello, Mona," Colin said in a voice drained of emotion.
He seemed to have shrunk in stature, and when he turned
to Sharon, the expression in his eyes conveyed total and
helpless loss. Sharon did not move but said, "I hope you'll
find your way, Colin."

Colin looked at her sadly, then turned and said, "Come,
Mona, it's time to go."

Sharon did not watch them leave together. She turned
her back, and when the door had closed, she felt Hannah's
hand on her shoulder. She still did not turn, and Hannah
said in a broken tone, "This is going to be so hard for you.
Your parents will be devastated—and the society columns

in the papers will have a field day!"

Sharon felt nothing. Devoid of all emotion, she said without turning, "One thing I know, Hannah—I'll never be put in this position again. Not ever!"

PART THREE

March–June 1935

★ ★ ★

CHAPTER THIRTEEN

CLAYTON TAKES A FALL

★ ★ ★

Leland Winslow leaned back in his chair and studied the beautiful landscape that lay before him. March had come in gently, and already the mild weather had coaxed the grass into a beautiful emerald green on the estate of Leland's good friend, Vernon Wells. The lawn was as level as a pool table, and Leland watched as a man on the far side of the lawn worked assiduously in a flower bed. Turning to his host, Leland said with admiration, "Vernon, I do believe you've got the most beautiful grounds in America."

Vernon Wells was a diminutive man in contrast to Leland's height. The only thing large about him was his head—and according to many, his oversized head was stuffed with more brains than the entire working force of the New York Stock Exchange, where he had made his fortune. Wells had a rather sharklike expression, and he now exposed his small, perfectly formed teeth as he said, "It should be. It cost enough."

Stirring in his chair, Leland's mind went back to October 1929 when Black Tuesday, the darkest day in American economics, hit. That had been more than five years ago, but he would never forget it. He thought of how he himself had nearly gone under, but Vernon had helped him, keeping him out of bankruptcy court. He pondered the last several bitter years of depression America had been suffering. A chill came over him at how close he had come to being out on the streets. He had learned of the tragic downfall of a distant cousin of his whom he had never met, even though both families lived in New York. Lewis Winslow had lost everything and been forced to take his family south to live on a farm in Georgia.

"Vernon, you might get tired of hearing it, but I think so often of how you saved my bacon when the stock market fell in twenty-nine. If it hadn't been for you, I'd probably be in the poorhouse." He flashed a smile at the smaller man. "I'll never forget that."

Wells waved his hand in a gesture of dismissal. "You don't need to ever thank me again. You've done that. It's ancient history."

"Maybe for you, but sometimes I still wake up in a cold sweat when I think of where I'd be if it hadn't been for you. I might have jumped off a building."

"No, I can't imagine you'd take your own life over money, Leland. And leave your family to suffer alone? You're a better man than that."

The air was filled with the smells of spring, the verdant earth releasing its odors that had lain frozen all winter long. With the snows gone, spring flowers were beginning to peep out from beneath the crust of dead leaves, proclaiming the advent of another year. From one of the ornamental pear trees close to where the men sat, a small brown bird began trilling a sweet sound.

"What kind of bird is that, I wonder?" Leland murmured.

"Song sparrow. I love them. Sweetest singing bird in the world. Not powerful but sweet. You know, that sparrow reminds me of your daughter. I heard her sing in church two weeks ago. Beautiful voice."

"I've always thought so."

"You know, I thought at one time she might take up singing as a career."

"Oh, that was just a passing fancy. Where would one of our social class sing? I couldn't see Sharon singing in a music hall or on Broadway."

"Opera perhaps."

"You have to be first class for that, Vernon. She doesn't have the voice for it."

"Well, she doesn't need it. She has her art. I read that story about her last month in *Life* magazine. I know you were proud."

"Yes, I was. Very proud indeed." The story had brought an avalanche of fan mail, which Sharon did not appreciate. She felt obligated to answer all the letters and had had to hire a secretary to take care of that unwanted chore.

"Is there a lot of money in art, Leland?"

"If you're at the top there is, and of course, Sharon's at the top now." He shook his head in wonder. "She refuses to take a penny of my money now that she makes her own, although of course, I'll be dividing everything between her and Clayton when Lucille and I are gone."

"How is Clayton these days? Still determined to be an architect?"

"Yes, he is. And he'll be a good one too. We're very proud of him. He was at the top of his class last year. He's only nineteen, almost twenty, so he's got a ways to go yet."

Leland found it very relaxing to sit quietly conversing with his friend. He had come here often in the last few lean years when he had struggled to bring his lumber business back to a profitable level. Very few people had the money to build these days, but somehow with Vernon Wells's help, he found businesses that could afford to buy lumber again and was recovering nicely from the sudden downslide. "We've got a problem at home," he said as he studied the man digging in the flower bed. "My gardener is retiring. Don't know how I'll replace him."

Vernon turned and exclaimed, "Now, isn't that just like the Lord!"

Vernon's comments sometimes confused Leland, and he raised his eyebrows with surprise. "What do you mean by that? What does the Lord have to do with it?"

"Do you see that fellow over there?" Wells indicated the man working in the flower bed. "His name is Morgan—Gwilym Morgan."

"What's that name again?"

"It's Welsh. G-w-i-l-y-m. It's the Welsh form of William, so everyone calls him William, except me. I call him Gwilym because I like the sound of it. Let me tell you, he's your man. I believe God put him here and then brought you here today so the two of you could meet."

Leland burst into laughter and reached over and squeezed his friend's thin arm. "So you think life is all laid out like a play, and all we're doing is acting out our part?"

"Not quite like that," Wells said, shaking his head. "But I do think God engineers circumstances for our good. Let me tell you about Gwilym. He's a cousin to my own gardener. Things are very bad in Wales, so he came over to this country to find work. My man asked about putting him on, and though we didn't need additional help, I agreed. But Ben tells me he's a fine gardener. Knows everything about every flower and could make grass grow on the highway. If I didn't have Benny, I'd hire him myself."

Leland looked with interest at the man digging across the lawn and said, "That would be fine if he would work out. Would you be sorry to lose him?"

"No, put him as the head of your grounds and turn him loose. Come along. I'll introduce you."

The two men walked across the emerald grass, and when they approached the flower bed, the digger turned. He was not a large man but very trim and fit. He wore dark brown trousers, a white shirt, and a tie. The idea of wearing a necktie in the garden amused Leland. The musical sound of

Wales was in his voice as he said, "It's happy I am to know you, Mr. Winslow."

"I understand you've come over from the old country recently."

"Yes, sir, and sad I was to have to leave. But Mr. Wells here has been very kind to my daughter and me."

"You have a daughter and a wife?"

"No wife, sir. I lost my dear wife two years ago."

"I'm sorry to hear it."

"She's with me every day," Morgan said simply and without any trace of embarrassment.

"My gardener is leaving me," Leland went on. "He's been with me for many years, but he's finally retiring. Would you like to come and work for me, see how we get on?"

"That would be fine with me, sir, but Mr. Wells must say."

"It'll be a great thing for both of you, Gwilym. Why don't you two talk terms, and then when you come back to the house, Leland, I'll beat you in another game of chess."

"Beat me in *another game*! You haven't beaten me in a month."

"Well, today just might be the day I'll lay you on the ground," Vernon said with a chuckle.

As Vernon walked back toward the house, Leland and Gwilym discussed wages and other circumstances concerning the job. "There's a cottage for you as well—not large, but it has two bedrooms and is well furnished."

"That sounds very fine. My daughter works at a hospital in Manhattan. She's training to be a nurse."

"Then we'll have to figure out how to get her to the hospital, but I'm sure we can work out something. Someone's always going into town and coming home. And there are taxis."

"Oh, I do have a car, sir. It's not in great shape, but we've learned to nurse that Model T Ford along."

"How soon could you come?"

"I could come tomorrow if that would satisfy."

"Indeed it would. I'll look for you then, William." He gave directions to his house and shook hands with the man, noticing that Morgan's hand was not large but felt powerful. Leland walked back to the house and joined Vernon, who was sitting at a table in the parlor in front of the chess game he had set up.

"Did you make the agreement?" Vernon asked.

"Yes, very satisfactory."

"He'll make that place of yours hum. You wait and see. Now, sit down and take your beating like a man."

★ ★ ★

Seana Morgan pulled the old Model T up to the small house that she and her father were renting and went inside. Her father turned from the stove where he was cooking, his eyes bright with excitement. "Very good news, daughter."

"Good news, is it, now? And what would that be?" The twenty-one-year-old had red hair and beautiful green eyes. Her face was oval, her features strong, her lips broad. She was not a Hollywood type, but she had a beautiful figure that even the starched white uniform she wore could not conceal. Her speech, like her father's, was rich with the lyrical Welsh accent. Putting down her purse, she came over and gave her father a kiss. "Well, are you going to tell me?"

"I've got a new job with a family named Winslow." He went on to tell her the terms, and she was pleased at the salary. "And the best thing is, it has a cottage that goes with it. We'll each have our own bedroom, and it's already furnished."

"Well, bless us all! Isn't that wonderful!" Seana's eyes shone. Never one to hold back her emotions, she kissed her father again, then twirled across the floor in a series of circles. "Now we'll make that house a bit of old Wales!"

★ ★ ★

Sharon looked out the front parlor window when she heard a car approaching. She had been reading a book while waiting for the new gardener and his daughter to arrive. The old Model T Ford backfired a couple of times before stopping in the driveway. The butler had the day off, so she opened the door herself and invited them in. "Good morning," she said with a smile, "You must be Gwilym Morgan."

"Indeed I am, ma'am."

"I am Sharon Winslow. My father asked me to look after you when you got here. My parents are in town on business."

"There's kind of you, Miss Winslow. This is my daughter, Seana."

Sharon turned to the daughter and said, "It's so nice to meet you, Seana." *What an attractive girl*, she thought. "Come along, and I'll show you to the cottage."

Sharon walked to the cottage while the father and daughter got back in the car. The cottage was on the edge of a group of oaks that grew high into the air, and she turned and waited until the pair got out of the ancient vehicle.

"There is beautiful, it is!" the young woman exclaimed, her eyes sparkling as she impulsively hugged her father. "You see how the good God takes care of us, Father?"

"Indeed I do."

The trio went inside, and both William and Seana showed their pleasure openly. The large main room had a small kitchen at one end with a gas cookstove, at which Seana exclaimed with delight, "No more ashes and smoke!" She opened the cabinets and found they were filled with dishes and plenty of cooking utensils. A round dining room table and four chairs rounded out the kitchen area. "This is fine indeed!" Seana said. "Wait you, now"—she smiled at her father—"see if I don't fatten you up like an old pig."

The rest of the room was comfortably furnished with a

leather couch, two easy chairs, and brass floor lamps. The walls were papered in a cheerful light blue pattern. The two bedrooms down the hall from the main room were across from each other, and both were surprisingly large and furnished with beds, dressers, and ample closets. The bathroom was immaculate.

"I hope you'll find it comfortable here," Sharon said.

"What kind of people would we be if we didn't find this comfortable? It's like heaven on earth, isn't it, Father?"

"It is indeed. Very luxurious, Miss Winslow."

Sharon thought of the opulence of the mansion she lived in and for a moment a strange feeling assailed her. *These people think this is a mansion. I've been spoiled beyond redemption.* She was enjoying the company of these two pleasant people. Turning to the girl, she said, "I understand that you're in the nursing program at City Hospital."

"Yes, indeed, and a fine hospital it is, ma'am."

"Have you wanted to be a nurse a long time?"

"Forever," Seana said with an intensity that seemed to fill the room.

"She had no chance in Wales to get any special training," Gwilym said. "You can look at her hands and see she worked like a man on the farm with me."

"You were farmers, then?"

"I was a coal miner in my younger days. Then I farmed the old home place, but there was no living in that, so I took a job working for a big landowner, caring for his grounds. Seana here, she worked right alongside of me." Affection was evident in Gwilym Morgan's face as he said, "She's a wonder of a girl, she is. That's the truth of it, ma'am."

"Well, I'm so happy you've come. Your reputation has preceded you, William. Mr. Wells says you're the second-best gardener in the world," Sharon said with a smile. "He thinks his own man, Benny, is the best, of course."

"I hope to please. It's good to be here in this amazing big country where a man can spread himself out."

Sharon started to leave, but when she got to the door, she

turned back and said, "I realize you're going to be very busy for a time, Seana, but there's a favor you might do for me."

"Anything at all, Miss Winslow."

"Perhaps you don't know that I'm a sculptor. I'm always looking for models, and I wonder if you would pose for a bust for me."

"A bust? What's that?"

"Just a statue of your head and shoulders, not full length."

"Of me? Well, devil fly off! Wouldn't that be something, Father?"

"I'd love to see such a thing," Gwilym said.

"Then we'll get together and talk about it," Sharon said. "I usually pay my models a little something, so that might help."

"No need to pay me," Seana quickly replied.

"We'll argue about that later," Sharon said as she left.

When the door closed Seana turned to her father and swept him into an energetic dance, leaving him no choice but to dance too.

"Whist, woman! You're going to make a dance hall out of our new home?"

"Yes, and a concert stage too. There'll be singing and dancing in this house, or you'll find me flat on the floor!"

★　★　★

As Clayton got out of the car, he started toward the house, then decided instead to check on his new stallion first. He was wearing his best suit, tailor-made for him, for he had been to a dinner given by the dean of his college to the more promising students. The light gray double-breasted suit fit his tall figure admirably. He was an even six feet, trim and athletic. He loved swimming and was a member of the swimming team. Now as he moved, it was with a lazy grace. When he got to the stable, he saw that the doors were open and walked in. He couldn't see very well in the semidarkness, but he still moved confidently down the familiar corridor of stalls. He saw someone shoveling industriously and called out, "Is that you, Mack?" Mack was the boy who usually took care of mucking out the stables.

"No, it's not."

At first Clayton thought it was a boy clothed in a pair of overalls, but now that his eyes were adjusting to the dark, he quickly saw his mistake. It was a young woman with enormous eyes and red hair that escaped from beneath her soft hat. "Who are you?" he asked.

"It's Seana Morgan, I am."

"Seana Morgan? Are you the new stable hand here?"

"Indeed I am not!" Her voice had a lilt to it that caught his attention, and he studied her more closely. She had creamy skin and was probably not yet twenty, he imagined. Her attractive figure was apparent to him even under the work clothes she wore.

"Well, whoever you are, you're a better-looking hand than Mack. I'm Clayton Winslow."

"Happy to know you, I am."

Clayton was intrigued by the girl. In truth Clayton had a history of being flirtatious with the attractive young women who worked in the house. It was harmless fun, for he had not had a relationship with any of them. Now he said, "It's nice to come home and find a beautiful girl taking care of my horse."

Seana did not answer. Leaning against the shovel in her hands, she studied the forward young man. She had been warned about Clayton by one of the maids, who had giggled and said, "He likes to steal a kiss now and then. He's not as bad as some, but he might give you a hug. Don't make anything of it."

"What's the matter?" Seana asked.

"You don't come from this country, do you?"

"No, I'm from Wales."

"Wales, is it? I always make a habit of welcoming newcomers to America with a kiss."

He put his hands on her shoulders and attempted to kiss her but suddenly found himself shoved backward with a surprising strength. He cried, "Hey—!" as he staggered back, tripping and falling flat.

As soon as Clayton hit the ground, he knew he had fallen right into the pile of fresh manure Seana had been shoveling. Anger and embarrassment mingled as he got up, covered in the mess. He grabbed for a handkerchief but knew that he made a ridiculous sight.

"Why, you little vixen! You can't do that to me." Clayton started toward her, but she lifted the shovel in warning, her eyes as cold as polar ice.

"Stay away from me or I'll knock you down again!"

Clayton smelled the rank odor of the manure that covered the back of his new suit. He gritted his teeth and said, "You're fired!" then turned and stalked away. He was not accustomed to having women reject his advances, and he burned with anger.

He left and tried to sneak into the house without being seen, but of course, he encountered several of the servants. He could hear them giggling as he passed by, which did not help his emotional state.

★   ★   ★

Sharon looked up as Clayton came into the parlor. "Why, hello, Clayton. I didn't know—"

"Sharon, where's Dad?"

"He's in town. What's wrong?"

"It's that . . . that girl!"

"What girl?"

"The one who's working in the stable."

"Oh yes, that's Seana Morgan. She's the daughter of the new gardener, William."

"Well, she's not working here anymore. I fired her."

Sharon saw that Clayton was angry to the bone. "What happened?" she asked.

"She insulted me."

"Insulted you? How?"

"Never mind. She's fired!"

Sharon said, "She can't be fired."

"Why not?"

"Because she doesn't work for us. Her father does. She's training to be a nurse at City Hospital. She was just helping her father."

"Then he's fired too!"

Ordinarily Clayton was pleasant and courteous, but sometimes when his will was crossed, he could flare out unexpectedly. "Here, sit down and tell me what happened."

"I won't sit down! That girl is insolent." He tried to put her off, but Sharon got the story out of him. And he finished by saying, "And she ruined my best suit! You're lucky I've changed out of it already."

"Clayton, she didn't shove you down for nothing."

"I was just going to give her a little kiss."

"I see. Suppose one of the servants tried to give me a little kiss."

He muttered, "That's entirely different."

"I've known for a long time that you've taken liberties with some of the young women who work here. I think it's terrible of you. They have no defense."

"I never hurt any of them. Just give them a little kiss or a hug."

"Well, this girl is not one of our maids. If you forced yourself on her, I think she should have hit you with that shovel. I thought better of you, Clayton."

For a moment Clayton stood there, his face burning. He started to speak but clamped his lips together, turned, and walked out without a word.

Sharon watched him go and shook her head. *He's a good young man, but he thinks too much of himself. I'd like to congratulate Seana, and I will if she ever mentions it.*

CHAPTER FOURTEEN

A KNIGHT IN DENIM

★ ★ ★

Sharon ate breakfast hurriedly, listening to her parents talk about their plans for the day. She took a good look at her father, who at the age of sixty-seven was still a handsome man. His hair was now fully gray, but it was still healthy and glossy. His body had grown only slightly stooped and somewhat thick.

Her father remarked, "William Morgan is one of the finest gardeners in the United States. I'm monstrously proud that we were able to get him."

Sharon bit off a bit of toast and chewed it. "Clayton doesn't care much for William's daughter."

"What's the trouble there?" Leland frowned. "He told me I should fire William because of her, but he wouldn't tell me what the problem is. What's the girl done?"

Sharon did not think it fair to go into the details, so she simply summed up the incident. "Oh, you know how Clayton is. He's been kissing the maids since he was sixteen years old. He doesn't mean anything by it, of course, but when he tried it with Seana, she rejected him. I think his pride was hurt."

"Well, I can't fire the best gardener in the country simply because Clayton's feelings are hurt!"

"Perhaps the girl doesn't know her place," Lucille offered, taking up Clayton's cause, as was her habit. "I haven't met her, but he says she's insolent."

At one time Sharon would have sympathized more with her mother's defense of Clayton. He had always been the darling of Sharon's life. While he was growing up, she had been like a second mother to him, but in the last few years she had become painfully aware that Clayton was a tremendous snob, and she was no longer so willing to defend him. "He needs to be more careful how he treats people, Mother, especially those he considers beneath him. He thinks his behavior shows his superiority." Getting to her feet, she said, "I've got to go into town to get some art supplies. I won't be back until late this afternoon."

She left the house and went directly to her studio to make a list of needed supplies. The mild March weather had turned brisk and blustery, and she pulled her coat tightly about her as she came back to get in her car. As she did so, she saw Seana coming out of the cottage and called to her, "Good morning, Seana."

Looking up, Seana smiled and waved. She came over and said, "You're going into town, are you, Miss Winslow?"

"Look, why don't you just call me Sharon. I'm not your employer."

"That would be nice. Sharon's such a beautiful name."

"So is Seana. I suppose people misspell it all the time."

"Yes, they usually write S-h-a-u-n-a."

"What does Seana mean in Welsh?"

"Actually it's a Gaelic name. It means 'gift from God.'"

"How lovely!" Sharon smiled. For a moment she hesitated, then said, "I'm sorry about the trouble you had with Clayton. My brother is too forward and a bit high tempered. He's spoiled, and I'm sorry to admit I did most of the spoiling."

Seana had grown cautious as Sharon brought up the subject of Clayton, but when she saw the woman meant no harm, she laughed and ran her hand through her red hair. "He was a bit out of line, but he lost his dignity when he landed in that muck. I didn't really mean to do that."

"I would probably have done worse. Hit him with the shovel, I suppose." The two laughed together, and then Sharon asked, "You want to be a nurse very much, don't you?"

"Yes. I've wanted it for a long time."

"And then you'll work in a hospital?"

"I hope I'll be able to serve God as a missionary." Her smooth brow wrinkled slightly as she went on. "What I'd love to be is a doctor, but that costs too much. So I'll be a nurse, maybe in China or Africa. I know it sounds foolish, but God has put this desire on my heart."

Sharon was charmed by the girl. She had a simplicity about her that was completely natural and unassuming. Yet there was a hint of temper in her wide-spaced green eyes and a firmness about her mouth. "Well, I must go. I hope you have a good day, Seana."

"And may the good Lord make the grass green beneath your feet, Sharon."

Sharon laughed as she got into her new Ford station wagon. She was proud to have her own car now, and the station wagon was certainly an eye-catcher. She loved the look of the glossy walnut and birch that formed the outer body. More than its appearance, though, Sharon was delighted to have a car large enough to haul around her art supplies. She started the engine and, waving to Seana, took the car down the drive at a fast clip.

★ ★ ★

By the time Sharon had finished all of her business in town and loaded the back of the car with art supplies, it was late afternoon and she was anxious to get back home. Seeing that traffic was heavy on the main highway, she turned off onto a dirt road. The shortcut was a serpentine affair that wove back and forth between farm fields that were vacant now, for it was too early for spring planting.

She had gone approximately half the distance to her home when suddenly the car lurched, and there was a clanging sound followed by a whirring rattle. The car immediately lost power, and Sharon only had time to steer it to the edge of the dirt road before it rolled to a stop with a shudder.

She knew nothing about what made cars run, but nonetheless she got out, pulled up the hood, and stared at the engine. "What in the world is wrong with you?" she said to the car impatiently. She could see nothing wrong, of course, and shook her head with irritation. She looked around, but there was no house in sight. It would be dark in half an hour, and she tried to think how long it had been since she had passed a house where she might call for help. Not remembering any close by, she decided the only solution was to start walking home. She had walked no more than twenty feet when a vehicle appeared in the distance coming her way. Relief washed over her, and she went back to stand beside the Ford with its hood still up. As the vehicle approached, she saw that it was an old battered truck with two men inside.

"It's probably too much to hope that one of them is a mechanic," she muttered. "But at least they could take me home, and I can have a wrecker come out."

The truck rolled to a stop, and the driver pulled over in front of the Ford and got out. He was a huge, bulky man, and on the other side of the truck a smaller man got out, slamming the door. As the two approached her, the smaller man said, "Won'tcha lookee what we got here, Jake."

The big man had a blunt face with battered features and close-set eyes. "We got us a lady here, Ed," he said, grinning broadly, revealing yellowed teeth. "A damsel in distress them romances call it, I think."

Sharon felt a touch of fear. They were rough-looking men. The smaller one had a face like a ferret, and both of them wore shabby clothes with threadbare felt caps shoved back on their heads.

"Do you think you could help me with my car?" Sharon ventured. "It made a strange noise and then stopped."

"We won't worry about that, sweetie. We got plenty of time," the big man said, winking at the other. "Ain't that right, Ed?"

"Right you are, Jake. Ain't nobody around for miles. Looks like we can have ourselves a party." He pulled a flask from his inner coat pocket and took a hefty swallow before shoving it toward Sharon. "Here, I hate to drink alone."

"No thank you. I need to get help," Sharon said, trying to keep her voice steady as she smelled the raw alcohol on the big man.

Suddenly Jake reached out and grabbed her arm. "We can take you to get help, but first we gotta have ourselves a little fun."

Fear raced through Sharon like a live wire as she frantically thought of how to escape these men. "Let me go!" she cried, trying to jerk her arm away. But Jake held on tight and laughed at her effort.

"Now, that ain't no way for you to behave. You oughta be grateful you weren't stuck out here all alone after dark. Ain't that right, Ed?" Jake said, leering and pulling her close.

"Sure, sure," the weasel-faced man laughed and tilted the bottle again. "We got us all night to have a good time together, ain't we, sweetie?"

Sharon had never known such terror. She was petrified, but she fought with all of her strength. The big man was as strong as a gorilla, and he held her tight, laughing crudely at her attempts to escape. He pinioned her against the truck and whispered vile things in her ear while she twisted and jerked, trying to get away. When he tried to kiss her, she managed to turn her face away, which only amused him more. He started pulling her off the road toward a grove of trees when a sudden roaring startled them all. They turned to see a motorcycle stopping in the road.

"Help!" Sharon cried as she struggled. "Please help me!"

The man shut off the engine and got off the bike. He was very tall and lean and wore blue jeans, a denim jacket, and a low-crowned Stetson. He deliberately removed his hat, revealing a full head of silver hair, took off his goggles, and carefully laid them both down on the seat of the bike. "You boys better scratch for it!"

Sharon staggered as Jake suddenly released her and put himself squarely in front of the newcomer. "Buster, I'll break your face if you don't get back on that bike and scram!"

"Let's not make a production out of this."

The man moved forward in a loose-jointed way until he stood in front of Jake.

Jake cursed and threw a punch that would have demolished the other man if it had connected. But the tall stranger simply jerked his head back, then whipped a tremendous blow that caught Jake in the jaw, driving the big man backward onto the ground. He started to get up, and without hesitation the newcomer kicked him in the jaw. There was a cracking sound, and Jake fell back and lay utterly still.

The tall man turned to Ed and said, "You want me to help you put him in the truck?"

Ed cast a frightened glance at the prostrate Jake and stammered, "Y-yeah, I guess so."

"All right—you take his feet. You'd better get him to a hospital. I think his jaw is busted."

Sharon watched her rescuer with growing relief, but she was still trembling as the two hefted the big man over the side of the pickup and rolled him in.

Without looking back, Ed got into the truck, slammed the door, and departed with a roar.

She watched the truck disappear over a hill, then turned toward the tall man as he ambled back to her. Now that the violent episode was over, he smiled calmly and said, "You all right, ma'am?" He spoke with a pronounced southern accent.

"Oh yes, I am . . . now. But if you hadn't come . ..." Her voice broke.

"I'm glad I happened by. What are you doing out here by yourself, anyway?"

"I was taking a shortcut to my home when my car broke down. My name is Sharon Winslow, by the way."

"I'm glad to know you, Miss Winslow. I'm Temple Smith. What seems to be wrong with your vehicle?"

Sharon turned to stare at the Ford. "I don't know. It made a loud bang and rattled and then wouldn't run."

Smith walked over and looked at the engine briefly. "It's a little hard to tell with it starting to get dark, but it sure sounds like you might've slung a rod out. Probably busted the block. I reckon you'll have to have a new motor."

"Oh my!" Sharon exclaimed. She felt helpless and was still not over the shock of the attack. "I don't know what to do."

Smith shrugged his shoulders. "I can go get help if you want to wait here."

"Oh no, I couldn't do that!"

Smith grinned, which made him look much younger than Sharon had thought he was at first. He did not speak loudly, but there was a strength in his voice. "The only other thing I can offer you, miss, is havin' you get on that motorcycle with me. Do you live close by?"

"Not very far, but I . . . I can't get on that thing!"

"Then we'll have to sit here until somebody comes."

Sharon hesitated, feeling trapped. "But I'm wearing a dress. I can't straddle a motorcycle."

"I don't reckon there's anybody out here who's gonna notice. I'll be in the front, so your modesty's safe. It's the best thing to do. Better lock the car and get your purse."

While Smith closed the hood, Sharon grabbed her purse out of the car and made sure the doors were all locked. When she turned she saw the man was already seated on the motorcycle. He kicked the starter, and the engine broke into a roar. "Get on behind me," he shouted over the raucous noise.

Feeling more like a fool than she ever had in her life, she hiked up her skirt and threw her leg over the machine. As she settled down behind him, Smith shouted, "Put your feet on the bars," he said, kicking with his heel. "And put your arms around my chest."

Sharon gingerly found the place for her feet on a pair of rods that jutted out and put her arms loosely around him, feeling absolutely ridiculous. "Now where do we go?" he asked.

"You go straight down this road for several miles. Then we'll turn off. I'll tell you when."

"All right. Here we go." The cycle moved forward, then picked up speed. "Better hold on tighter."

The wind was tearing at Sharon's hair and blinding her. She turned her head to one side and of necessity held the man tightly. She was embarrassed to have to be so close to a man she didn't even know, but this was an emergency.

Sharon directed Smith to her house and finally cried out against the wind, "There's the drive that leads to my house."

"Right!"

Sharon began to relax as the bike slowed down. "This is it," she said, and Smith stopped the motorcycle in the driveway. An unfamiliar man stepped out of the house, and she wondered who it could be. Before she could get off the bike, there was a blinding flash.

"I guess that there feller got a good picture of us."

Sharon felt her face burning. Her dress was hiked up, exposing her leg, and she knew her arms were still around Temple Smith when the camera went off. She dismounted quickly and awkwardly as she heard her father's voice.

"Sharon, what in the world!"

Sharon was more embarrassed at what had just happened than at her strange appearance on a motorcycle. "Who was that man, Dad?"

"Oh, a reporter from one of the Hearst papers, trying to get a story about you. I had just sent him away and here you show up like . . . like this!" Leland was looking wild-eyed from the motorcycle to the tall cowboy.

Sharon quickly explained. "My car broke down, Dad, and Mr. Smith came along just in time to help me."

"I'm very much in your debt, then, Mr. Smith. Please come inside. My wife will want to thank you as well."

"That's not necessary, sir," Temple drawled.

"Oh yes, it is. Please come in," Sharon insisted.

She started for the house, and Smith fell in beside her father. When Leland asked him how he had happened along, he simply said, "I was just eatin' the breeze when I saw your daughter having trouble."

"Well, I'm very glad you did. I thank you for taking the time to stop."

As soon as they were inside, Sharon found her mother waiting. "I was looking out the window watching that horrible reporter leave. He took your picture."

"I know it, Mother, but there's nothing I can do about it." She turned toward Temple and said, "Mother, this is Mr. Temple Smith. My car broke down, and he came to my rescue."

Lucille was looking the man over, obviously noting the cowboy clothes and high-heeled cowboy boots that made him appear even taller. "We can't thank you enough, Mr. Smith."

"Why, it was nothin' at all, Mrs. Winslow."

"Look, we're about to have supper. Why don't you join us, and you can tell us all about this little adventure."

"Be proud to. I'm hungry as a bear."

After Sharon and Mr. Smith had a chance to wash up, Sharon directed her guest into the dining room, where the table was already set. Sharon and Mr. Smith sat across from each other, which gave Sharon a chance to observe the man more carefully. His silver hair was very attractive—glossy and slightly curly. His eyes were a blue that Sharon had never seen, almost electric. She saw that his hands were scarred and showed signs of hard labor, and she also noticed the tip of his little finger on his left hand was missing. His face was quite unusual. His skin was tanned to a deep mahogany, which made his teeth appear very white. His nose had been broken, and deep vertical creases surrounded his lips. He did not speak like an educated man, but neither did he seem to be ignorant.

After the cook brought in a platter of roast beef and several bowls of vegetables, Sharon said, "I ought to tell you a little more of the story, Mother and Dad. When my car broke down, I was accosted by two men who were drunk and threatening me. Mr. Smith came and stopped just in time to keep me from harm."

"Did they give you any trouble, Mr. Smith?" Leland demanded.

"One of them put up a little argument, but we thrashed it out." Temple lowered his right eye in a wink at Sharon.

"It was more than that," Sharon supplied. "He had to use force."

"Against both of them?" Leland asked.

"Aw, they weren't really all that tough, Mr. Winslow. One good blow and they hightailed it outta there."

Sharon's parents were greatly relieved at Mr. Smith's rescue, which in their eyes was nothing short of heroic. They had a few words of admonishment for Sharon, however, telling her that this was why they didn't like her out "gallivanting around" by herself and that she was never to venture off the main highway again. Sharon took their words stoically and without argument, for in truth she was quite shaken by the incident and had inwardly vowed never to be alone on that road again.

The rest of the meal went off in a relaxed and pleasant manner, but Sharon was aware that her father was trying to find out more about the stranger who had done them such a service. Smith was not terribly forthcoming with details of his life, however, and all that Leland could determine was that he had apparently traveled extensively around the United States and to some foreign countries as well.

After the meal, Smith rose and said, "That was a fine meal, folks. I appreciate it." He turned to Sharon. "If I were you, I'd get that car hauled in soon. Otherwise, you might find it stripped clean. If you like, you can call a wrecker and I'll go meet them at the car and take care of the details."

Sharon said, "Oh, that is so nice of you! But I hate to trouble you."

"I've got nothin' better to do."

Sharon said, "Wait here, then." She called a wrecking company, then ran to find her purse. Coming back, she pulled out some bills. "You'll have to pay for the wrecker, and here is something for your trouble. This doesn't cover what it's worth, of course, but please accept it as a token of my appreciation. I'm so grateful to you."

Sharon expected Smith to argue against taking money, but he quietly accepted the bills, folded them without looking, and stuck them into his pocket. "I'll have them take the car to the nearest Ford agency, and you best call them in the morning to explain what the trouble was."

"Thank you, Mr. Smith. I can never thank you enough."

"Don't mention it, Miss Sharon." Smith nodded, put his Stetson on, and stepped out of the door. She watched as he mounted the motorcycle and roared out of the driveway.

When she got back to the dining room, Leland said, "If that fellow hadn't come along, you would have been in terrible trouble. Maybe it's not such a good idea for you to be driving around all alone."

"I can't do that for the rest of my life, Dad. I've never had a problem before."

Leland knew he wasn't going to win this argument with his daughter, so he changed the subject. "He's an odd-looking man, isn't he, with that silver hair?"

"But he doesn't seem all that old," Lucille mused.

"No, and he's very strong and quick," Sharon added. "Well, I think I'll go relax in my room now. It's been a tiring evening. Good night, Mother. Good night, Dad."

Sharon went up and showered and then tried to read, but she could not concentrate, for the experience had shaken her. She knew exactly how close she had come to terrible disaster. Finally she went to bed, and as she lay there, she thought about Temple Smith. *What an unusual name. I wonder if I'll ever see him again.* A part of her wanted to see him again, but he was obviously a workingman and outside of her social circle. Still, she owed him so much. She eventually drifted off, but it was a broken sleep, troubled by disturbing dreams.

★   ★   ★

When Sharon came downstairs in the morning, she found her father waiting for her with an odd look on his face and the newspaper in his hand. "Bad news, daughter."

"What is it, Dad?"

"Look at this."

Sharon took the newspaper he handed her, and her heart sank when she saw the picture. There was Temple Smith in his Stetson and goggles with her right behind him on the motorcycle, her skirt pulled up to her thigh and hugging the man with what appeared to be great enthusiasm. The caption read: "Miss Sharon Elizabeth Winslow, noted sculptress and heiress of the Winslow fortune, arriving home last night from an escapade with an unidentified companion."

"Oh, Dad, this is terrible!"

"Yes, it's pretty bad. I've called the newspaper to complain, but of course, it's too late to do anything about it. That Hearst bunch will do anything to sell papers. They aren't much interested in the truth."

Sharon knew that her life would be miserable for a time at least. She'd had her picture in the paper before, but there had always been some dignity to it. Now, however, her heart sank as she foresaw the snickers and covert whispers that would follow her wherever she went.

"Well," Leland said, "you're all right. That's the main thing. And this will pass in time." His face was grim as he waved at the newspaper. "It ought to be against the law for a man like Hearst to print pictures and a false story like this. But it's not. It'll sell a few papers, and what does he care how it hurts someone?"

CHAPTER FIFTEEN

LOVE IS *PEOPLE*

★ ★ ★

Sharon entered the Calvary Baptist Church in Manhattan—the church she had attended all her life—and felt that everyone was staring at her. In truth only a few were staring, and these few Sharon tried to ignore as best she could while she sought out conversations with friendlier acquaintances. She knew the stares had to do with her picture in the paper, and for this reason she had stayed home for the past couple of weeks, avoiding any social contact and unwanted questions. But on this Sunday morning she had decided it was time to show her face and ignore the gossips.

Most of the people she greeted kept a discreet silence about the embarrassing photo, but the same couldn't be said for the church busybody, Mrs. Susanna Parker, who had never left a thought unspoken in her life. Mrs. Parker rushed over to say, "Oh, I saw that dreadful picture of you in the paper! I know you must be sick over it."

"I'll survive, Mrs. Parker."

"You poor thing! These newspapers! Someone ought to put that man Hearst in jail!"

Sharon made her escape as quickly as possible and

entered the sanctuary, where the service was about to begin. She made her way awkwardly past several worshipers to reach an empty seat in the middle of a pew at the back of the crowded church. When she sat down a shock ran through her as she saw she was sitting next to Temple Smith. He was not wearing a suit, as most of the other men were, but simply a white shirt with no tie and a denim jacket. Sharon nodded and faced resolutely away, wondering if he had come to church just to see her. How did he know which church she attended? she wondered. Perhaps they had mentioned it at dinner the night he had rescued her. She could not say for sure, but she was so accustomed to thinking in terms of people trying to get something from her that her mind was naturally suspicious. She had not seen Smith since the night of her rescue. She had expected him to call but never heard from him. She had only heard from the Ford agency, which had called the next day to say that the car had been brought in and would be repaired under the terms of the warranty.

The pastor preached an eloquent message on Matthew 25:40, "Inasmuch as ye have done it unto one of the least of these my brethren, ye have done it unto me." He stressed the dire needs that existed in parts of New York City. "The Depression has been going on for over five years now," he said soberly but with great intensity, "and the Church of Jesus Christ is not to sit idly by. This beautiful building we are in is wonderful indeed, and I love to worship here. But we must decide once and for all if the church is to be a window display with everything in order—or if it is to be a field hospital, going out to where there are hungry, hurting people."

Sharon listened to the sermon intently, though aware of Temple Smith to her right. She loved the pastor, for he was a fine man. Dr. Thomas Snyder, a man with a national reputation as a writer and speaker, had been her minister for ten years, and she trusted him implicitly. She listened attentively as he said, "I intend to go out to the streets and do what I can for those who need help. I'm sure some of you will want to join me. If this is a ministry you'd like to be involved with, I'll ask you to meet me in the prayer room after the service."

Sharon found herself deeply moved by his challenge, and as the service concluded, she made her way out of the pew and to the prayer room as quickly as she could. Only two couples were there when she sat down, and then the door opened and Temple Smith walked in, carrying his Stetson in his hand.

"Good morning, Miss Winslow," he greeted with a smile.

"Good morning, Mr. Smith."

"Don't you reckon as how we could go by Temple and Sharon?"

"Why . . . yes, of course."

"Good." He took a chair. "I admire this preacher. I've never heard anyone preach better."

"Have you been here before?"

"Yep, the last two Sundays. A friend of mine recommended it. If I was a settled man, I'd join this church. But I never know where I'll be next."

Sharon wondered about Temple's life but had no time to pursue this. Dr. Snyder walked in and seemed pleased to see anyone there at all.

"I didn't expect a great deal of response, but I hope there'll be more as we go along. Why don't we wait a few minutes and see if anyone else arrives." Eventually about a dozen people showed up, and Snyder commended them all for their compassion. "All right, I have done a little organizing here. We're going out two by two just as Jesus sent His disciples out. You husbands and wives will probably want to go together. And the rest of you can choose a partner."

"Miss Sharon and I know each other, Preacher. I reckon we might make a pretty good team."

"Fine," Dr. Snyder said. "I don't believe I know your name."

"Temple Smith. I'm not a member here, but I've visited

three times now, and I'd like to help."

"I'm glad of that." Dr. Snyder went over some of the details. "I have the names here of a number of families with various needs. I'll talk with each team separately, pray with you, and send you out. You can start anytime."

The pastor prayed briefly, shook hands with everyone, and then they filed out.

"I'm excited about this," Temple said cheerfully to Sharon as they left the prayer room together. "When do you want to start?"

"I don't know. What do you think?"

"Tomorrow be all right?"

Sharon wished fervently she had not gotten herself into this after all, but there was no way out now. "Yes, that will be all right."

"Fine. Let's make sure the pastor will be here tomorrow morning and then we can set a time." They conferred with Dr. Snyder and agreed on eight o'clock.

Sharon left the church, glad that Temple did not try to accompany her. She drove home, completely confused about what she had done. After lunch, she walked for a time around the grounds. She was admiring the new plantings and changes William Morgan had done when she was interrupted by Seana.

"Been to church, have you, Miss Winslow?"

"Yes, and you too, I suppose?"

"Oh yes. My father and I found a fine chapel very close to here. It's small, but the preacher there is a man of God."

The two women talked about their churches, Seana with great enthusiasm. Sharon found herself telling Seana that she had volunteered to work with the poor in the city, and Seana was delighted. "There is wonderful, it is! And it's God working in you."

Sharon was not accustomed to being on quite such familiar terms with God, but she saw that this young woman was.

"I'm not sure I can do it. I've always been willing to give

money, but I'm afraid I'm a bit of a coward when it comes to talking to complete strangers about God."

"The good Lord himself will be in you and with you. It's a fine thing you're doing, Miss Winslow, and God will bless you in it."

★ ★ ★

Sharon drove her car downtown early the next morning, and when she passed the church looking for a parking spot, Smith waved at her from the curb on his motorcycle. "I thought we might ride the bike," he drawled, "but your wagon here will be much better." She saw a gleam of humor in his eyes and knew he was teasing her.

"Much better," she agreed.

"There's a parking place down in the next block I can see," Temple said, pointing. "I'll wait for you here and we can go see what Dr. Snyder's got for us."

Sharon parked the car, and the two went into the church together, where the secretary admitted them to Dr. Snyder's office. He got up at once and greeted them, pleased to see them so early. After a time of discussion and prayer, he pulled out a note card from a box and said, "This is the family I'd like you two to see. I don't know them personally, but one of our members gave me their name. I understand the man of the house is ill and there's great financial need."

Temple took the card and asked, "Where's the rest of them?"

"The rest of what?"

"The other cards. You're not going to limit us to one family, are you, Preacher?"

"Not at all," Snyder said with a smile. "I assumed most of our volunteers would want to start with just one family. Here, you can have all you'd like."

Sharon watched Temple take several cards, and when they left Dr. Snyder's office, they walked back to her Ford and got in. Temple read the name of the family Dr. Snyder had spoken about first. "Mr. and Mrs. Anthony Pappagallo." He read the address and said, "Do you know where that is?"

"No, not really."

"I'll direct you, then. I've been studying the city, so I know it pretty good."

Following Temple's directions, Sharon saw a part of New York she had never seen before. The tenements on the Lower East Side were like another world to her. On this warm April day, clothes were hanging out to dry on every balcony, and the streets were filled with yelling children and peddlers of all sorts.

"Pretty busy place, isn't it?" Smith said. "Look, I think that's it right over there." Sharon pulled into a parking place, and he got out. When Sharon joined him, he said, "Come on. We'll see what we can do." A boy no more than twelve was walking by, and Temple said, "Hey, buddy, do you know where the Pappagallos live?"

"Sure. Right in that building on the third floor. Do you know them?"

"I will in just a few minutes. Here, go buy yourself a soda pop." He handed the boy a coin and grinned as the youngster ran off. "Nobody ever gave me money when I was his age. I enjoy giving kids an unexpected treat. Reckon we'd better get on with our business."

Sharon moved reluctantly as they climbed the steps and entered the building. The odor of rotting cabbage and stopped-up drains and moldy dampness repelled her, but Temple did not seem to notice. He spoke cheerfully as they climbed the narrow stairway to the third floor. Seeing several unmarked doorways, he said, "Reckon we'll just have to ask where they are."

He knocked on a door, and a short, wide woman opened it.

"Good morning. I'm looking for Anthony Pappagallo."

"He'sa down there at the end of the hall."

"Thank you very much, ma'am. And a good morning to you."

The two went to the end of the hall. He knocked on the door, and a dark-haired woman opened it. "Mrs. Pappagallo?"

The woman looked frightened. "What is it?"

"My name is Temple Smith and this here lady is Miss Winslow. We're from the Calvary Baptist Church. Understand one of your family members is sick and there are some financial problems. We're here to help in some way if we can. Reckon we can come in and talk?"

Maria Pappagallo looked even more frightened. "We no do anything wrong."

"Why, of course not. Is your husband here?"

"He's in the bed. He'sa sick."

Smith smiled at the children who had gathered around the woman. "Well now, what fine kids you've got!" he exclaimed.

The children were handsome with curly black hair, large brown eyes, and olive complexions, but they were far from clean. There were five of them—one a baby just starting to crawl. They all watched the visitors with big, frightened eyes.

"My Tony he'sa back here," the woman said as she opened the door wider and beckoned them to follow. "He needs a doctor, but we have'a no money."

"Reckon we'll see about that." Temple followed the woman into a room at the end of the hall. Sharon waited at the door, feeling embarrassed and out of place. She could see that the big man in bed was very sick. She watched as Temple went over and shook Mr. Pappagallo's hand. He introduced himself cheerfully and said, "We're gonna get a doctor out to see you, Tony. Don't you worry now, and don't worry about the kids. We'll see that they're taken care of— them and your wife. Would you mind if I prayed for you?"

Tony Pappagallo lay there as if dazed. There were large

circles under his eyes, and he had a bad cough. "I guess not," he muttered.

Sharon listened as Temple prayed briefly, then said good-bye. When he shut the door, he said to Maria Pappagallo, "What do you need most?"

"Need? We need *everything*!" Tears formed in the woman's eyes. "Mr. Williams—the landlord—he'sa gonna throw us out."

"Are you behind on the rent, Mrs. Pappagallo?"

"Yes. Tony no able to work now for nearly a month. We have'a no money."

"You tell me where Mr. Williams is. I'll take care of that."

Sharon stood helplessly by as Temple got the landlord's address and said, "We'll be back soon with something nice. You kids like candy?"

The children stared at him, and the older ones nodded.

"All right, then, I think we can help with that. Come along, Miss Sharon."

"Where are we going?" Sharon asked as she almost ran down the stairs, attempting to keep up with him.

"We're gonna find this slum landlord and take care of this rent business."

The landlord lived in another neighborhood, a much nicer one. He was bowled over when Temple blew into his office and demanded, "Do you have a tenant named Pappagallo? How much is their rent?"

"They're behind. They owe me twenty bucks."

"Here, I've got the money, Temple," Sharon said.

Temple took the cash, counted out some bills, and said, "Here's the back rent, and here's rent for the next two months. I'll need a receipt."

Williams stared at the tall man in surprise. "Sure. Glad to do business with you."

They left the office, and Temple said, "Now the fun begins. Let's find us a grocery store."

They found an Italian grocer around the corner, and Temple insisted that Sharon pick out the food. "I don't know what Italians like to eat except spaghetti."

"They need fresh fruit and vegetables and meat."

Sharon forgot herself for a time, and before long they had collected two huge baskets full of food. "This ought to keep them from starving for a few days. Now, let me throw some candy in with that."

They left the grocery store and had started back to the apartment when they passed an Italian restaurant. "Let's stop and get them a hot meal," Temple suggested.

"That would be nice," Sharon agreed.

Temple led her inside, and they ordered enough food for a small army. Once again Sharon noticed he made no attempt to pay for it, so she did, but that was something she did not mind doing.

When they got back to the apartment, it took several trips to carry the groceries up. They took the hot food first, and Sharon stayed inside and helped Mrs. Pappagallo put the food out as Temple carried the rest of the groceries up the three flights. The woman's eyes brimmed with tears of gratitude.

When the food was in place, Sharon said, "Don't worry about the rent, Mrs. Pappagallo. It's paid for the next three months, and I'll have a doctor come by and see to your husband."

Mrs. Pappagallo began to cry in earnest, and Temple went over and put his arm around her. "We're doing it all in the name of Jesus, Mrs. Pappagallo. God loves you. And we'll be back."

As they left the apartment, Sharon felt exhausted. She could not understand why she was so tired, but she soon discovered that their workday was just beginning.

"It's time for the next call," Temple said excitedly. "Come on."

* * *

Except for a brief stop for lunch, Temple was untiring in his attempts to help people that day. By the time they arrived back at the church and pulled into a parking place, Sharon leaned her head back and said with a sigh, "I'm so tired I could drop. I don't know if I can do another day like this."

"You've done fine," Temple encouraged her. "I know it's hard for you, Sharon, but you did great. Are you free tomorrow? There are a lot more families we can help."

"I have to work tomorrow, but perhaps I could the day after." Sharon hesitated, then said, "Look, Temple, I'm not much good at this. Why don't I just furnish the money and let you do the actual visiting?"

Temple cocked his head to one side and said softly, "Sharon, love is what these folks need—and love is more than money. Love is *people*."

Feeling rebuked, Sharon said quickly, "All right. Eight o'clock here at the church day after tomorrow?"

"Yep."

"You're some lady, Miss Sharon Winslow," he said with a smile that seemed to engulf her. He got out of the car, and she watched as he mounted his motorcycle, kicked it into action, and flew off down the street with a wave.

Sharon was ravenous by the time she got home, but the family had already eaten supper. She went into the kitchen and asked Mabel to heat up some leftovers. She was half done with her meal when Clayton came in and sat down across from her with a cup of coffee, asking her about her day. She carefully detailed it for him and told him, "I'm so tired, but it's such a good thing to do."

"I suppose it is," he said, "but seeing how tired you are, couldn't you just hire this fellow Smith to do it?"

"It wouldn't be the same thing."

Clayton shook his head and left his sister to join his parents in the parlor, where he expressed his concerns about Sharon's relationship with "this cowboy" Smith. "It's not a good thing, is it, her going around with this fellow? He's a rough character, isn't he? I'm not sure he's safe."

"He did Sharon a great service," Leland said with a shrug, referring to her rescue from the dangerous thugs. "And I'm rather proud of her for going out and helping the poor, if you want to know the truth."

Clayton was frustrated that he could not get his parents to agree with him. "She's always gone overboard about one thing or another," he muttered, "and now I'd say she's gone overboard about religion." Having said his piece, he went to the stable to take an evening ride on his stallion.

★   ★   ★

Two days later Sharon went out again with Temple to visit the poor on Manhattan's Lower East Side, and so as not to wear Sharon out, Temple agreed to finish earlier that afternoon. As they relaxed over a cup of coffee in a small café overlooking Central Park, he asked her a number of questions about her artwork, and she said on impulse, "Why don't you come out and see what I do in my studio?"

"All right. I will."

All the way home that afternoon Sharon wondered if she had done the right thing, but it was too late to take back her invitation. She found Temple Smith a fascinating man. As her brother insisted, some might consider him a rough character, but she also found him strong and capable as she had watched him in action helping the poor. She had also seen his compassionate nature as he talked with great concern to the people they met and showed special attention to the children. Once he had picked up an ailing toddler, holding her as gently as any woman would. He rarely seemed to have any money but was comfortable with letting Sharon take care of the expenses that came along.

When she got home she pulled up in front of her studio, and Temple, who had kept pace behind her on his motorcycle, parked the bike and hooked his goggles over the handlebar.

"Come on in," Sharon invited.

Daylight came streaming through the skylight, and when she showed him her work, he appeared very interested. He made few comments until she came to the study of the soldier.

"I really like this one," he said. "How'd you get all the details right?"

Sharon stared at him. "How do you know they're right?"

"I wore one of these for a couple of years."

Sharon turned to him with new interest. "You were in the war?"

"Sure was."

"Do you think much about those times?"

Temple shrugged. "Best not to dwell on them. It was pretty bad."

She suddenly felt the need to talk. She had never had the courage to talk to any soldier who was in the war, not wanting to hear any horrific details. But now as she saw him studying the figure of Robert, an impulse prompted her to say, "Let me take you out to a favorite place of mine to eat."

"Suits me. I'm hungry."

The two left together in Sharon's station wagon and went to a quaint restaurant in a small town nearby, which Sharon enjoyed visiting by herself at times. As they were about to enter, Sharon glanced at Temple and realized he was not dressed properly to dine out, even in this small-town restaurant.

"Oh, Temple," she said, embarrassed. "I just realized you don't even have a tie on. I could have borrowed one from my father."

"Not to worry," Temple said with a grin. He fished down into his jacket pocket and came up with what looked like a black string. Tying it around his neck, he said, "There. Now I'm proper enough for anyone."

Sharon could not help being amused. As it turned out, the maitre d' glanced briefly at the denim jacket, cowboy hat, and string tie, and without further hesitation, showed them to a private table by a picture window overlooking a charming garden with a goldfish pond and lighted fountain in the middle.

They happily talked until the meal was brought, at which time they bowed their heads and Temple asked a simple blessing.

"This is perfect," he said as he cut into his steak, done rare as he had requested.

In their conversation she found that Temple had been everywhere and done everything. "Will you tell me a little bit about the war?" she asked. "I had a dear friend who was in it."

Temple looked up quickly, studying her for a moment. "He didn't make it back?"

"No, he didn't."

"There were good men there and bad men. But when we went over the top, we all went together. I never asked a man's background when we faced the enemy."

He talked for some time about the war, and somehow she found it comforting. They progressed onto other subjects, and she asked, "Do you have a family?"

"You mean am I married?"

She saw his face change and she nodded.

"Yes, I was married—to a dear woman named Heather. I met her in London."

Sharon did not speak, seeing that this was a hard story for him to tell as he grew still and seemed to debate about his next words.

"I brought her here, and we had three good years. But then she died in childbirth."

Sharon clearly saw the pain on his face. "And the child?"

"He died too. He would have been a fine boy."

Sharon thought then of her own loss and immediately realized how self-centered she had been. *I've been grieving as if I were the only person ever to lose a loved one, but Temple's loss is so much greater than mine!*

CHAPTER SIXTEEN

OUT OF THE PAST

★　★　★

The May sky was a perfect azure, Clayton noted with satisfaction as he looked up at the lazily drifting clouds. A flight of blackbirds wheeled overhead, turning perfectly together. *I wonder how they do that,* he thought. *It's like all those birds share one brain.* He smiled at his own foolishness, then bent over the worktable he had set up on the verandah so he could enjoy the fresh fragrance of the spring day.

Looking down at the large sheet of paper he had pinned to the top of the table, he saw an ant crossing it, bearing a burden. Food, he supposed. Leaning down, he examined the tiny insect and waited until it reached the edge. The ant seemed reluctant to get off, so Clayton nudged him with the tip of his finger. "I believe you're lost, little boy," he said. "You'd better get back to your family." He watched the ant crawl across the table, then down a leg, still bearing his burden. "You ants—all work and no play. And, by george, that's what I feel like! It's been a tough year."

Clayton took a drink of his iced tea and then arched his back to relieve the stiffness from bending over the worktable for several hours. The school year was over, and with a sigh of relief he realized he didn't have to go to another class this year. He loved school and was very successful in his studies. In fact, all of his professors said he was destined for greatness. But as much as Clayton enjoyed his classes, he was glad to be free for a while. He was looking forward now to his summer plans, complete with parties, travel, swimming, and tennis.

His first job before relaxing, however, was this project that his mother had started and been unable to finish. She had not been feeling well and was resting. The doctor said her heart was not as sound as he would like and recommended that she keep to her bed for a time. Lucille's illness troubled Clayton. He had just turned twenty this month, and it was the first time he had encountered a serious problem in his life. He had experienced his share of broken hearts over various young women who interested him but had recovered quickly from each one as there was always someone else anxious to fill the role of Clayton Winslow's sweetheart. Being healthy, strong, and handsome in addition to being wealthy had allowed him to lead a very easy life. He lived in a manner that pleased him and took the good things he had inherited for granted. Aside from an occasional twinge of conscience when he saw real suffering, such as ragged men selling apples on street corners to feed their families, Clayton was satisfied with himself and with life.

His reverie was broken when he heard his name called. He turned around and saw Sarah Mellon, the woman he planned to marry, coming out of the house. The niece of the famous Andrew Mellon, she was rather short and one day might have a serious weight problem like her mother, but for now she was well shaped and attractive. She came over to give him a light kiss. Her round face, brown eyes, and brown hair looked very pretty with the light green dress she wore, accented by jade earrings and a large jade ring on her right hand.

"Your sister told me you were out here. I thought I'd

stop on my way into the city and see if you wanted to come with me."

"I'd better not. I stayed up most of last night working on this new landscape plan, and I want to show it to the gardener. I moved out here this morning because it's so beautiful today. Here, let me show you what I've done."

Clayton enthusiastically explained the drawing, outlining the new flower beds, pond, and fountains with his forefinger. His mother had decided she wanted changes made in much of the grounds, but she had barely gotten into it when she had fallen ill. Clayton had told her, "Don't worry, Mom. You go to bed and get well, and I'll do the landscaping. After all, I *am* an architect—or will be someday."

He turned to his girlfriend. "It's going to be a new place, Sarah. It really is."

"I can't tell much from a picture, but I know it will be beautiful."

He leaned over and gave her a hug and tried to kiss her, but she turned her lips away so that he kissed her on the cheek instead. She was not terribly affectionate, but she was pretty, and her family, the Mellons, had no end of money. She had not given him a definite yes or no to his marriage proposal, but Clayton had enough confidence to know that one day she would. His mother was already planning the wedding, and he had had to remind her, *"It's the bride's mother who does all that. You'll have to wait until Sharon marries before you get to make all the decisions."*

"I'll tell you what, Sarah," he said. "I've got to go give William these plans. Do you want to come with me?"

"Sure, I'm not in a big hurry."

"Great. It's a nice day for a walk." He unpinned the drawing and rolled it up, and the two made their way across the grounds. "I don't see William," Clayton commented. "He's usually around at this time of day."

They were passing the shed that housed the gardening equipment when Sarah said, "Look, there's a woman working on that tractor. Can't you afford to hire men?"

Clayton glanced in the direction she gestured. "That's Seana Morgan, William's daughter. She's not hired to work here, so I don't know what she's doing with that tractor. But maybe she knows where her father is."

As the two approached the shed, Seana turned. She was wearing a pair of greasy coveralls and had a spot of grease on her cheek. Her red hair was tied up and mostly hidden under a white-billed cap.

"A good morning to you," she greeted.

"Hello, Seana. This is Miss Mellon. Sarah, this is Seana Morgan."

"It's glad I am to greet you," Seana said, "but I'm sorry I look such a mess." She shrugged and held up her greasy hands.

"That's all right. It's nice to meet you too," Sarah said. "You know how to work on tractors?"

"Oh, a bit. Enough to keep them going."

"I'm looking for your father," Clayton said. He was ill at ease, for ever since Seana had shoved him into that pile of manure, he had felt she was secretly laughing at him.

"He's gone to get a load of fertilizer, and then he's going to stop off and get some parts for this beastly machine. Would you be wantin' him to do something on the grounds? I have two days off from classes, so I'm helping around here."

"No, we're making some changes in the landscape. I want to go over them with him."

"Changes? What sort of changes?"

"Almost everything." He hesitated, then said, "Look, I'll have to talk to your father, but I could give you an overview, and he can look the drawings over and get back to me." He unrolled the paper, stretched it out on a workbench, and held down one end. He had begun to explain the proposed changes when he was suddenly interrupted.

"You can't be doin' this," Seana said.

Both Clayton and Sarah stared at her. They weren't accustomed to being told they couldn't do something.

"I can't do what?"

"You can't make a pond here. It won't work where you've got it."

"What are you talking about? That's where I want the pond."

"Have you been out and walked over the grounds?"

"Of course I have." Actually he had not gone specifically to look at the grounds before making his plan, for he believed he knew the estate very well.

"You can't make a pond here. The elevation's too high."

"Then I'll build a dam or something," Clayton said stiffly.

"A dam it is now! Aren't you a creative architect? This place needs to look natural. Not like a government project."

Seana touched another spot on the sketch. "And magnolia trees! They don't grow in this climate. I should think you'd know that. They're a southern tree."

As Seana continued to point out other features that wouldn't work well, Clayton's face grew hotter. This girl could anger him more than anyone he had ever met. He snatched up the plan, rolled it up, and said huffily, "I'll talk to your father when he gets back."

"Right you are. He'll tell you the same things I did. And a good day to you both."

Clayton stalked off with Sarah running to keep up. As soon as they were out of earshot, she demanded, "Why do you put up with help like that? You should have discharged her on the spot!"

"I can't discharge her. As I told you, she doesn't work for us. She just helps her father."

"She's a wild thing, isn't she, running around in a pair of coveralls? And that red hair, it's completely impossible!"

Clayton shrugged. "Yes, she is a pain, but when she's dressed up, I have to admit she's rather attractive."

Sarah stopped abruptly. "Oh, you think so?"

"I . . . I just mean she's presentable enough," Clayton quickly said, wishing he could take back his careless comment, for Sarah could be bitingly jealous. "Of course, most of the time, she's either wearing coveralls or grubbing around in her father's old clothes. Except when she's always wearing one of those ugly nurse's uniforms."

Sarah's back was stiff. "I'm glad you find the help attractive. Come on. I've seen enough of the gardens for one day."

⋆ ⋆ ⋆

"I'll tell you, sis, that girl is impossible. I wish she'd stick to her nursing and stay out of my business."

"She hasn't been shoving you into any more piles of horse manure, has she?" Sharon could not help teasing Clayton, but seeing him glare at her now, she tried to appease his anger. "I'm sorry, Clayton. It wasn't the end of the world, and Seana didn't mean to do it."

The two were in Sharon's studio, and she was wearing her white work smock, her hands covered in white dust from the plaster of Paris she was mixing. She continued to knead the mass as she spoke. "What has Seana done now?"

"I took the plans for the new landscaping down to show William, and he wasn't there, but Seana was. She was tinkering with a tractor and had grease all over her."

"I didn't know she was a mechanic."

"I guess she can do anything. In any case, I showed her the plans, and she found something wrong with everything I pointed out. Imagine! Her telling me how to draw up a landscape plan!"

"What did she say was wrong with them?"

"For one thing, she said the elevation wasn't right to put in the new pond where I want it."

"Is she right?" Sharon asked.

"Now, don't *you* start!"

"Well, is she? Have you checked it out?"

Actually Clayton *had* gone out and walked over the grounds and discovered that Seana was indeed right. He had already decided on another location for the pond, but he was too proud to admit his error. He continued to speak rather testily, explaining the other features the woman had found fault with.

"Why do you get so angry? Is it because she's right?"

"No, it's her attitude."

"Hmm. Her attitude has always been good around me. I think you bring out the worst in her. She probably thinks you're pompous and likes to poke little pins in you to deflate you."

"Do you think I'm pompous?" he demanded.

Sharon hesitated. "Sometimes you get a little too conscious of your own importance, Clayton. We've talked about that before. You were that way when you were a boy. I love Mother and Dad, but a lot of their attitudes about high society have gotten into you."

"Sis, you know that status is important. Family is important."

"The families of poor people are important too. Like those families Temple and I have been visiting on the Lower East Side. That's such a terrible place to live. But Tony and Maria Pappagallo love their family and each other as much as we do. Yet most people of our social upbringing wouldn't give Tony Pappagallo the time of day. I wish you'd learn to look at yourself in this light. Your attitude is going to cause you problems down the road, and I think you know it."

"I'm glad you've got such a high opinion of me."

"You know I love you dearly, Clayton. I always have, and I always will. But because I love you, I don't think I should keep silent about your faults."

"Then maybe I ought to tell you a few of yours."

"Maybe you should." Sharon waited, but Clayton dropped his head. When he lifted it, he was trying to smile. "You're right, sis. I do get pompous, and I hate it when I see that in other people. So let Seana puncture me. Maybe it'll be good for me."

"Show her your other side. Have you apologized yet for trying to kiss her?"

"No."

"I think that would be a good place to begin."

Clayton laughed. "All right, sister dear. I'll do that. She'll probably knock me down with a shovel, but I'll do it because you asked me to." He watched her for a few minutes as she continued to work with the plaster. Finally he asked her what she was doing that afternoon.

"I'm going downtown again with Temple. We're going to visit some of the people we've been seeing on the East Side."

"You're spending an awful lot of time with this fellow Smith. Who is he anyway?"

"Oh, just a man who cares about people."

"You don't know anything about him, really. Where does his family live? What do they do?"

"There you go again."

"Now, wait a minute. It's not wrong for a fellow to inquire about the man his sister's dating."

"I'm not dating him. We're working together for the church."

"It looks to me like you could just give money."

"That's what I thought, but Temple looked me right in the eye and said, 'Love is more than money. Love is *people.*'"

"Well, somebody has to pay for the groceries and doctors and everything else. Does he have any money?"

Sharon felt uncomfortable. "I don't think so."

"Do you pay for everything?"

"I have a time or two." She did not want to elaborate on that subject. "It's easy to give money, but to actually go out and help people involves much more of yourself. It's rewarding. I feel like I'm serving God for the first time, Clayton. I wish you'd come with us sometime."

Clayton shook his head. "That's not for me. And I want you to be careful."

"Don't you like Temple?"

"I don't know him. He sounds like a workingman, and we move in different worlds."

"I suppose that's true."

"I just don't want you to get to liking him too much, Sharon. He doesn't fit in our world." Clayton put his arm around her. "After that picture of you and him on the motorcycle, all kinds of gossip has been going around."

"What do they say?"

"They say you're in love with a bum."

"That's foolishness!"

"I'm glad to hear it. You go on with your church work, then, but watch yourself, sis. You're in a vulnerable position."

"You don't have to worry about me and Temple. I'm too old for romance."

Clayton shook his head. "I don't believe that for a minute. You haven't been very lucky in love, but if you could find a good man—"

"I'm past all that," Sharon insisted. "Now, you go on and tell Seana you're sorry."

★   ★   ★

The Pappagallo children swarmed Sharon as she and Temple entered the family's new apartment. After Sharon had paid for medicine and a doctor's help, Tony had recovered quickly and returned to work. She had paid all their expenses in the meantime, and she and Temple had helped them find a better apartment for their family. She sat down and gave out candy to the children, and they clamored for her attention while Temple talked to their mother.

"Things are looking much better now, Maria, aren't they?" Temple said with a smile.

"Oh, Mr. Temple, you wouldn't believe'a how wonderful it is. Tony he ees back to work, and we have plenty to eat and live in this nice'a place." She reached up and touched his cheek. "It's all your doing, you and Miss Sharon."

Temple turned to look at Sharon, but she was busy with the children and had not heard their conversation.

"She's such a good woman," Maria said as they watched her playing and laughing with the children. "Why you no marry her?"

"Maybe she wouldn't have me." Temple shrugged.

"Don't be foolish. Any woman would have a handsome man like you."

"I think you need glasses, Maria. Anyway, we gotta be going."

"I'll tell Tony you were here. He'll be sorry he no get to see you."

The two left the apartment, and when they were outside, Temple said, "Those kids sure love you. You have a way with them."

"I haven't been around children much except for Clayton, and that was a long time ago."

"Some people have a way with kids and some don't."

Sharon did not know how to answer this. As they walked to the car, she looked at her watch. "It's getting late. I think I'd better get home. Will I see you tomorrow morning at church?"

"Sure thing, and . . . I've been thinking . . . maybe after church we could take in a ball game. I'd enjoy having some company."

She didn't answer, and when Temple looked at her, he was troubled by her expression. "What's wrong?"

"Oh, nothing."

"Sure there is. I can tell you're trying to hide something. Don't you like baseball?"

"Oh, Temple, it's just that . . . I have a memory about going to a ball game that makes me sad."

"How can a baseball game make you sad?"

"Only because Robert took me to a game once. I'd never been to one. It was one of the things he did for me that got me out of my sheltered life."

"That sounds like a good memory."

"I guess it really is. I just don't want to spoil it by going to another game."

"That was a long time ago. This is another day, another game. I wish you'd go with me. I get a little lonesome going by myself."

Sharon turned to look at him. As Clayton insisted, he was a rough character—like a machine intended for hard use. She was used to men who were polished and genteel, but there was none of this in him. She liked his smile, but she had noticed that at other times his face held elements of sadness. And yet she remembered the ease with which he had fought off her attacker, and she noticed now a C-shaped scar just to the right of his eyebrow and wondered how it had gotten there. Despite his roughness, there was an endearing quality in him she could not explain.

"Well, do I pass inspection?"

For some inexplicable reason, Sharon was suddenly flooded with memories of Robert. She remembered the ball game and how she had sat beside him eating a hot dog. She remembered the love they had shared, and tears came to her eyes, unbidden. She was horrified to feel them rolling down her cheeks. She fumbled for a handkerchief, but Temple pulled out his and gave it to her, saying gently, "It's all right to cry. I do it myself sometimes."

"I don't believe that!"

"When I lost Heather I did."

Sharon looked at him, stunned.

"I think it's fine that you still remember Robert. I probably would have liked him, and I'll bet he would smile if you went to another baseball game."

Sharon smiled at that thought, knowing for certain that Temple was right. Robert had been that kind of a man. He would not want her to punish herself, and he would have approved of her going to a ball game with this unusual man who had come into her life.

"All right. But I'll warn you, I know nothing about baseball."

"All you have to do is yell, and I'll tell you when to cut loose. The Yankees are playing the Red Sox. We're sure to see a good fight when those two get together. We can leave right after church tomorrow and have our lunch at the stadium. I'll get us some good seats."

★   ★   ★

The next day Temple and Sharon sat together at church, and after the service they both drove to Yankee Stadium, she in her station wagon with Temple following on his motorcycle. For once he did not expect her to pay, and at the stadium ticket window he fumbled around and pulled some bills out of his shirt pocket. He never carried a billfold like other men, just loose money in whatever pocket was handy.

He led her up into the stands and said, "Here we are. Right behind first base. It's the best place to sit. You can see each pitch clearly."

As they sat down she mentioned that Babe Ruth had pitched for the Red Sox during the game she'd seen with Robert, and she asked if Ruth would be playing today.

"Gee, kiddo—you weren't kidding when you said you don't know much about baseball, were you?" Temple said with a grin. When she shrugged he explained. "The Red Sox sold Ruth to the Yankees in 1920 for a paltry sum. And now the Yankees beat them every time! They call it 'the curse of the Bambino.' In fact, Ruth did so well for the Yankees that this stadium we're in is called 'the house that Ruth built.'"

"Wow," she said, looking around the impressive stadium. "So we'll see him play for the Yankees today, then?"

"Not so fast," Temple said. "He's playing for the Boston Braves this year, but I just saw in the paper today that he's retiring for good. Baseball is losing its greatest player ever!"

Sharon enjoyed learning more about the game and found

herself getting involved with it, though she did not know the fine points as Temple obviously did. Munching on a mustard-covered hot dog, she was intrigued by one of the Yankees who was obviously a favorite of the fans.

"What do you know about Lou Gehrig?" she asked. "The fans seem to love him."

"Highest-paid player in baseball," he said, shelling a couple of peanuts and popping them into his mouth. "The Yankees are giving him a whopping thirty thousand this year! He deserves it. He's one of the greatest players in the game."

Sharon was pulling for the Yankees—perhaps because it had been Robert's favorite team, or perhaps because she enjoyed watching the popular Gehrig. She sat up and took special notice when Gehrig came to bat in the bottom of the eighth inning with the bases loaded, two outs, and the score tied two to two. When the first pitch came, Gehrig did not lift his bat, and the umpire signaled, "Strike one!"

Sharon was so excited she jumped to her feet and surprised even herself by yelling, "Why, you idiot, you're blind as a bat!"

Temple pulled her back, laughing. "Hey, calm down."

"Calm down? Didn't you see that was a ball?"

"It's whatever the umpire calls it. If the ball is ten feet over the batter's head and the umpire calls it a strike, it's a strike. Nobody ever won an argument with an umpire."

A second pitch came and the umpire called it a strike. "What's with that stupid umpire!" she declared.

"Don't worry, kiddo. It's only a game, you know."

The pitcher wound up and let the ball go a third time. Gehrig uncoiled like a steel spring, and everyone in the ball park heard the crack of the bat.

"That's outta here!" Temple shouted, now jumping to his feet. "That's four runs! They have it in the bag now!"

Sharon leaped up too, and as the ball cleared the fence, she jumped up and down, screaming, "Thataway, Lou! Thataway!"

She turned to Temple and in her excitement threw her arms around him. He hugged her back for a moment, but then she pulled away, embarrassed. "I'm sorry. I didn't mean to do that."

"No need to be sorry," he said with a smile.

They found themselves locking eyes, not able to look at what was happening on the field. There in the middle of Yankee Stadium, with the crowd around them going mad over Gehrig's home run, Temple threw his arms back around Sharon and kissed her. Taken completely by surprise, she returned his kiss, feeling the heat of reckless emotions. As he responded to her, she sensed his intense loneliness and desire for her, even in the midst of the yelling crowd. But then she came to her senses and quickly pulled away. "Don't ever do that again!"

Temple smiled in return. "It takes two to make a kiss like that," he said evenly.

Sharon grabbed her purse and whirled around, shoving her way through the crowd toward the exit. He followed her out to her car in the parking lot, where he grabbed her arm to stop her before she got in.

She pulled her arm away, saying tersely, "Good-bye, Temple."

"Wait, Sharon. Let's talk. Didn't you enjoy yourself?"

She hesitated, then said, "Yes, I enjoyed myself, but I'm sorry about the way it ended."

"I'm not," he said. "That was the first time you let yourself escape from the secret place you hide in, Sharon. I'm happy to know there's a real woman living behind the face you put on. It's good to be passionate about life . . . and to let it show now and then!"

She just stared at him because she had no answer, then again said tersely, "I have to get home. Good-bye."

"Good-bye, Sharon. I hope I'll see you again."

She got in the car without a word and drove off. She saw him in her rearview mirror watching her leave and felt tears stinging her eyes. She was furious—not with Temple so much as with herself. She could not understand what had happened. The two were so different, and yet she had yielded to his embrace like a ... *like a wanton woman!* she thought. She had felt desire and was ashamed of herself.

While she drove home she thought back over the day—sitting next to Temple in church, enjoying conversation over a hot dog, experiencing the thrill of the game. She was thinking about the kiss when she got home and met her father in the foyer, his face ashen. .

"What is it, Dad?" Sharon said, her concern causing her to quickly forget the uncomfortable scene with Temple.

"It's your mother," Leland said. "She's taken a turn for the worse. I'm afraid it might be influenza."

Sharon stood momentarily speechless. She knew how deadly the flu virus could be, remembering how millions around the world had died of the Spanish flu after the Great War.

"There isn't a minute to waste, then, Dad. Call Dr. Evans at once!"

CHAPTER SEVENTEEN

THE PROMISE

★ ★ ★

Dr. Melvin Evans stood in the center of the Winslows' parlor, a frown on his bearded square face. He was a short, stocky man with legs like stumps. He looked more like a wrestler than a physician, but he was one of the finest physicians around. He spoke in a harsh, raspy voice that belied his compassion for the sick. But his concern was evident as he stood before the Winslow family.

"I'm afraid Mrs. Winslow isn't doing as well as I would hope. This flu could turn into pneumonia, and with her weak heart, that would not be good at all."

"She doesn't like hospitals," Sharon said, a tremble in her voice. "She's always been afraid of them."

Dr. Evans nodded. "I know. She begged me not to make her go there."

"But shouldn't she go if she's this sick?" Leland asked anxiously. "I want the best for her."

"It's a choice you and she will have to discuss. She's so set against it that it might hurt more than help. Actually," he said, shrugging his beefy shoulders, "I think she'll be just as well off here at home. I don't mean to frighten you, but there's really nothing that can be done for an illness like this in a hospital. If she needed surgery, then of course hospitalization would be required. But what she needs now is peace and quiet and rest—and the very best nursing. Probably around the clock."

"I'll be here all the time," Sharon said quickly.

"You can't watch after her twenty-four hours a day, Miss Winslow," Evans said. "You should consider hiring a nurse to help you."

"Could you recommend some good candidates?" Leland said.

"Of course, I have several I'm familiar with." The doctor gave them half a dozen names, including that of Seana Morgan.

"Seana Morgan! Why, she's the daughter of our groundskeeper here," Leland said with surprise. "Is she good enough?"

"I would say she's the best of those I've named. I've had constant contact with her at the hospital. She helped me once before with a very difficult patient in a private home. She has a very good reputation."

"So you think she would be suitable for this job?" Sharon asked.

"Certainly! She's firm but very comforting to patients. That means a great deal, you know, Miss Winslow. Sick people need comfort for the soul almost as much as they do medication for the body. Yes, if she's available, I would recommend her strongly."

"Let's see if she's willing to do it, Dad," Sharon said at once.

Leland nodded. "Very well. I'll call the hospital and try to engage her right away."

Dr. Evans was pleased by their decision. He packed up his equipment, assuring them he would make as many calls as necessary. As he picked up his black bag and jammed his derby down over his head, he said, "I'll feel better with Seana Morgan on the job. If she has a fault it might be that she's a little over-religious, but for some patients that's good. I think your mother is one of those who might profit by it."

Sharon showed the doctor out and then stood by the doorway of the study while her father called the hospital. She could tell by her father's end of the conversation that things were going well.

When he hung up the phone, he turned to Sharon and said, "Everything's set. Seana will start first thing in the morning."

Together they went to Lucille's bedroom, where Clayton was sitting in a chair at the bedside. Leland took his wife's hand and told her that the doctor had suggested she have nursing care at home. He explained that Seana was highly recommended and that she would start the next morning.

"You hear that, Mother?" Clayton said. "You're going to have a fine nurse. Seana and I will have you back on your feet in no time."

"Thank you, dear, that's so good to know." Lucille was pale, and her voice was weak. "I hate to be so much trouble."

"Trouble?" Leland said, leaning over and kissing Lucille on the brow. "There's no such thing as trouble where you're concerned, my dear. We'll have you out of this bed before you know it!"

★ ★ ★

When Seana arrived early the next morning, Sharon greeted her and took her up to her mother's room. Clayton had been with his mother for the last three hours and now turned over the responsibility to Seana. He went downstairs and moped around the house, too worried about his mother to feel like doing anything. He loved his mother dearly, even though he knew she had shamelessly spoiled him. All of his life he had been able to go to her with any problem. Now he worried that she would not recover.

He walked aimlessly about the house, going outside from time to time. It was a beautiful June day, but he had no eye for the beauty of the grounds. He did pass by the spot where the new pond was to be located and thought about his disagreement with Seana. The argument had rankled him, and Sarah had asked him several times since then if he still found the red-haired daughter of the groundskeeper attractive. Clayton had wished fervently he had never mentioned such a thing.

At noon Clayton went into the kitchen, where Mabel fixed him a chicken-salad sandwich. He had little appetite and ate only half of it, then nibbled at an apple. After finishing he went upstairs to his mother's bedroom and knocked quietly. The door opened and Seana came out quickly and shut the door behind her. She was wearing a white nurse's uniform, with white stockings and white shoes, and her face was framed by the wealth of red hair. "What is it, Mr. Winslow?"

"I want to see my mother."

"I'm sorry. You can't see her right now."

Instantly Clayton grew stubborn. "She's *my* mother. I can see her if I want to."

"She's resting now, and she doesn't need to be disturbed. You can see her later."

Clayton's lips drew together tightly. He was unaccustomed to being challenged, yet somehow this woman seemed to do so constantly. She was watching him with her full attention, and he noted that her eyes were a peculiar green that seemed to have no bottom. He also could not help noticing the rich curve of her mouth. Her rosy complexion was fair and smooth, as beautiful as Clayton had ever seen.

As for her figure, the light that came through the window at the end of the hall was kind to her, showing the full, soft lines of her body not concealed by the austere nurse's uniform. He saw her willfulness in the set of her jaw and the hint of pride in her eyes, and the fragrance that hung about her was intoxicating. He found her a powerfully attractive girl, but he was determined not to let that show.

Clayton stood resolutely and shook his head. "Seana Morgan, you must get up every morning saying to yourself, 'Now, how can I find a way to irritate Clayton Winslow today!'"

The hint of a smile tugged at the corners of her mouth and showed in the tilt of her head. "That's right. I spend all of my spare time thinking of ways to frustrate you."

Clayton laughed shortly. "I guess that's why you're such an expert at it. How's my mother?"

"She's the same as she was when you saw her this morning. She's very weak, and she needs complete and total rest and no aggravation."

"And you think I aggravate her."

"You have been known to aggravate people."

Clayton flushed. "I've been working up to tell you—" He broke off, unable to find the words and then shook his head. "Look, Seana, I got off to a bad start with you, and I've been meaning to tell you I'm sorry that I offended you the first time we met in the stable."

"Well, there is nice you are!" Seana smiled fully then, exposing brilliantly white teeth. "I've been wanting to tell you that I didn't mean to shove you down into that mess. I just wanted to get away from you." She put out her hand like a man would. "All right. We're square on that."

He took her hand and noticed that it was surprisingly strong and not as soft as most women's hands. "You're quite a versatile person—fixing tractors, working in the garden, nursing. Your hands are a working woman's hands."

Seana lifted her eyebrows. "You're not holding my hand, are you?"

Clayton instantly dropped her hand and laughed softly. "I suppose I was, but please don't shove me down again. I didn't mean anything by it."

The two stood in the hallway, speaking quietly so as not

to disturb the patient. "Would you care to join me for a cup of coffee?" Seana asked.

"That sounds good."

They went down to the kitchen, where Mabel poured them each some coffee. He took his with cream and sugar, and Seana drank hers black. They sat down at the kitchen table while Mabel continued her work at the counter. With the warm sunshine streaming through the window, they both relaxed. Clayton asked, "It's a bit strange your being here, isn't it? I mean of all the nurses in New York and there you are waiting in the wings."

"I think God put me here."

Clayton stared at her. She had spoken of God as normally as if she had spoken of her father.

"You really believe that, don't you?"

Seana's eyes flew open wide. "Well, bless you, of course I believe that! Do you think God created us and put us here and then left us alone to go our own way?"

"As a matter of fact, I suppose I have thought something like that."

"Tell me this: when you have a son, is that what you'll do with him? Just shove him out the door and say, 'Don't bother me with your problems'?"

"I hope not."

"Well, devil fly off, I hope not too!" Seana sipped her coffee. "God made us each one different, but He's as interested in you, Clayton Winslow, as if you were the only human being in all the world. He designed you before you were even born, and He knows every thought you ever had or ever will have—as well as every deed good or bad—and His desire is for you to conform to the image of His Son Jesus Christ."

Clayton sat absolutely still. He had never been preached at like this before! There was a hidden fire in this girl that refused to stay inside. Her eyes spoke as she looked at him steadfastly, and every line of her body showed that she fully believed what she was saying.

"I've just never had that kind of religion."

"Everybody's got religion of some kind. I suppose the old Scratch himself has some."

"Old Scratch?"

"That's what they call the devil back in Wales. Listen, you don't need more religion. You need Jesus."

"I believe in Jesus, of course."

"Do you trust Him with all your heart and soul? Do you love Him with everything that's in you?"

Clayton wished fervently that he had not come downstairs to have this cup of coffee! He nervously twisted the cup around and finally met her eyes. She was watching him intently. In meeting her glance, he suddenly found her a rather provocative challenge—not the simple daughter of the family's groundskeeper but a complex and unfathomable individual. He noticed that as she leaned forward speaking of Jesus, her breath came quickly and color ran freshly across her cheeks.

"I'll tell you what," she said. "I'd like to give you some suggestions for how to act when you go up to see your mother."

"I think I know how to act with my own mother."

"Perhaps you do, but let me encourage you to tell her good things. Tell her she's going to get well. Read some of the promises out of the Bible."

"We're not that kind of a family, Seana."

"I believe you're going to be one day."

Her confidence took Clayton by surprise. "Why do you think that?"

"Because my dad and I are praying that you will find Jesus precious." She sipped her coffee and said, "Now, that's the end of my sermon for the day. Tell me about building towers and bridges."

Clayton found this much easier than the intense conversation that had preceded. He was surprised at how quick the girl was. She knew little of architecture, but he found himself explaining his pet theories.

After a few moments she got up, saying, "I must get back to your mother. Maybe you'll tell me some more about your buildings later."

Clayton rose and said, "When do you think she'll wake up?"

"I'll come and get you when she does." She smiled and then said, "You're not as bad as I thought you were at first, Clayton Winslow. You have a good heart—toward your mother, at least." She smiled, and he noticed again the dimple that appeared on her right cheek. "You're going to be a good man after you let God take charge of you."

Clayton watched as she turned and left the kitchen; then he heard Mabel say, "I guess she cleaned your clock, didn't she, Mr. Clayton?"

Clayton nodded. "I guess she did, but you know, it wasn't all that bad, Mabel."

★　★　★

After three days Lucille took a turn for the worse. Dr. Evans came at once, and after examining her, he met with the family in the parlor again. "I'm not optimistic. With her heart condition, the prognosis isn't good."

"Is it pneumonia?" Sharon asked, dreading to say the word.

Evans stroked his beard and refused to meet her eyes. "I don't want to frighten you, but she's very close to it."

"Should she be in the hospital?" Leland demanded.

"I don't think so."

"But what can we do?" Clayton asked almost desperately. "There must be something, Dr. Evans."

"We're doing all that human beings can do." Evans started to say something else but then clamped his lips together. He looked almost stern, for he did not like to see disease get the better of his patients. He lifted his hands in a strange gesture. "We'll have to depend on God, I think."

★　★　★

Clayton could not forget the doctor's words: *"We'll have to depend on God."* He had never had to consider such a thing. His family's wealth had insulated him from much of the world's harshness. But now he knew that death could stalk the grounds of the millionaire as well as the tenements on the Lower East Side.

All day long he fretted and could not concentrate on anything. When evening came, he sat silently at the dinner table. His father and sister were disheartened too, barely touching their food. They finally broke up, and each quietly went his separate way.

Clayton listened to the radio for a time, but was not even aware of which program was on. He was thinking of his mother. He tried to read for a while and then went to bed and tossed and turned. He tried to convince himself that he was going to sleep, but he could not.

He got up and put on his robe and slippers. He walked down to his mother's room and cautiously turned the knob, trying to make no sound. As the door cracked open, he heard someone speaking, and when he pushed the door open slightly, he expected to see Seana talking to his mother. Instead he saw that the girl was on her knees beside the bed. As he moved closer he could hear her words.

"O Lord, this woman is beyond the help of doctors and medicine, but she is not beyond your help, for with thee, O Lord God Almighty, nothing is impossible. I pray, O God, that you would manifest your glory and heal her body. Let your mercy shine forth and be a living witness to those in this house that you are the Lord God Almighty and that you are worthy of all our love and all our devotion. . . ."

Clayton listened spellbound as she prayed on and on. The prayer was like nothing he had ever heard. At times Seana grew almost demanding. He heard her say, "O God, you have spoken in your Word, and I stand on it. Now,

Lord, you have to fulfill your Word as you always do. And I'm expecting that you're going to do exactly what I'm asking—and that is to heal Lucille Winslow."

At other times she prayed in a language he did not know but suspected was Welsh. There was a lilt to it, a different cadence from English.

Once he heard a sob in her voice. He was shocked when she stretched out full-length on the floor and cried, "O God, you are my hope and my trust! Heal this woman, I plead. I can do no more than beg you, Lord, for I know you are merciful."

Clayton quietly left and shut the door, emotionally stirred in a way he had never been in his life. Here this girl who was practically a stranger to his family was crying out to God with such fervor! He went back to his room and sat down on his bed, unable to get her prayers out of his mind. He knelt beside his bed, something he had not done since he was a small boy, and began to pray. There was no eloquence in it, and he spoke to God rather awkwardly. When he could think of nothing else to say, he got into bed and stared up at the ceiling. "God, I wish I could pray like Seana, but I guess I'd have to be a better Christian than I am. So please, God, hear her prayers if you won't hear mine."

★ ★ ★

He slept fitfully, tossing most of the night and awakening at dawn. He got up and went downstairs, where he found Seana speaking with Sharon. Seana turned to Clayton at once, her eyes bright. "Your mother had a good night's rest, and when she woke up this morning, she was so much better. Her fever is gone, and her pulse is almost regular now."

"She's going to be all right?" Clayton whispered.

"Yes, thanks to the living God, it looks like she's going to be all right."

Clayton felt as if the weight of the world had been lifted from his shoulders, and he felt tears come to his eyes. He quickly turned away and mumbled, "That's wonderful, Seana."

CHAPTER EIGHTEEN

THE TROUBLE WITH BEING RICH

★ ★ ★

"I've never seen anything like it. It usually takes people weeks to recover from a thing like this."

Dr. Evans was standing beside Lucille, who smiled up at him, her face glowing with new color. "I really feel able to get up, Doctor."

"We'll talk about that tomorrow. I suppose in the meantime you could use the wheelchair."

"That would be so nice. I'm tired of this bed."

Clayton, who stood behind the doctor listening, said nothing. He was remembering Seana's prayers for his mother and wondering if he was observing a miracle. Like Dr. Evans, he found it hard to believe his mother's recovery had anything to do with prayer. Now he heard Dr. Evans say, "Your heart is more regular than it's been in years, Lucille, but I still want you to take care of yourself." The doctor turned to Leland and said, "You watch her now; make sure she doesn't try to do too much too soon."

"I'll watch her like a hawk, Doctor," Leland said.

Dr. Evans smiled down at Lucille. "I'll come back and check on you tomorrow, but you mind your nurse."

"Yes, Doctor, of course."

As soon as Dr. Evans and his father left, Clayton drew a chair up beside the bed and sat down. Seana was freshening up after a long night with little sleep. "You gave us all quite a scare, you know."

"I know, dear. I'm so sorry to be such a bother."

"How could you be that?" Clayton took her hand and kissed it. "You look marvelous. You've got color in your cheeks, and your eyes are clear, and the doctor says your heart is doing fine."

"I'm so grateful to be well, son."

Clayton held her hand for a moment longer. "Do you remember much about when you were at your lowest point?"

"I remember thinking I was going to die. I was only barely conscious, but it seems I remember hearing Seana praying for me."

"She probably was."

"She's such a dear young woman. She cared for me so marvelously."

"Now we're going to get you stronger so you won't need a nurse."

"Do you suppose I could have some breakfast?"

"Of course. I'll go see to it."

Clayton went downstairs to the kitchen and had Mabel prepare a tray for his mother. When he took it up to her, he saw that Seana had returned and was bending over the bed washing his mother's face with a cloth.

"And a good morning to you, Mr. Clayton Winslow."

"Good morning, Seana. How does the patient look?"

"She couldn't look better."

Clayton sat with his mother while she ate a good breakfast, and then Seana shooed him out, saying it was time for him to leave. He left the room but waited in the hallway until Seana came out. "She looks great, doesn't she?" he said.

"She's had a healing touch from the Lord God."

"Seana, I have a confession to make."

"Only one?"

"Well, one in particular. Last night when my mother was so bad, I couldn't sleep. I came down to see how she was, and when I opened the door, I heard you praying."

"Did you, now!"

"Yes. I never believed much in things like that. Our family prayers were pretty perfunctory, I guess."

"But now you must believe. Perhaps your mother was ill so that you and your father and your sister could see the power of God."

"Perhaps."

He wanted to inquire more into the matter but found it hard to speak to her. "I know I've apologized for my behavior when I first met you in the stable, but I keep thinking of it, so let me tell you again how sorry I am."

"You don't have to apologize every time you see me! You told me you were sorry, and I said I was sorry, so now it's buried. That's the way it is with our sins when we come to Jesus. God takes all of our sins and puts them in a bottomless sea and puts up a No Fishing sign."

He could not help smiling. "You know, I think apologizing to you might be the hardest thing I've ever done."

"You're not good at admitting you're wrong, are you, Mr. Clayton?"

"Just call me Clayton. No 'mister.' No, I'm not."

Seana had a look of compassion in her fine green eyes. "That's the trouble with being rich. You never have to say you're wrong."

"That's not so."

"I think it is. It's only when you're flat on your back and there's nowhere else to look but God that you really feel the need to pray."

"I've been wondering how you could pray for my mother like that. You're not even related. You hardly knew each other."

"I asked God to give me a burden for her, and He did,"

she said simply. "It was clear that she needed someone to pray for her, and I seemed to be the likeliest candidate. It's what's called intercessory prayer when we can pray for others like that. You should try it sometime."

He could not get over Seana's boldness. "I actually did pray for my mother last night. But I could tell when you prayed you really believed God was going to heal her."

"You're making progress, you are, Clayton," Seana said with a smile. "Now, be off with you. I've got work to do, so you go design a bridge or something."

★ ★ ★

"Where in the world are we going, Temple?"

"We're taking a vacation. We need a break, a little relaxation."

Sharon was on the back of Temple's motorcycle, holding on to him tightly. She thought back over the last two weeks, amazed that her mother was well again and that she was together with Temple again. In the face of her mother's brush with death, Sharon had turned to him for comfort. Despite her embarrassment and anger over their kiss at the ball park, he was the only person she wanted to be with in the midst of her family crisis. He had been more than willing to come to the Winslow estate when she called and offer his emotional support. During the last week the two had taken up their visits to the poor again and had been visiting a family named Ramsey whose youngest child had just died. The family had no money for a funeral or burial, and Sharon had privately helped them with that.

As they bounced over the roads on the motorcycle, Sharon remembered watching Temple talk with Mr. and Mrs. Ramsey, impressed with how gentle he was. Despite his rough-looking exterior, he had a compassion she had rarely seen in a man—or a woman either, for that matter.

"Why, this is Coney Island!" Sharon exclaimed as they

pulled into the parking lot of the famous park.

"Sure is," Temple said as he stopped in a suitable parking spot. "Have you ever been here?"

"Not for years and years. My dad brought me here with my best friends for my sixteenth birthday."

"Wow! That *has* been years! It's a great place to be a kid again. Let's pretend we're sixteen years old."

"I can't even think back that far."

They bought a book of tickets for the rides, which they found were all going at full speed. "How about that one?" Temple said. "The Octopus."

Sharon looked at the Octopus with apprehension. Its cars were mounted on eight long steel arms that went around and up and down. The cars swiveled as the arms turned, spinning too violently for her liking.

"I'm not sure about that one."

"There's only one way to get sure about it, kiddo. Let's try it! Come on."

Sharon reluctantly followed. She got into the seat with Temple settling in beside her, and the attendant fastened a thick wooden bar in front of them. She grasped it nervously. "I'm not sure this is such a good idea."

"I am. When you're on one of these things, you can't think about your troubles—you're too busy wondering if you're gonna die soon!"

Sharon flashed him a worried look as the ride started up and she found herself being thrown around. She bounced off the side of the car, then against Temple. He put his arm around her and held her tight, laughing. "I'm your safety belt. Just trust me!"

The ride was exhilarating, and Sharon discovered that she liked it after all.

"That was fun!" she said as they tumbled off together, dizzy and laughing.

"Let's do the roller coaster next." Temple grabbed her hand, and they headed to the roller coaster like a couple of schoolchildren.

Sharon actually enjoyed it more than Temple did. When they pulled out of one of the steep dives, she turned to him and saw the strain on his face. "Come on. This is relaxation," she teased. "I'm the one who's supposed to be scared."

"I keep wondering what would happen if this thing went off the track."

Sharon had wondered that too but had dismissed the thought. "Don't be afraid," she kidded him. "As Seana would say, 'What is to be will be.'"

After several more rides, Temple bought some cotton candy and two candied apples. Eating the sticky treats in the summer heat, Sharon shook her head helplessly. "You need a shower after eating these things."

"We could take a dip at the beach," Temple said with a grin.

"No thanks," Sharon said quickly. There was no way she would even dream of wearing a bathing suit in public!

Sharon could hardly believe what a good time she was having. All the stress of the last two weeks had simply melted away, and she felt a release of the spirit as she and Temple laughed like children. She knew she should be acting more dignified. Women her age did not run around amusement parks with abandon, but for once she really didn't care what anyone else thought.

They came to the Ferris wheel, and as Sharon got in a car, she saw that Temple was whispering something to the operator. When he sat down beside her, she asked, "What did you say?"

"Oh, just meddling. I always think I have to run everything. That's my gift."

"What did you tell him?" she demanded.

"I'm allowed to have a few secrets, aren't I? Just enjoy the ride."

Sharon did enjoy the ride, but after three turns, when their car reached the top of the enormous wheel, the ride stopped, causing the seat to rock alarmingly. The view was breathtaking, but as she peeked over the side toward the ground, Sharon said nervously, "Whew! I feel like we're sitting on nothing." It was a long way to the ground, and the laughter and shouts of children sounded muted from this distance.

"It's nice up here," Temple said. "Maybe we'll just stay here for a while."

Sharon swung her head to look at him. "You told that man to do this, didn't you?"

"Yes, I did. He won't let us down until I give him a signal."

"Why in the world would you do that?"

Temple put his arm around her shoulder and pulled her against him. "Because I wanted a private moment to tell you how much I've come to care for you. I never thought I'd care for anyone again after I lost Heather, but God's given me a great love for you, Sharon. I want to marry you, and I want us to spend the rest of our days together."

He drew her to him in a fervent but tender kiss, and Sharon forgot for a moment where they were. Feeling the strength of his arm around her and his lips on hers, she savored the sweetness and surrendered herself to him. She clung to him as the car swayed, with the muted sounds of the crowd reaching her as if from a distant planet. Suddenly the rashness of the moment gripped her with fear, and she put her hand on his chest and pushed him back. "No, Temple. This is wrong. I can't marry you. I'm past that now. I'll never marry anyone."

"Why, Sharon? You're wasting your life. God has so much more for you."

"I'm not wasting my life. I'm doing good things. I don't need . . ." Her voice trailed off, for despite her words and protests she recognized a desire for love coming alive in her that she had thought was long dead and buried. Still in his embrace, she trembled and shook her head. "I can't do this, Temple. I just can't be the woman you want me to be."

Temple said nothing more, just signaled to the operator

to bring them down. They got off the ride together in silence and made their way out of the park. Sharon fought back the tears that threatened to embarrass her further. She could not believe that she had ruined another wonderful day with Temple! But maybe he was the one who kept ruining things by pushing her to be something she simply could not be. Why couldn't he understand that? She was forty years old. Certainly too old to marry now. Yet she craved his friendship and enjoyed the closeness they shared. And she *had* returned his kiss. . . .

★   ★   ★

It was evening when they arrived back at the Winslow estate. The sun was setting in a glorious display of color, and Sharon could not bear to send Temple away. She invited him to walk with her out on the grounds. Perhaps they could come to some understanding. They paused to look out over the new flower beds Clayton had designed, but she saw little as she pondered the nature of their relationship and where they should go from here.

Temple was the first to break the silence. "Every time I think of you, Sharon, a song from my childhood comes to mind. May I sing it for you?"

Sharon nodded and listened to his strong baritone voice lift on the evening breeze as he sang the sweet lilting melody:

"There's a harp that is silent, whose strings were of gold,
And whose song, as the jasper, was clear,
Oh, its cadence so rare was of beauty untold
As it fell like a charm on the ear.

"There's a lute that is 'reft of its beautiful strings—
It is shattered, and silent, and still,
And the song that once rose as on glorified wings,
Now no longer our senses can thrill."

When he stopped, Sharon let the tears she had been holding back freely fall. "That's beautiful, Temple. What does that song mean to you? Why does it remind you of me?"

"I would think that's obvious, Sharon. You are the most beautiful creature alive to me—like a golden harp that was designed for the angels to play. But the strings are silent now, and the beautiful music can't be heard because you won't allow yourself to be the woman God made you to be. You're like a silent harp—hiding away in this beautiful castle in the country that no one else can see." He swept his arm around the magnificent grounds. "But more importantly, you've hidden your God-given melody inside of yourself."

She started to object, but he shook his head to stop her. "Oh, you let it out a little here and there. Through your art . . . through visiting the poor and giving your money. But that's only a part of what God wants, Sharon. He wants *you*. He wants all of you. He wants you to be the wonderful instrument He has created, on which He can play beautiful melodies for all the world to hear. He didn't make you to be a silent harp—for others only to look at but never to be played." He looked at her with eyes that were almost sad. "Am I making any sense to you?"

"Maybe . . ." Sharon said quietly. "But what . . . what does that have to do with us?"

"You're as silent as the harp in that song. And what good is a silent harp to anyone?"

"Silent?" she came back. "I don't know what you mean by that. I'm not a harp and I'm not silent!"

"God made you a woman, and a woman is not meant to be alone. A woman needs a man and a family. But you won't allow that in your life because you've made an idol of Robert—and I'm sure he would have hated that."

"That's . . . that's not so!"

"It *is* so, Sharon. And that other fellow who was after your money—he betrayed your trust, and now you've built a wall around your life so that nobody can get close enough to hurt you. You live behind your wall of money, hiding from the things you really need." Finally he said, "You're like a silent harp, a beautiful instrument that is of no use to anyone because it's not fulfilling the very thing it was created for."

"No . . . no, don't talk like this, Temple! I *am* trying to live the way God wants me to. You're not being fair to say these things."

He studied her face. "Why won't you marry me, Sharon? I know you love me, and I love you more than words can say. Is it because of money?"

The question struck her with the force of a blow as he touched a sensitive spot deep within her. A sense of shame came over her as she realized this was indeed the reason she was holding back her feelings for Temple and not allowing herself to surrender fully to his love. She could not deny that the difference in their attitudes toward money had influenced her thinking.

"You've got the wrong idea about money. Money is not what makes a man—or a woman—valuable to God. It's only people who think money is so important."

Sharon had heard all she cared to. Wiping the tears from her cheeks, she whispered, "I can't see you anymore, Temple. This is never going to work between you and me."

He sighed and gazed into her eyes. "I won't talk anymore about marriage, but don't expect me to stay completely out of your life."

Sharon was secretly glad he didn't agree to go away for good. "We can be friends, then. But let's not talk any more of marriage."

He took both of her hands in his. "I won't . . . I promise. But I also promise to be here listening when that silent harp wakes up and begins playing her very own melody!"

PART FOUR

September–October 1935

★ ★ ★

CHAPTER NINETEEN

LELAND'S SECRET

★ ★ ★

"Mr. Wright will be just a few more moments. Would you please take a seat, Mr. Winslow. He won't be long."

"Yes, I'll wait."

"There's the latest paper in case you haven't seen it."

"Thank you." Leland sat down in the blue velour chair and picked up the paper. The photo under the September 16 date on the front page showed the new German flag, just unveiled this week. "The *swastika*, a symbol of prosperity and good fortune," the caption explained. To Leland it simply looked like a hideous broken cross. With growing concern lately, he had read the news filtering out of Europe over the remilitarization of Germany and the rise of the Nazi Party. He felt in his gut the world would someday regret that they were allowing Germany to re-arm, but he also felt helpless to do anything about it. Most Americans gave little thought to what was happening across the Atlantic, and Leland himself had his own business troubles to contend with.

He glumly searched through the paper, finding very little that was promising. The Depression still held the nation in an iron grasp, and the result of the ongoing financial woes was that Leland had arrived at the First National Bank of New York to beg for a loan. During the last six months he had seen a dramatic downturn in his business and had lost millions. The decision to seek a loan had come hard for him, but it had to be done.

"Mr. Wright is free now, Mr. Winslow."

"Thank you."

Getting up from his seat, Leland placed the paper on the coffee table and walked through the large door into the office of Daniel Wright. The bank president got up from his desk and came over to offer his hand. "Hello, Leland. Good to see you."

"Daniel. How are you?"

The two men exchanged pleasantries, but Leland sensed a tension in the face of the tall man. He had banked at this institution for years, and their meetings had always been pleasant, but today he felt a constraint in the countenance of Daniel Wright. Finally Leland found the courage to ask, "What about the loan, Daniel?"

Wright hesitated, apparently searching for the right words, and Leland felt a coldness close around his heart. He hastened to explain his position. "This downturn has happened so suddenly. I know we can come back from it with some help. The trouble is all of our equipment is outworn. New techniques have come along. If we can just restructure and get new equipment, I know we'll be all right."

"I hope so, Leland. You've been a faithful supporter of this bank for years, but the meeting didn't go well." Wright looked at his desk and bit his lower lip. "I did my best to get the committee to approve your loan, but in the end they declined. These are very hard times for everyone. I'm sure you understand that."

A silence fell across the office as Leland absorbed the bad news. "All right," he said wearily. "I know you did your best."

"These things can change quickly," Wright added. "I've

seen loans denied one month, and the next month there's an entirely new feeling. I'll work on the committee man to man. We'll try again in a few weeks. Try to keep your head up."

"Thanks, Daniel. Well, I guess I'll be going."

As the door closed behind Leland, he heard Daniel say aloud, "There are times when I *hate* being a banker!"

★ ★ ★

That evening over supper, Daniel Wright found himself telling his wife about the meeting with Leland Winslow. "I hated to turn him down," he said, "but we did some investigating, and the Winslow lumber business isn't what it used to be. Leland took a pretty bad beating when the market fell in twenty-nine, but he did pull out of that all right. Now this trouble is perhaps worse than the first."

"You mean he's going to lose his business?"

"I'm afraid it could come to that."

Ethel digested this, and when supper was over, she went right to the telephone to call her closest friend, Mary Mellon. It was very unusual for her husband to reveal something spoken in confidence in his office; therefore she took it as a sign that she should warn her friend. When a woman answered, Ethel said, "Is that you, Mary?"

"Yes, you should know my voice by this time, Ethel."

"I had to be sure. I'm going to tell you something in absolute confidence. You must promise not to tell anyone about it and certainly not where you heard it."

"Of course. What in the world is it?"

"It's about Leland Winslow. . . ." Ethel quickly gave the facts, then ended by saying, "It's really wrong of me to tell you this, but if I had a daughter thinking of marrying a certain young man, I'd want to know about the state of his inheritance."

"I'm so glad you called me. I'll never breathe a word of this to anyone."

"Do you think Sarah will listen to your concern over the fortunes of the Winslow family?"

"I hope so. We all like Clayton, but this sounds serious. It could lead to social disaster for us if Sarah were to marry a young man who's about to be bankrupt. I'll have a talk with her, and I'll of course keep your name out of it. Thank you so much for calling, Ethel."

"Let me know how it turns out."

"I certainly will. Good-bye."

★   ★   ★

"You wanted to see me, Dad?" Clayton said as he entered his father's study. "What's wrong? You look worried."

Leland had kept his secret for months now, but he could no longer keep his business problems from his family. They would have to know sooner or later. He stalled a moment by asking, "Has Sarah decided yet whether to marry you?"

"No, she's still walking a tightrope." He shrugged. "One day it's on, the next it's off."

Leland could not understand young people these days. When he had fallen in love with his wife years ago, he had felt intense emotional turmoil. Clayton seemed to feel none of this. Leland shook his head and launched into the matter at hand. "I want to talk to you about the business, son. I hate to be the bearer of evil tidings, but the Depression has finally caught up with us."

Clayton knew very little about the inner workings of the Winslow lumber empire. It had been assumed that he would one day inherit his father's business, but he did not show much interest in learning about it and had little grasp of the overall operation. "What's wrong, Dad?"

"The Depression is what's wrong. People aren't building

houses, and when people don't build houses, Winslow Industries loses money."

Clayton saw the weariness and concern in his father's eyes. "You're really worried about this, aren't you?"

"Clayton, I might as well tell you." He rubbed his face. "We may lose the business—and even this house."

Clayton could not fathom what his father had just said. The family business was just a given in his life, something he had always taken for granted—like the sun rising in the east and setting in the west. He had been a rather thought-less young man, which was not altogether his own fault. His parents had always provided everything he needed, and never had his father given him the slightest hint that any-thing was amiss. The Depression had closed thousands of businesses, but Clayton had never considered the possibility that the economy would affect his own family. "I didn't know things were bad for us."

"I didn't want to worry you, son—and don't say any-thing to your mother or your sister. This is just between us for now."

"Is there anything I can do?"

"At this point it looks as if the only thing we can do is pray. I went to the bank today, and they turned me down for a loan that would have saved the business."

"Turned you down! But, Dad, you've banked there for a millennium!"

"I know it, and the president's a good friend of mine. But all loans have to be approved by a committee, and the com-mittee didn't feel we'd be able to repay such a large sum. What I wanted to do was update everything. We've fallen behind in machinery, equipment—virtually everything—and without a loan there isn't much hope."

Clayton could not control his thoughts. They fluttered through his head like bats in an attic. "You know, Dad, I've always taken things for granted."

"I know you have. You're no different from the way I was at your age. We'll try our best to pull through, son."

This was cold comfort to Clayton, and as he left, he wondered, *Is there any way I could make it on my own?* The thought frightened him, for he had never done anything on his own. His parents had provided everything, and as he walked through the mansion that he had assumed would always be there, he was shaken to realize that none of his surroundings were necessarily permanent.

What will Sarah think about this? he wondered. *Her family has plenty of money. Should I even tell her?*

★ ★ ★

As Sharon and Temple came out of the church the following Sunday, they found the sun shining brightly. "It's going to be warm today, Temple."

"Yes, that's all right with me. I like hot weather. I hate the winter. Winters were pretty mild in Oklahoma, where I grew up, but I can do without these New York winters. Give me the heat any day."

"Did you go to college there? In Oklahoma?"

"I never went to college. I went to war instead."

The crowd was filing along the street on either side of them, and when they reached Sharon's car, she said, "I don't see your motorcycle."

"No, I walked."

"Oh. Can I take you someplace?"

"Sure. You can take me to the zoo."

"To the zoo?"

"Sure. When's the last time you went to the Bronx Zoo?"

Sharon tried to think. "I don't know. I was no more than ten or eleven years old."

"Time you went back, then."

She had been seeing Temple regularly all summer. After their discussion about marriage three months ago, he had kept his promise to never mention it again, and she was relieved. She enjoyed their friendship and wanted to keep it on that level, and she assumed he felt the same way now.

"Come on," Sharon said. "I'll drive, but you'll have to tell me how to get there."

"Okay. We can grab some hot dogs at the zoo."

They got in the car, and as they drove along, they discussed the morning's sermon. Their pastor had preached on the story of the rich young ruler from the nineteenth chapter of Matthew's Gospel. He had reminded them of Jesus' admonition that "It is easier for a camel to go through the eye of a needle, than for a rich man to enter the kingdom of God." Temple grinned at her. "I imagine that stirred some feelings among all of you rich people."

"I've never understood that Scripture passage," Sharon said thoughtfully. "Do you really think Jesus was saying that everybody ought to sell *everything* they have and give it to the poor?"

"No, I don't think that at all. I think some of the Bible is descriptive and some is prescriptive."

"What does that mean?"

"It means sometimes the Bible simply describes the situation. Like in this case, Jesus told this *particular* rich fellow that he needed to sell everything, but I don't think that applies to everyone with money. And some parts of the Bible are prescriptive—for instance, the command that everyone needs to be generous and give to the poor."

Sharon was always cautious in speaking with Temple about money. She did not know how he got by, for he seemed to have no regular hours or a job. He had none of the trappings of wealth, and yet he never seemed to want things.

"I've often thought about the biggest giver in the whole Bible," he said. "Do you know who that was?"

"No, I guess I don't."

"You'll find her in the Gospel of Mark, chapter twelve. It tells about a poor widow who put two mites into the offering plate—which was like a quarter of a penny. The religious leaders had all put in lots of money, but Jesus told His disciples that the poor widow had put in more than all of them! They were astonished, of course, but Jesus explained that the rich men had given out of their abundance and had plenty left for themselves. This poor widow had put in everything she owned. She had given it all to God." His voice was filled with admiration. "Of all the people in the Bible, I think I admire that poor woman the most—and we don't even know her name."

Sharon was silent for a moment. "That passage troubles me."

"Why is that?"

"It seems so . . . so irresponsible! I mean she had to eat. Maybe she had children. It doesn't seem like she could afford to give away everything she had. Especially when there were rich people to give and keep things going."

"I think rich people miss out on something," Temple replied. "This woman knew she didn't have enough to take care of herself. When she threw it all in, it was like saying, 'All right, Lord, I've given you everything. I'll starve if you don't feed me and take care of me.' Now, that's what I call faith."

Sharon did not like the implications. She herself had become a liberal giver through the church, but this story seemed to negate her own gifts and make them seem like not enough. She had always ignored such teachings from the Bible. "I still think it doesn't seem right."

"So do you think the widow starved to death?"

"Why . . . I don't know! I've never thought about it."

"I don't think so. I think God *did* take care of her. And I think she found one of the greatest pleasures in all of life."

"What's that, Temple?"

"Giving sacrificially. That's a joy most rich people will never know. I mean if you've only got a dollar, it doesn't seem like much to give the whole dollar. But suppose you've got a million dollars. How many people do you know who would give all of it and leave themselves with an empty account at the bank?"

"That wouldn't be . . ." She could not finish, for she somehow felt fenced in.

"Sharon, when was the last time you sacrificed something? When you had to do without something because you had given everything you had?"

. She did not answer but kept her eyes on the traffic in silence as she drove. She turned a corner and then angrily blurted, "I don't understand you when you talk like this! God gave us common sense, didn't He?"

"I don't think God is looking for common sense. I think He's looking for faith. If Moses had used common sense, he would never have gone down to Egypt to get a million slaves set free from a powerful pharaoh. If the first disciples had had common sense, they would never have followed a crucified Christ and allowed themselves to be persecuted and killed for their belief. Common sense is all right, I suppose, but the Bible says without faith it's impossible to please God."

Sharon drove silently again, and when they arrived at the zoo, she parked and turned to him. "Come on. That's enough serious talk for today. Let's go watch the monkeys. They remind me of you!"

★ ★ ★

The conversation was much more lighthearted while they were at the zoo, and they enjoyed watching the animals as well as the other people. As they left, Sharon said, "It's been such fun."

"We'll have to do it again. We didn't get to see nearly all of it."

"All right. We will."

Sharon drove back to the church, where Temple insisted that she drop him off. She realized that she didn't even know where he lived, but apparently it was within walking distance of the church. Again she wondered about all her unspoken questions. "I'll see you tomorrow," she said, assuming they would make their usual Monday rounds on the Lower East Side.

"No, not tomorrow. Not for a while, Sharon."

"What do you mean?"

"I've gotta go away for a time."

"But you'll be back, won't you?" Sharon was surprised at this turn of events and at her own reaction to the announcement. She did not want him to go away.

"I really can't say when or if I'll be back."

Sharon drummed her fingers against the steering wheel. Then it hit her. She turned her gaze on him and demanded bluntly, "Is it a woman, Temple?"

He nodded solemnly. "Yes, it is."

His direct answer left Sharon speechless. She knew she had no right to feel possessive. She had made it plain enough to him that day in her garden that there could never be anything serious between them, but now she was deeply disturbed that he had another relationship. "I know I have no right to pry into your private life, but is this woman someone . . . someone very close to you?"

"Very close indeed. I love her with all my heart."

"Then why did you talk about marriage to me this summer? Has this all happened since then?" Sharon's tone was sharp, and anger was rising in her.

"Why, Miss Winslow . . . I believe you're jealous."

"Don't be ridiculous!"

"Actually, there's no need for jealousy. I've got to go see my mother in Oklahoma. She's sick, and I need to be with her."

Sharon felt like an idiot. "I'm so sorry. Is she very ill?"

"I hope not, but I'll have to go see. And I don't know how long I'll be gone."

Knowing the truth of the matter, Sharon now wanted to help, and a thought occurred to her. Not wanting to offend him, she said carefully, "I know it's expensive traveling. I'd really like to help with your expenses." She took some bills out of her purse and handed them to him.

He took them and studied them as if they were rare and curious items. "You have a good heart, Sharon." He tucked the bills into his shirt pocket and stepped out of the car. "Good-bye," he said simply.

"I hope your mother does well."

"Thank you." Temple hesitated for a minute and then appeared almost ready to say something. Sharon looked at him eagerly, but he only said, "I hope I'll see you again." He turned and walked away without looking back, and Sharon felt a sense of loss she could not explain. As she started the car, she tried to put Temple Smith out of her mind, but she knew that was not going to be possible.

CHAPTER TWENTY

LUNCH AND A SERMON

★ ★ ★

The restaurant was crowded, and Clayton wished that Sarah liked less ostentatious places. The Colony on Sixty-second Street was her favorite place to eat, largely because it was also the place to be seen. Nothing was too good for the clientele. Clayton looked over the menu and frowned. He could barely pronounce some of the names: vichyssoise, pompano en papillote, pheasant aux huîtres. It was as if the cooks were afraid to serve ordinary food.

"I don't see why they can't just have roast beef and potatoes," Clayton complained.

Sarah gave him an amused look. "You can get roast beef at any old restaurant, but you're not going to find delicacies like eel ragout—or tripes à la mode de Caen."

"Well, who wants that anyway?" he griped.

"Why are you so hard to get along with today?"

"I don't know. Just grumpy, I guess." Clayton tried to cheer himself up by reading the wine list. It was pages long, with eighty-five different champagnes alone. As they sat waiting for their food, Sarah commented on various celebrities passing by. She was not particularly impressed by

Doug Fairbanks, Junior, but she did point out that several members of the Rockefeller family were eating there.

Clayton tried to hold up his end of the conversation, but it was difficult. He couldn't stop thinking how pretty Sarah looked tonight. Her silk gauze dress with a black-and-white print had a rounded neck and loose sleeves that came to a point at the elbow. The dress seemed to float about her as she moved, turning this way and that so as not to miss seeing any famous personage.

From time to time the patrons were treated to a display of culinary pyrotechnics when waiters brought out flaming food skewered on swords. "Look at that," he said, shaking his head in disgust, "they've even got hot dogs on flaming swords."

As they were having their dessert and coffee, Sarah said tentatively, "I hear your father's business is in trouble."

Clayton looked at her, startled. "Wherever did you hear that?"

"Oh, I don't know. Things like that get around."

He shrugged. "Well, things have been better."

"Do you think your father will be able to save the business?"

"Of course!" Clayton was not as certain as his reply sounded, and he suddenly turned serious. "I want to do something with my life, Sarah."

"What do you mean? You *are* doing something. You're going to college."

"No, I want to do more than that. I may drop out of college and go to work in the business. Dad needs my help."

Sarah was quiet for a moment. She was not accustomed to dealing with such problems. In her circle there were no business failures. For people like the Rockefellers and the Mellons, the government would have to fail before they'd lose their money.

After thinking about it, she said primly, "That seems the appropriate thing to do."

Her reply caused him some anxiety, and he asked, "Will

263

this affect your decision one way or the other about marrying me?"

"Of course not! Don't be foolish," Sarah said, laughing. She stood up and pulled on his arm. "Come on. Let's dance."

★ ★ ★

Despite what Sarah had told him over their fancy lunch, Clayton was glum. He knew her parents would never allow her to marry into a family that was going down financially. Mulling this over as he drove home from the Mellon mansion, he was surprised that it did not trouble him all that much. He had thought at one time that he was in love with Sarah, but now the thought of not marrying her was an acceptable possibility in his mind.

It was late afternoon when he arrived home, and he saw William sitting out in front of his cottage. On a whim, Clayton walked over to say hello to him.

William Morgan got to his feet and took his pipe out of his mouth. "Good day to you, sir."

"You're taking the day off?"

"Just resting a little. I'm about to put in that new bed of roses your mother wanted."

"A little late in the year for that, isn't it?"

"Yes, but I think we can make it work."

Seana stepped out of the cottage wearing a simple green dress. Her braided hair was pinned up in a circular design, and it gleamed in the sunlight like the sun's corona. "Good afternoon to you, Mr. Winslow."

"Hello, Seana. You're not in your uniform, I see. Are you off today?"

"Yes indeed, and I'm going to hear a great missionary speak tonight. I expect you'll be going as well."

"Me? No, I hadn't planned to."

"Your own relative, and you're not going?"

"My relative?"

"There's a foolish man, you are. Reverend Barney Winslow, the famous missionary from Africa, is speaking at the Calvary Baptist Church tonight."

"Oh, I didn't know he was in the States. I've never met him but I guess he's the half-cousin of my father—or something like that."

"Well, shame on you for missing an opportunity to hear him preach. I've got to go now. I don't want to be late."

"He's preaching this evening?"

"Yes, at six o'clock for a missionary gathering. I've just got time to get there."

An impulse seized Clayton. "Let me go with you."

Seana smiled warmly. "All right. That would be fine."

"You listen carefully now to what the reverend says," William said, removing his pipe again to speak. "I'll hear about it when you come back."

Seana leaned over and kissed her father. "That you will."

The two young people walked down to the garage and got into Clayton's car. He pulled it out and stopped it in the driveway, turning to her. "I don't know what's gotten into me all of a sudden. You don't suppose I'm getting religion, do you?"

Seana smiled at him, a light of humor dancing in her eyes. "No harm it will do you," she said. "But you don't need more religion. You need Jesus."

Clayton laughed and shook his head. "I guess I don't know the difference, but maybe I'll learn."

★　★　★

Clayton and Seana arrived right at six o'clock and were met at the door by a tall man with white hair. "It's pretty full, but I think there are still seats up in the balcony."

"But I'm a relative of Reverend Winslow," Clayton said quickly.

"Is that so? In that case, there are two remaining seats for important visitors right on the very front row. Come along."

The service had just started as the two walked into the sanctuary. The congregation was singing heartily, and as soon as they found their seats, Seana picked up a hymnbook from the rack and found the page for "Are You Washed in the Blood?"

"I don't think I know that one," Clayton said.

"You'll pick it up." She joined the others on the third verse in her rich contralto voice, which seemed to rise above those around her. She sang with fervor and intensity throughout several hymns.

When the singing ended, the minister made some announcements and then introduced the speaker.

"We're proud today to have Reverend Barney Winslow with us. Many of you have heard him speak before, and I trust all of you are familiar with the great pioneer work he has done in Africa." He went on for some time in glowing terms, then with a sweep of his hand, said, "Come, Brother Winslow, and give us your message."

Clayton had heard his father and other members of his family speak of the man, so he knew what to expect. The tall man with silvery gray hair was deeply tanned from his many years in the African sun. Though he had to be in his midsixties, he seemed as healthy and vigorous as a man half his age, and his voice rang out strong and clear.

"After that introduction," Barney said with a smile, "I feel like a pancake that's had syrup poured all over it." He paused for the laugh and then looked out over the congregation. "Before I preach, I want to tell you how very grateful I am to all of you who have come tonight. Many of you have supported our work in Africa to carry the glorious Gospel of Jesus to the peoples of that continent. So I thank you in the name of Jesus." He paused and opened his Bible. "The book of Acts has a message in it for all of us. I'm reading from Acts 1:8: 'But ye shall receive power, after that the

Holy Ghost is come upon you.' I am sure you know the story. Jesus had died and come out of the tomb and now appeared to His disciples. They were waiting, not knowing what to do. But here, just before He left to sit at the right hand of His Father, He gave them this promise: 'Ye shall receive power.'"

Winslow looked out over the congregation, searching out individuals. Clayton felt vulnerable and exposed as the preacher's eyes met his. It was as if Winslow were speaking directly to him. "The one thing everyone needs is not money or popularity or fame," Winslow said, his voice lifting to fill the sanctuary. "The one thing we all need is power. Power to live. Power to serve. Power to praise. We need to step out of the pitiful condition in which many Christians live and lay hold on the power of God." He pointed to the lights hanging from the high ceiling. "These lights that are burning overhead have no power in themselves. A wire runs from each one to a switch box. From there another wire runs to a pole outside. And from that pole more wires run to a great dynamo that creates the power. Many, many Christians have disassociated themselves from power, and therefore, their lights are not shining. But, friends, Jesus himself is that power. When we are connected to Him, we will not be powerless!"

Clayton listened intently as Reverend Winslow spoke. He had never seen a preacher so full of enthusiasm, and he turned his head slightly to look at Seana. She was entranced. Her lips were slightly open, her eyes fixed on the figure who moved around the platform with the grace of a much younger man.

The sermon went on for forty-five minutes, and every moment of it was packed with verses from the Old and New Testaments and with thrilling stories of life in Africa. And throughout it all, the name of Jesus was always on Barney Winslow's lips.

"Every time I preach I assume that God has someone within the sound of my voice who needs this power. Perhaps many of you would say, 'I'm not a strong Christian. I'm a weak disciple.' Well, there's no reason for you to be. I'm going to ask you to get up out of your seats and come down here to the altar and ask God for His power! There's no power in me, but there's power in Jesus." He hesitated, then went on, "I believe God is speaking to someone here about giving his life as a missionary. Come and we'll pray about it."

Winslow turned the pulpit over to the song leader, who announced a hymn title and page number. Clayton rose to his feet, fumbling with the hymnbook, and was shocked to see the aisles suddenly full and scores of people kneeling at the altar rail. He had never seen such a fervent response from a congregation, and he watched Reverend Winslow move from person to person, praying for each one. Clayton noticed that some had tears running down their faces, and he found himself strangely moved. Again he stole a glance at Seana and saw that she too was weeping. He took out his handkerchief and handed it to her. She murmured her thanks and wiped the tears from her face.

They sang for a long time, it seemed to Clayton, and then the service was concluded.

"Do you think we could meet him?" Seana asked. "After all, you *are* related."

"I don't see why not. Nobody's with him at the moment." Clayton and Seana walked over to the missionary, and Barney Winslow turned to greet them. He put out his hand to Clayton and said, "Good afternoon, brother."

"I'm glad to meet you, Reverend Winslow. I'm Clayton Winslow. I'm a relative of yours. My father's name is Leland."

"How good it is to meet a family member here," Barney said, smiling broadly. He turned to Seana and something changed in his face. "And how are you, my sister? Walking in the love of Jesus?" he asked gently.

"Oh, Brother Winslow, my heart's so full!"

"I can see that." Winslow reached out and took Seana's

hand. He held it for a moment, then closed his eyes and prayed, "Oh, God, I can see that your daughter here has a heart to serve you. She loves you, and I pray that you will guide her through the very door that you would have for her. Be with my kinsman here as well. You know his heart, Lord. I know how you long for him to serve you and to love you, and I pray that he might find you precious. In the name of Jesus I ask it."

Clayton did not know what to say. His eyes suddenly stung, for no one had ever prayed for him like this. Huskily he said, "Thank you, Reverend Winslow."

"Tell your father I'd love to see him while I'm in town. And the rest of your family. Do you suppose they would come with you to the service tomorrow?"

"I'll see what I can do."

Others were waiting to speak with the missionary, so the two turned away to leave the church. As they stepped outside, Seana turned to Clayton, her face filled with joy. "Wasn't that wonderful! I've never heard a man preach like that."

"Neither have I," Clayton admitted. "He believes every word he says."

"How proud you should be that he is of your blood."

"Yes, I guess I am."

The two walked to Clayton's car and drove home. When he stopped in front of the house, he said, "Let's go in the kitchen and get a bite to eat and some coffee."

"But my dad will want to hear about all that happened," Seana protested.

"We'll go tell him in a bit. Come on. I want you to tell my parents about meeting Barney Winslow."

"All right, then. I will."

Clayton and Seana went inside and stepped into the parlor, surprised to find Sarah Mellon there with Clayton's parents. Clayton noticed that Sarah's lips were pale as she kept them tightly closed. "Oh, Sarah," he said, "I didn't know you'd be here."

"I can see that."

"We've just been to hear Reverend Barney Winslow preach," Clayton babbled. "I believe you know Miss Seana Morgan."

"We've met."

"If I'd known you were coming, we could have all gone together." Clayton was aware of the gloom that Sarah cast on the scene. She was obviously angry, and he tried to placate her. "We were just going to have some coffee and a snack before Seana went home. Come in and join us, Sarah. We'll tell you about the service."

"No, I really must be going," Sarah said coldly. "Good night, Mr. Winslow, Mrs. Winslow."

"I'll walk you to your car," Clayton offered.

He followed Sarah outside and said, "Look, I know you're upset, but there's really—"

"I believe you said once you found that girl attractive. I can see you still do."

"Look, Sarah, there's nothing—" But Clayton's words were cut off as she slammed the door. "I'll call you tomorrow," he said. But he got no answer and Sarah sped off down the driveway. He turned to go back inside, feeling as flustered as he ever had in his life. He found Seana waiting for him. "Come on," he said. "Let's forget about the snack. I'll walk you home."

"All right." She walked alongside him until they reached the cottage, and then she turned to him and said softly, "I'm sorry about all that."

"Oh, she'll get over it."

"She's very jealous, isn't she?"

"Yes, she is a bit." The stars overhead cast down a silver light, and he studied her face for a moment. They were standing close enough together that he could smell her perfume. She looked serene in the starlight, but he realized suddenly there was a fire in her that made her a lovely woman, a lively spirit behind the cool reserve of her lips.

Seana smiled, a gleam of humor in her eyes. "Aren't you going to try to kiss me?"

"N-no . . . I don't think so. I learned my lesson," Clayton said, startled and amazed at how easily this girl could knock him off balance.

"There's no pile of manure here for me to push you into," she said as she swept her arm at the manicured grass. "It's kind you were to go with me to hear Reverend Winslow. It was a wonderful night—but I am sorry about your lady."

"I'll see you tomorrow, Seana."

"You won't come in?"

"No, I've got to go try to explain to my parents."

Seana stopped smiling. "Good night, then." There was something in her voice he could not identify—perhaps a longing or some other emotion she was holding back.

"Good night." As he moved away, he heard the sound of the door close and thought of what an unusual night it had been. He had been moved and stirred by the sermon—and now in a different way he had been stirred by Seana, who was so different from any girl he had ever known.

CHAPTER TWENTY-ONE

A TIME TO LOVE

★ ★ ★

Sharon looked up from the bust she was working on, and one look at her father's face told her that something was bothering him. "Hello, Dad." She put down the wooden spatula and wiped her hands on a towel. "Sit down and we'll have a cup of coffee. I need a break anyway."

"All right."

Sharon poured two large mugs from the coffeepot she kept on a hot plate and handed one to her father. She sat down across from him, and when he did not speak, she said, "What's troubling you? I can see something's on your mind."

"I was always a pretty good poker player, which means I've been able to cover up what I think—but I guess I've lost that ability somewhere along the line." Leland sipped his coffee, holding the cup in both hands, and slipped back into silence.

A thought struck her. She leaned forward and asked abruptly, "You're not worrying about me, are you?"

"I am a little. Your mother and I always have, I guess."

"You mean because I've never married?"

"Yes. We had always assumed you'd get married and have a family." Leland stirred uneasily in his chair. "To tell the truth, we've been worried about your seeing so much of Temple Smith. You're not really getting serious about him, are you?"

Sharon could not meet her father's eyes. She turned away and studied the painting on the wall as if she had never seen it before. The silence grew longer. "I can't tell you how I feel, Dad. I don't know myself." She waited for her father to protest, but she saw that he had no intention of saying more. "What's really troubling you?" she asked, anxious to change the subject.

He sighed. "It's financial problems."

Her eyebrows lifted with surprise. Her father had never spoken with her about any sort of problem in his business. She had always assumed that things were going well, for she had lived an affluent life and never lacked for anything material. "Is it really serious?"

"I'm afraid it is, Sharon. I've never discussed these things with you, but during the last several months I've lost millions. I've been struggling to keep the company going, but it's been getting worse. I had planned to revamp the whole organization, but I needed a sizeable loan to accomplish that, and the bank turned down my loan application."

"How could they do that? You've banked with First National and Mr. Wright for years!"

"It wasn't Daniel's fault. He wanted to okay the loan, but the committee refused." Leland swirled his coffee around and stared into it as if it would reveal some secret to him. Finally he lifted his head and shrugged. "There's always a chance I can still pull things out, but if I go broke, I want you to be ready for it. I've already talked to Clayton, but don't tell your mother. She doesn't need this extra worry."

Sharon reached over and put her hands over her father's. "It's all right, Dad. We'll come out of this."

Leland mustered up a smile. "I wonder what it would be like if we lost everything. There was a time when your mother and I had nothing, but then as the business prospered, you got spoiled. We all got used to money and the things it could buy. That's why some men jumped off of buildings when they were down to their last million back in twenty-nine."

Sharon gave her father what assurance she could, and the conversation gradually turned less serious. When he left, she went to the window and stared out at the opulent grounds, thinking of how she had never had to worry about money. She reflected on her father's statement, *"I wonder what it would be like if we lost everything."* Then she thought of Temple Smith. He apparently had little, yet he was one of the most well adjusted human beings she had ever met. She thought about the days they had spent together and whispered, "I don't know how I feel about Temple. I wish I did!"

She went back to work but was troubled all day about the conversation she had had with her father. She knew it would crush her mother if the family lost all their money and their place in society. While Sharon worked she tried to imagine what that would be like, and to her surprise, she realized that money wasn't all that important to her. Of course, she had a good income now from the sale of her pieces, so if her father went broke, she would not be destitute. And the loss of social prestige meant absolutely nothing to her. In fact, not having to worry anymore about their place in society would bring a sense of relief.

Her thoughts were interrupted when Clayton came in to bring her the mail. "Hi, sis."

"Hello, Clayton. You going out?"

"I'm afraid so. Here're the letters for you." He was wearing a dinner suit and looked handsome but rather miserable.

"You look beautiful," Sharon said with a grin. "If you drop dead, we won't have to do anything to you. What kind of a party are you going to?"

"The same kind I always go to with Sarah. The kind where people show off and drink too much."

"Then why are you going?"

"Because that's what Sarah likes to do." Clayton struck his hands together impulsively, betraying his impatience. "I hate these things! Sometimes I think I'd rather dig a ditch than go to another one of them."

Sharon studied her brother, thinking what a handsome young man he was. *But he doesn't seem to know it, which is a good thing.* Aloud she said, "Seana told me about your going to hear Barney Winslow."

"Yes. You know, he is really something! I went back to hear him again by myself."

"Really? I wish you had asked me. I'd have liked to hear him."

"The meetings are over now, but I'll tell you, sis. Listening to that man, I was proud to be a Winslow. Why, he's done everything. Do you know he even killed a lion with his bare hands when he was a young man?"

"That sounds impossible."

"It's not, though. He didn't tell the audience about that, but after the second service I talked to a fellow who travels with him and he told me about it. The Masai over there even call him the lion killer."

"I'll bet Seana liked him."

"She sure did. We went up after the first meeting and met him, and he prayed over her. And I'll tell you it really meant a lot to her."

"She's a sweet girl, isn't she?"

"After she stopped pushing me into piles of manure, I kind of got a different view of her." Clayton managed a grin. "I'd better be on my way to this wonderful party."

"Have a good time. Maybe you and I ought to go out and celebrate something tomorrow."

"Celebrate what?"

"I don't know. The fact that we're alive and well and healthy. So many people in this country are suffering. It makes me feel bad sometimes. We have everything, Clayton."

He grew serious. "You're right about that, and I don't do

a thing to deserve it." He shook his head, then straightened up. "Well, we'll go out and do the town tomorrow."

"Have a good time tonight."

"I won't do that," he announced grimly as he left.

Sharon glanced through the mail Clayton had brought her. She was pleased to see a letter from Temple. She thought about how much she had missed him and how deeply he had gotten into her life. She opened the single sheet and read it quickly:

> Good news here, Sharon. My mother is doing very well. I plan to stay on for a little while longer just to be sure. To tell the truth, I've enjoyed being with her again. She's a wonderful woman, and I know you'd love her.
>
> I hope things are going well with you. I just wanted you to know that I haven't forgotten what I said to you that evening we talked in the garden. I hope you haven't either. I'm still waiting to hear the beautiful music you're going to make someday!
>
> With all my love,
> Temple

The short note stirred Sharon, and she was touched that he would sign the letter *With all my love*. She sat down and read it again, trying to find more in it. She liked the fact that he was close to his mother. She knew Temple Smith had never been a mama's boy, but he had a genuine affection for his mother that pleased her. She had heard someone say once, *"See how a man treats his mother, and you'll see how he treats his wife."*

She put the letter aside and worked late into the afternoon before being interrupted when Hannah Fulton came in.

"I'm sorry to disturb you at your work," Hannah said as soon as the two had exchanged greetings. "I thought you'd be done by now. We haven't seen each other for a while and it seemed like a good time for a chat."

"No need to apologize. I'm through for the day. Why don't we go to the kitchen and have Mabel fix us some supper? Everyone else had plans to eat elsewhere, so I thought I'd see if there were any leftovers from yesterday."

Hannah agreed, and twenty minutes later the two were eating fried chicken and cole slaw in the smaller of the mansion's two dining rooms.

"I got a letter from Temple today," Sharon told her friend. "He's with his mother in Oklahoma. She's been ill."

"I hope not seriously."

"No, he says she's fine now." Sharon hesitated, then said, "I don't know what to do, Hannah. Temple says that he loves me."

Hannah turned her full attention on Sharon. "And what about you? How do you feel about him?"

"I don't know. I . . . I just don't know. I haven't had the most successful life where men are concerned." She detected the tinge of bitterness in her own voice and quickly added, "I don't mean to complain, but it makes me wonder if I can really care for any man."

"If you love the man, marry him."

"But I'm afraid, Hannah. I'm afraid of making the wrong choice."

"Are you afraid he might be after your money?"

"I don't think so, but I just can't be sure."

Hannah put down her fork and took a deep breath. "I love you, and I want to say something very bluntly. You lost your first love when you were young, and you've let that tragedy affect you. And then after you nearly gave your heart to a man who was not worthy, you built a wall about yourself. But you're not too old now to get married and maybe even start a family. If you feel something for this man, don't waste the woman that's in you. The Bible says there's a time to love, and this just might be your time."

Hannah's words troubled Sharon, and she was glad when her friend left. She sat for a long time pondering their conversation, but the more she thought about it, the more confused she became.

★　★　★

Sharon was in her room starting to get ready for bed when her father burst through the door without knocking. "Clayton's been in an accident!" he shouted.

She jumped up. "Is he hurt badly?"

"I don't know. Your mother and I are going to the hospital. I think you'd better come along."

"Yes, of course."

She rushed downstairs and grabbed her coat. The chauffeur was in the car waiting, and her father cried, "Don't waste any time. Get us to the hospital quickly."

Sharon tried to get more information, but her father knew nothing. "I just got a call from Dr. Fremont that he's there at City Hospital. Let's hope he's all right."

★　★　★

Dr. A. J. Fremont was one of the finest doctors in New York City. He looked more like a business executive than a doctor. His hair was silver, and he had piercing blue eyes and a soothing voice.

"Now, let me put your mind at rest," he said as the Winslows stood before him. He was wearing a green smock with short sleeves, and his arms looked muscular. "Clayton isn't critical, but he's been seriously injured."

"What happened?"

"You'll have to get the details of the accident from the police. It'll be in the report, but medically he's going to be all right."

"What's wrong with him, Doctor?" Sharon demanded.

"He's got some broken ribs and his right wrist is broken, both of the big bones. His leg was badly cut, so he'll be in a wheelchair for a time. He's going to need a lot of care."

Relief washed over all three of the Winslows, and Lucille

said, "Can we see him, Doctor?"

"Right now he's still out from the anesthetic. It'll be a while before he comes around."

"Will he have to stay in the hospital long?" Leland asked.

"I think he should stay for a few days, and then he can probably make it at home with some good nursing."

"We had Seana Morgan take care of Mother when she was ill," Sharon said. "She's one of your nurses here."

"Yes, I know Seana well. She would be fine if she's available."

★　★　★

The world was a great pool of blackness, but from somewhere far away Clayton heard voices. Slowly they became more distinct, and he opened his eyes and saw his parents standing beside his bed. He tried to speak but found his lips were very dry. When he did manage a few words, his voice was a whisper. "Hi, Mom, Dad."

"How do you feel?" Lucille said. She gently pushed his hair back from his forehead.

"Terrible."

"You're going to be all right," Sharon said from the other side of the bed. She leaned over and gave him a quick kiss. "You had a bad accident, Clayton."

"I feel like I was beaten up with sledgehammers," Clayton whispered.

"You were very fortunate. The car was totally demolished."

"What about Sarah?"

"She was thrown clear. Got some scratches and bruises, but she's all right."

"Thank goodness."

Clayton closed his eyes, and the three thought he was asleep. But in a few seconds he opened them again. "I don't want to stay in this hospital. I hate hospitals."

"You'll have to stay for a few days, son," Leland said. "But we'll take you home as quick as Dr. Fremont says it's okay. You'll have to have some nursing."

They could all see that Clayton was in some pain as he grimaced and said, "You know, when I saw there was going to be a wreck, I got an instant course in life. I've always heard that your whole life flashes before you in a situation like that." He lifted his right hand and stared at the cast, then reached over with his left and grabbed Sharon's hand. "I'm no one to be giving advice, but don't miss out on a minute of life, sis. We don't have that much time."

Sharon felt a sudden sense of urgency in his words. She thought about her conversation with Hannah and whispered, "I'll try, Clayton."

* * *

The accident changed the household almost completely. They all recognized from the police report that it was a miracle Clayton wasn't killed instantly. When he was brought home from the hospital, a room on the first floor was prepared for him, and Seana was there to help get him settled in. The ambulance driver helped bring him in on a stretcher, and when they put him on the bed, he groaned involuntarily.

"Careful there," Seana admonished. "This is no sack of potatoes you're moving!" She got Clayton settled and dismissed the ambulance team.

"You're feeling pretty bad, I can tell that. I'll give you something for the pain."

"I've never felt so helpless. I can't even turn over by myself."

"That's why I'm here. Now, we've got a job to get you well again."

"You know, I told my mom and dad that just before I had the wreck, my whole life flashed before me. And you know what I thought of what I saw?"

"What did you think?"

"Not much," Clayton whispered. He looked up and tried to smile. "You've done something with your life, but all I've ever done is spend money and have fun."

"Well now, we'll have to talk about that, won't we?"

★   ★   ★

Clayton slept well that night, due mostly to the medication Seana gave him. When he woke up, she was right there, and he was surprised at how easily she could move him around. She pulled him up into a sitting position, putting pillows behind him. Although it was painful, he tried not to show it.

After she helped him with his breakfast, she put the dishes aside and came back with a basin of hot water. "Now it's time for your bath."

"Couldn't that wait until I get well?"

"No, it can't. Now, lean forward." She stripped his hospital gown off and washed him as impersonally as if he were a block of wood. After she washed his upper body, she yanked the sheet up, washed his legs, and then handed him the washcloth. "There. You take care of the rest of it while I get your shaving things."

"You're not going to shave me!" he said with alarm.

"You don't intend to grow a long beard, do you?"

Clayton finished the washing, and when she came back with fresh water, she worked up a lather with his shaving brush in a businesslike manner and lathered him up. Taking the straight razor, she came at him abruptly.

"Have you ever shaved anyone before?" he asked anxiously.

"Many a time back in Wales." She put her hand on his head, turned it to one side, and then paused, a flash of humor in her eyes. "Of course, they were all dead men."

"Dead men!"

"Yes, we did our own funerals over there, and I shaved many a corpse. Not a one of them complained," she said, her lips turning upward in a smile.

Clayton laughed heartily, even though it hurt him. "All right. I'm glad to have an experienced barber."

Seana shaved him competently and then dabbed shaving lotion in her hand and smoothed it over his face. "Now you're all nice. Smooth as a baby's bottom."

Clayton hardly knew how to react to her. "You have a way with words—and with patients. I'm glad you're here, Seana."

"It's getting you well I'm here to do. And then no more car crashes."

"I'll do my best, but with a nurse like you, it's not really so bad."

"And what will you have me do now? You've got all day."

"Maybe you could play some music or read to me."

"All right, but I get to choose the music, and I get to choose the book."

CHAPTER TWENTY-TWO

THE OPEN DOOR

★ ★ ★

As September gave way to October, Sharon found herself getting more and more confused about her feelings for Temple. Both Clayton's accident and her conversation with Hannah had caused her to spend some time reflecting on her life, yet she was uncertain of where her feelings were leading her.

Late one Thursday afternoon she had given up on work and was sitting in her studio in the overstuffed chair reading a book. She discovered that she had read the same page twice without making any sense of it when she heard a familiar sound. A distant roar that seemed to swell as it drew nearer pulled her head up. Jumping out of the chair, she ran to the door and outside. As she saw the motorcycle approaching, her heart surged with gladness, and she realized that she would always feel that peculiar kind of joy whenever Temple Smith came into her vision. She ran forward as he braked the cycle, threw the kickstand down, and came off in one easy motion.

"Temple!" she cried and ran toward him. He had taken off his Stetson and goggles and turned just in time to find her running toward him, a smile on her face and light dancing in her eyes.

Sharon surprised herself by throwing her arms around him, and he lifted her off her feet in a bear hug and kissed her soundly.

Temple released his hold and she stepped back, her face flushed. "Well now, I reckon absence makes the heart grow fonder," he said with a grin.

"I . . . I'm so glad to see you."

"So I can tell."

Flustered, Sharon reached up to tuck a curl back in its place, knowing that her face was pink. She had never shown such outward affection to anyone, not even Robert that she could remember. "How's your mother?" she asked quickly.

"She's fine. I wish you could meet her, Sharon. She's the best woman in the world."

Sharon was still embarrassed over the greeting she had given him and laughed shortly to cover it. "That will make it hard on your wife if you always feel like that."

"I don't think so."

Sharon waited for him to speak again, but his gaze was fixed on her in a penetrating way. He had the bluest eyes she had ever seen, and they seemed to swallow her as he took her shoulders and pulled her closer. She did not resist, and at that moment it seemed to Sharon that she had ceased to be the same woman. She could not explain it even to herself, but a wall had suddenly fallen that she had built over the years, and she stood helpless before him with an unfamiliar weakness that she found not at all unpleasant.

"Sharon, I'm not a young man anymore. I don't have as much time as I once did—so I'll come right out and say what I have to say."

Sharon could not move from his gaze. She felt his strong hands squeezing her shoulders and saw the determination that was so much a part of him. "What is it, Temple?"

"I love you, and I want to spend the rest of my life with you." He hesitated, and she saw in him a vulnerability she had never noted before. He had always seemed so strong and self-sufficient, but now there was a strange pleading in his eyes she could not miss. "I want someone to lean on," he went on. "Someone to be with me always. And I want someone I can support when she needs it. That's what marriage is—two people so close that when one of them hurts, the other one knows it and comes rushing to the rescue."

Sharon whispered, "That's what I've always thought too, but I could never say it."

"I know I love you, Sharon, so either have me as a husband—or tell me that you don't love me and you can never marry me."

Time seemed to stand still for Sharon. She had thought constantly about Hannah's words, *"Don't waste the woman that's in you."* She reached up and put her hands on Temple's shoulders, conscious of the hard, lean muscles beneath them. In her mind's eye she saw a flashing image of a pair of balances, and she knew that the decision she made in this instant would control the rest of her life. Then another image came of a woman she knew was herself walking down a long empty road. It was a lonely picture. But then she saw a third image of herself walking that road with Temple by her side—only the road wasn't lonely anymore.

"Can you give me a little time, Temple?" she whispered.

"I don't have time, Sharon. Neither do you." He hesitated, then said gently, "I'll come back tomorrow. If you'll have me, I'll be the happiest man in the world. If you won't, I'll be okay, but I'll always know that I missed something true and wonderful and good." He kissed her firmly on the lips, then turned and walked away.

Sharon watched as he mounted the cycle, kicked it into a roar, and without looking back wheeled the machine and shot down the driveway.

She watched him go, feeling like a wounded, dazed soldier. She had never had such turmoil in her spirit, and with a sob she turned and ran to the house. She dashed past the maid, who stared at her in amazement. Sharon knew that tears were streaming down her face, but she didn't want to speak.

She went up to her room but could not rest, so she walked the floor. She was still there an hour later when Ruth came to tell her that dinner was ready.

"Tell them I don't feel well—that I'm not coming down."

"Yes, Miss Sharon."

Sharon moved to the window and stared out as darkness fell on the manicured lawn. The moon was already visible, but she took no joy in the crescent shape.

"I'm so confused," she cried aloud. "God, show me what to do!"

★　★　★

Sharon awoke with a start, completely bewildered until it all came rushing back. She had paced endlessly and then knelt and begged God to show her what to do before collapsing on her bed and falling into a fitful sleep.

She heard a light tapping on the door, as if someone were tapping with their fingernails.

Sharon rose and fumbled for the light before opening the door. When she found Seana standing there, she said, "Is it Clayton? Is he worse?"

"No, it's something else. Can I come in and talk to you?"

Sharon was still not completely awake but murmured, "Yes. Come in." She allowed Seana to come inside and shut the door. "What is it?"

Seana seemed uncertain, one of the few times Sharon had ever seen her like that. "Are you in some kind of trouble, Seana?"

"No, it's not that. You may think I'm strange, but ... from time to time God puts a burden on my heart to pray for someone. When that prompting comes, Sharon, I have to pray until it's lifted. Sometimes it takes a long time, days maybe, and I fast and seek God."

Seana's voice was barely above a whisper, but there was an intensity in it as she said, "Tonight God put you on my heart. I prayed and prayed, and God gave me a word to say to you. I know you may not believe in things like this, but I feel God has something He wants me to tell you. You are having difficulty, aren't you?"

"Well . . . yes, I am."

"I thought you might be when you didn't come down to dinner tonight."

"What do you think God wants you to tell me?"

"It's a Scripture verse from the book of Revelation. A single sentence."

"What is it, Seana?"

"'I have set before thee an open door.' That's in the third chapter of Revelation, verse eight. I wasn't sure at first if it was just my imagination, but after I prayed some more God assured me that I should tell you, and He also gave me the words, 'Do not fear to move through it.' I'm not sure what that means, but I had to tell you."

Sharon stood still as the words sank into her spirit. "'I have set before thee an open door. Do not fear to move through it.'" She could hardly speak but managed to say, "Thank you, Seana. I believe that *is* from God."

As soon as Seana left, Sharon went to her bed, feeling weak. She fell beside the bed and cried out, "God, don't let me do the wrong thing. Show me what to do. . . ."

★ ★ ★

An hour after dawn Temple stopped his cycle in front of the Winslow mansion and put the kickstand down. He paused for a moment, letting the engine idle. He had slept little, and now as he sat looking at the house, he felt depressed and empty. He raced the engine briefly and thought about leaving—then shrugged his shoulders and cut the switch. He had not gone more than a dozen steps toward the house when the door opened, and Sharon stepped outside. She looked tired, and yet when she came closer, he also saw a peaceful light in her eyes. She stood before him and put out her hands. He took them and waited.

"I want to be your wife, Temple, and I want us to be together always."

Temple felt as if something had exploded within him. He had been afraid that she would come out and tell him good-bye forever. He smiled and drew her into his arms, and she came willingly. He held her close, breathing in her sweet fragrance, certain that his desire for her would never fade.

He kissed her then, and when he lifted his head he said, "Are you sure you want to marry me? You don't know very much about me."

"I wasn't sure until last night, but God gave me assurance. I believe in you, Temple. Nothing you can do will shake that."

"All right, then. Are you ready to tell your parents?"

"Yes. I know they'll have some trouble with this, but let's get it over with."

"If this is what God wants, He can work it out."

The two found Leland and Lucille having breakfast. Sharon said, "I'm glad you're up, Mother, Dad. We have something to tell you."

Apprehension appeared on their faces as they looked up and saw Sharon holding Temple's hand.

"I know this may come as a shock to you, but Temple and I love each other, and we're going to get married."

Lucille gasped and Leland patted her hand and rose to his feet. "Are you certain this is right for both of you?"

"I've never been as sure of anything in my life," Sharon answered.

Leland turned to Temple. "Do you love my daughter?"

"More than I could ever say, sir."

Leland paused, at a loss for words. "Can you support a wife?"

"I know this is hard for you," Temple said slowly, "but Sharon will never know anything but love and kindness from me. As for supporting her, she'll never miss a meal as long as I'm alive. I know you wanted a different kind of man for your daughter, but I think God has given us to each other. I hope you'll learn to accept me."

Sharon looked up at Temple proudly. There was much that she didn't know about him, but that did not worry her, for she trusted him implicitly. She prayed that her parents could learn to trust him as well someday. She left Temple's side and went over to kiss her mother's cheek. "I'm so happy, Mother. Please try not to be upset."

Lucille studied her daughter's face. A long moment passed, and then with a hand not quite steady, she touched Sharon's cheek. "If this is what you want, then this is what we want for you. I can see the happiness in your eyes." Lucille's long illness and brush with death had changed her, and no longer did society's expectations hold first place in her life. "We'll have to begin making wedding plans and talk about dates."

Sharon laughed with joy as she reached for the hand of the man she loved. "I'm sorry, but I can't take another big wedding, Mother. I'd like to get married in this house if you'll let us—and as soon as possible. What do you think, Temple? Could you be ready in two or three days?"

"How about Monday morning? Is that soon enough?"

She beamed as she bobbed her head vigorously.

Leland was grinning. "You remind me of me," he said. "I was the same way when I was a younger man." He put his hand out to Temple, and the men shook hands firmly. "God bless you both. I'm glad to welcome you to the family, son."

Temple gave Leland's hand another shake, then went over to where Lucille sat. "I want you to meet my mother, Mrs. Winslow. You two are a great deal alike. I know you're going to get along."

CHAPTER TWENTY-THREE

THE BRIDE

★ ★ ★

"There's the music for your cue," Leland said with a smile. "Are you ready, dear?"

Sharon thought back to when she was a little girl. She saw herself going to her father with some hurt she had suffered, asking for his sympathy. Now as she stood dressed in her wedding gown, she knew this would be the last time she would turn to him for her needs. *I'll have Temple from now on,* she thought. "I'm ready, Dad."

"You look absolutely beautiful, Sharon." Leland's quick glance took in her simple, sleek, white silk wedding dress. Sharon wore a bridal cap trimmed with orange blossoms and carried a bouquet of orchids and roses. He saw a pristine beauty in his daughter that seemed to have emerged with her decision to marry. He had learned during the past three days since Sharon and Temple's startling announcement that the well of joy in her had reached overflowing. As he looked into her eyes, he saw the deep happiness there. "Come along," he said. "I hope I don't trip and fall down the stairs. I've got to stay on my feet long enough to give you to your husband."

Sharon took her father's arm, and they left the bedroom and advanced to the top of the beautiful curving stairway. As they descended in time to the music, she took in the small group that was standing in expectation. She had decided to have the wedding in the large foyer at the foot of the stairs, which had enough room to seat thirty people. Her mother had invited mainly family members and very close friends, including Hannah Fulton. She also caught a glimpse of Seana and her father, both of whom stood by the wall. Sharon lifted her eyes and saw Temple standing beside the minister. Her husband-to-be was wearing a navy blue suit, which picked up the color of his light blue eyes, and a dark maroon tie with a starched white shirt. He stood tall and straight, and their eyes met as Sharon reached the bottom of the stairway and advanced to where Temple and Reverend Snyder waited.

"We have gathered here this morning for a celebration—the joyous union of Temple Smith and Sharon Winslow," Reverend Snyder began. "The family of God has instituted the ordinance of marriage so that a man and a woman need not be alone. . . ." Sharon listened attentively to Reverend Snyder's words, and when he said, "Who giveth this woman?" she heard her father say, "Her mother and I give her freely." She turned and kissed her father, seeing a hint of tears in his eyes. He turned and went to sit beside her mother, while Sharon joined Temple in front of the minister.

The ceremony continued, and Sharon did her best to concentrate on the words being spoken, storing them in her memory to reflect on throughout the coming years. At the minister's instruction, she faced Temple and felt his large, strong hands around hers. A seriousness marked his features—yet at the same time an unmistakable happiness.

"Do you have the ring?"

Sharon looked into Temple's eyes as he said, "With this ring I thee wed."

She placed a ring on his finger and repeated the words, "With this ring I thee wed."

Then they pledged their vows, and Sharon felt a quiet joy, conscious that this was the moment she had been waiting for all of her life.

"By the authority vested in me, I now pronounce you husband and wife. You may kiss the bride."

Temple put his hands on her shoulders and pulled her gently toward him. Sharon lifted her face and felt his lips touch hers. When he lifted his head, he said, "I love you, Sharon—forever."

"And I love you too, husband," she whispered.

They made their exit to the triumphant sound of the piano, which had been moved into the foyer for the occasion. They headed to the large dining room, which had been set up with several tables to receive the guests.

Temple exploded with a deep sigh. "Whew! That was harder than going over the top back in the trenches."

Sharon flashed a look at him, not sure if he was serious. "Was it that hard to take a wife?"

"No. I was just afraid you would change your mind at the last minute," he teased.

Sharon reached up and touched his cheek. Her voice was soft as she whispered, "I'll never change my mind, sweetheart."

He leaned forward and kissed her, and then a hubbub of voices overwhelmed them as family and friends came in to congratulate them.

★ ★ ★

After following a narrow crooked road for what seemed like a long time, Temple stopped and waved at the scene that lay in front of them. "There it is. Your honeymoon cottage."

They had enjoyed a festive luncheon with their wedding guests before driving all afternoon, and now the sun was dipping low in the west. Sharon leaned forward in awe. "It looks like something that might be on a calendar or a painting. It's beautiful!"

The valley was rimmed on three sides with rising foothills, and the trees' autumn colors glowed in the waning sunshine. The lake reflected the yellow, crimson, and gold of the trees on the perfectly still water. A dock pointed the way to a wood cabin, weathered and silvered by time, with a roof of cedar shakes. An enormous rock chimney rose at the gable end, and even as Sharon took in the scene, she saw two deer grazing not twenty feet away.

"It's not the Waldorf-Astoria, but it should do as a honeymoon getaway."

Sharon was delighted. "Who does it belong to?"

"To me. Or rather, to us now."

"You own this?"

"I bought the land a long time ago, and I built the house too, mostly with my own hands. It's been my secret place for years. It's where I come to unwind. Come on. I'm anxious for you to see it. You'd better like it 'cause you're stuck here for as long as I can keep you."

Sharon reached over and took his hand. He squeezed hers, then took the wheel and drove down the steep road, saying, "When it rains too much it's impossible to get a car in here. Maybe we'll have floods and have to stay here for a year."

Sharon laughed, for she saw that Temple was enjoying showing his special place to her. She wondered where he had gotten the money to buy it but assumed that land this far away from the main roads had come cheap.

When they stopped in front of the cabin, he got out and came around to open her car door. "I'll get the suitcases later," he said. "I want you to see the inside."

Sharon walked toward the door and waited until he unlocked it. He shoved the door back, then said, "I like old customs."

He swept her up into his arms and walked inside, turning her around so she could see the interior. He held her as easily as if she weighed nothing as she studied the cabin. "I had it cleaned up and stocked with groceries. Do you like it?"

The large room had an enormous stone fireplace at one end with a rack full of split firewood beside it. In front of the fireplace was a large brown leather couch that looked big enough to sleep on. Two chairs flanked the couch, and small wooden tables sat next to them. The floor was pine with colorful woven rugs at strategic places.

On one side of the room picture windows allowed the fading sun to throw its beams into the gleaming kitchen. A small round table with four chairs defined the dining area, and along the walls were shelves containing books, magazines, and a collection of carved wooden figures.

"Let me down," she said. "I want to see this." When she got to her feet, she walked around exclaiming, "It's beautiful!"

"You like it? I've spent a lot of time out here. I hope we'll do the same together. Come on. I'll show you the bridal suite."

Sharon followed him to the door on the wall opposite the windows and stepped inside before him. The bedroom was also very large. A double bed dominated the room, and the only other furnishings were a dresser and a desk. Temple pointed out the door that led to the adjoining bathroom. One wall was nothing but windows, allowing the light to flood through.

"You'll be spending a lot of time in here. I hope you like it."

Sharon turned quickly and saw Temple trying to stifle a grin.

She flushed and said, "Proud of yourself, aren't you?"

"Come on. Let's take a walk by the lake."

They left the cabin and walked along the shore of the lake. Darkness was falling fast, and he held her hand as if he were afraid to let her go. And she held his, glad for the strength of his grip.

"Do you come here a lot?"

"Yes, I built it after I lost my wife. I've spent a lot of good hours here. It's the quietest place I know."

A flock of geese rose from a cove, making a miniature thunder with their wings. Sharon watched them as they rose into the air and disappeared into the fading light. She felt full and at rest. "This is so peaceful," she said quietly.

"Yes, it is. I hope you don't expect company, because there won't be any. Or there usually isn't. Come on. Let's go back and cook supper."

He started to turn, but she held him and drew him back. Putting her hands on his chest, she said, "I needed someone so bad, Temple. I have for a long time."

He put his hands over hers and kissed her lightly on the lips. "Well, you have me as long as I'm around."

★ ★ ★

Sharon had openly confessed that she was no cook at all, but Temple proved to be a very good cook. He took pains to please her with their first supper together, fixing pork chops, fried potatoes, corn and tomatoes, and biscuits.

When they sat down to eat, Temple bowed his head and asked a simple grace. "Lord, we thank you for this food, and I thank you for this woman and pray that I may always be a good husband to her."

"And I pray, Lord, that I may be a good wife to Temple. And I thank you for this place. Amen."

Temple reached out and lifted his glass of milk. "It's not champagne, but let's toast the bride and groom." He waited until Sharon lifted her glass, and they touched them, making a slight tinkling sound. "To love," he said simply, "and to the beautiful harp that is no longer silent."

"I've thought about that song so much," Sharon said after they had sipped their milk. "I'm not sure I understand it completely, but I love it. Would you sing it for me again, darling?"

Looking into her eyes, Temple softly sang the lilting melody:

"There's a harp that is silent, whose strings were of gold,
And whose song, as the jasper, was clear,
Oh, its cadence so rare was of beauty untold
As it fell like a charm on the ear."

"You'll have to write a new verse," Sharon said with a smile. "A verse that tells how the harp begins to play again."

"Yes, I think it is playing a lovely melody now." Temple spread some butter on a biscuit and took a bite. "You married me without knowing much about me."

"I know you love me, and that's all I require."

They finished eating, then washed the dishes together. When the last dish was done, Sharon felt nervous. "I think I'll take a bath before I go to bed," she said.

"You go ahead. I'll read for a while."

Sharon gave him a quick glance but could read nothing in his face. She went into the bedroom and shut the door, and for one moment stood there breathing rapidly. A fear came over her, but she did her best to shove it away as she unpacked her clothes and put them in the dresser. She had bought a few new clothes, mostly things for out-of-doors, for Temple had warned her about the isolation of their honeymoon cabin. But she had bought new lingerie as well. Reaching into the suitcase, she lifted out a shimmering white nightgown of pure silk. Giving her head a slight shake, she moved into the bathroom.

She took a hot bath, dried herself, then slipped into the nightgown. It clung to her figure like a second skin, and as she brushed her hair, she wondered if she would be what Temple expected. She had no experience with men, but Temple had been married, and she was nervous lest she prove somehow inadequate.

Moving into the bedroom, she slipped under the covers

and lay there, her mind active with private thoughts.

She heard the door open, and Temple entered. He shut the door and went into the bathroom, and after a while she heard the water running.

She noted that he was singing again, and then after what seemed like a short time, he came out. She had her eyes closed, but she could tell he had turned the light off. The bed sagged then, and as his shoulder touched hers, she turned to face him. "Temple," she whispered, "I don't know how to be a wife—but I love you."

His arms went around her, and she felt his rough palm on the smoothness of her cheek. "I love you, Sharon, and when two people love each other, everything will find its place." She threw her arms around him and held him close. Feeling his arms tighten about her, she thought, *This is my husband—I'm not alone anymore!*

CHAPTER TWENTY-FOUR

SEANA'S RULE

★ ★ ★

Clayton carefully rolled out of bed one chilly October morning and looked out the window at the brilliant fall colors. He was recovering well, but he still had to move slowly. In the month since his accident, the cut on his leg had completely healed, but the cast would remain on his right arm for another couple of weeks. The doctor had told him his ribs would take quite a while longer to heal completely. He found satisfaction in the fact that he was now able to dress and shave himself, and Seana had pronounced him sufficiently recovered that she could return to her work and studies at the hospital.

After getting dressed, Clayton went downstairs and found his mother alone in the dining room. "Good morning, Mother."

"Oh, Clayton, sit down. I know you're still having a lot of discomfort."

"Not bad at all," he said cheerfully. "I think Seana's prayed me out of most of it."

"She's a pleasant girl. And an excellent nurse."

"She's a taskmaster—that's what she is," Clayton said

with a grin. He sat down at the table, and when Mabel brought him a plate of ham and eggs and toast, he began eating enthusiastically. He had lost a little weight as a result of the accident but had already regained some of it. "I'm going to the office today to see if I can help Dad."

"Oh, Clayton, you're not ready for anything like that!" his mother said.

"Sure I am. I'll move slowly, and this wrist here is going to be a problem for a while, but it's something I want to do."

"Your father has talked to you about the troubles at the business, hasn't he?"

Clayton quickly looked up. "Yes, but I didn't think he had told you."

"He didn't want to worry me, but he told me two days ago. It sounds serious indeed."

"It is, but we'll get through it somehow. Since the accident has kept me from going back to classes this fall, I promised Dad I would do whatever I could to help with the business."

"I'm not sure there's much you can do. We may have to sell this house."

He was surprised to hear his mother say this and even more surprised that she did not seem overly troubled by the thought. "Maybe it won't come to that, Mom. Dad says since the bank turned down his loan request, he has applied for several smaller ones at other banks. Anyway, I want to help, even if it's just to give him moral support."

"All right. Don't stay all day, dear."

"I won't. I'm going by Sarah's too."

Lucille was greatly disappointed in Sarah Mellon, for the young woman had made only two brief visits to see Clayton during his long recovery. Both times she had seemed rather distant, but Lucille expressed none of this, only saying, "Give her my best wishes."

"Of course, Mom."

* * *

After spending some time at the office, Clayton drove up to the Mellon mansion overlooking Central Park. When the butler showed him into the drawing room, Sarah received him in a lukewarm fashion. It had not been difficult on her two brief visits to his home to sense that she was not pleased with him. The two sat on opposite love seats facing each other, and Clayton felt uneasy. "I've decided to go work with my father, Sarah."

"Oh, so you're not going back to college?"

"Not until things with the company are settled."

"So things are not any better with your father's business?"

"No, it's quite possible that it will go under."

"I see. That's really too bad, Clayton."

He heard a tone in Sarah's voice that had not been there before. There was a formal quality to it, almost as if she were deliberately placing a distance between them. He knew how much the Mellons stressed money and social position, and now he said rather coolly, "Even if we don't lose the business, it's going to be a long, hard struggle to come back. That's what we're asking God to do for us, though."

"I see."

The brevity of her reply caused something to turn inside him. He had fancied himself in love with Sarah, but now as he sat there facing her, he understood that whatever he had once felt was now gone. They had never been formally engaged, and suddenly he was very grateful for that. He made up his mind. "Things are going to be a lot different for my family."

"Yes, I suppose so." Sarah rose and said curtly, "Maybe when you get things all sorted out you can call me. We can have lunch or something."

"That would be nice," he replied politely as he rose,

realizing he was being dismissed. "Well, I must be going. Good-bye, Sarah."

"Good-bye, Clayton."

She made no attempt to touch his hand or receive a kiss. The two stared at each other for a moment, both of them knowing their relationship had ended. "I wish you well, Sarah," he said quietly before turning and leaving the house. Once he was outside and walking toward his car, he tried to feel hurt but discovered with mild surprise that he could not. Instead there was only a sense of relief. As he got into the car and pulled away, he knew he was leaving something behind that he had once valued very much.

★ ★ ★

"Clayton, you shouldn't be trying to work."

"I'm not going to be much use anyway, but I do want to learn more about the business." He grinned at his father and shook his head. "Don't worry about me. I'm mending together pretty well. Now, I want you to treat me just like a brand-new clerk, Dad. Bawl me out when I do something wrong."

"I'll certainly do that."

Leland was inwardly very pleased that Clayton had decided to throw himself into the work of rebuilding the company. Perhaps something good had come out of the accident after all. It had been the dream of his life that the two of them would work together, but up until recently, Clayton had shown little interest in the business. As he went over some of the rudimentary facts of the business with Clayton, he discovered that his son was sharper than he had known. He was perceptive and evidently had learned something at college.

"I believe we can bring the company back up to where it once was in the industry if we can just get the loans we need." Leland shook his head and added soberly, "But somehow I've got the feeling that the First National Bank is never going to approve a loan."

"Have you tried any other avenues?"

"Oh yes. I've put in applications at several other banks, but people are afraid these days. This economic climate has made businessmen cautious. They're hanging on to their money pretty tightly."

"I suppose most banks want a sure thing."

"That's it exactly."

Clayton hesitated, then asked, "Is there any hope at all that First National will eventually come through with the loan?"

"I have one more meeting with them. Why don't you go with me and we'll make a special plea to the board."

"Mr. Wright is on our side, isn't he?"

"Yes, he is, and he's tried hard to influence the loan committee in our favor. But he's not very hopeful. As a matter of fact, he's as much as told me that I'll have to look elsewhere."

The two men continued their discussion about the business for a while. "Say," Leland said, "I got a call from Sharon yesterday. She and Temple are returning from their honeymoon today."

"I wonder if Temple could be of any help with the business."

"I really don't know, and I don't think Sharon knows either. But if he wants to work here, I'm going to give him an opportunity."

"What does he do for a living?"

"All I know is that he worked as a roughneck in the oil fields in Oklahoma as a younger man. I think he's moved around a lot since then trying different ventures."

"I like him a lot, Dad. I think he'll be good for Sharon."

"You know, I do too. Sharon is happier than I've ever seen her. It took her a long time, but she finally found the right man."

"While we're on that subject, I might as well tell you

Sarah and I are no longer together."

"What happened, son?"

"I think I'm just not the kind of man she wants."

"Nor the kind of man the Mellons want either. They don't want a son-in-law with financial problems. Perhaps it's just as well. Are you troubled about it?"

"You know, I'm not. Not a bit. Right now what I want to do is see Winslow Industries back where it used to be. Right on top."

★ ★ ★

"I'll be glad to see Mother and Dad and Clayton again. Clayton seems to be doing well from what they've told me on the phone."

"That's good news." Temple glanced at Sharon, then smiled and reached over and put his arm around her. "You're sitting very close beside me, woman. Is that on purpose?"

"I was pretty sure you wouldn't mind."

"You're right about that. But if you were sitting any closer, you'd be on my other side." Temple laughed as she made a face at him. "That harp is certainly not silent anymore. I never expected to have such an ardent bride!"

Sharon flushed and tried to pull away, but he only held her closer. "You're everything a man could want, sweetheart."

Sharon leaned against him, and the feeling of safety and security was very warm and real to her now. "I'm very happy, Temple," she said quietly.

"I intend to keep you that way for the rest of your life." He held on to her, and they talked quietly. After a time he said, "You're worried about your dad, aren't you?"

"Yes, he says the business is in terrible shape. Clayton has been working with him, though. That's good news."

"Maybe I can help too."

Sharon turned to smile at him. "Maybe so, dear." She reached up and captured his hand that lay on her shoulder. "I think poor Dad's going to need all the help he can get."

★ ★ ★

The frogs had begun their twilight chorus as evening came closing in. Clayton sat on a bench beside the new pond at the Winslow estate and admired the way William had made the plantings blend in. He had to admit this was the perfect spot for the pond, and now the whole family enjoyed sitting here enjoying the scenery on warm days. The water was absolutely still. Not a breath of air was stirring, and the surface was like a mirror.

"What are you doing here all by yourself?"

Clayton turned, surprised to see Seana coming toward him along the pathway. "Hello, Seana. Sit down and help me solve the problems of the world." He waited until she sat down beside him, and he asked her about her day. She told him what they had talked about in class that morning and about some of her patients at the hospital. He knew she loved her work, and he liked that in her.

"How are things at the office?" she asked.

"Not good."

"It's sorry I am to hear it."

"Life gets complicated, doesn't it?" Leaning over carefully, Clayton picked up a small stone and tossed it toward the pond. It struck the still water with a plop, sending rings rippling out from it. "Look at those nice, perfect circles, Seana. I wish life were as simple as that. If you throw just one stone, everything is nice and even. But when you throw another one . . ." He picked up another stone and threw it. It landed near the spot where the other had hit and sent out its own pattern of circles. "Look how that messes up the first circle. When you throw two stones, the water gets all confused."

"I know one thing. You could throw a dozen stones out there, and God would know every circle just like He knows all of our problems," she said with a smile. "There are millions of people in the world, and God knows exactly what each one of them is thinking. He knows all they've ever been through and all they ever will think. He knows every act and every deed of every single one of us."

"That's hard for me to imagine."

"That's because you're not God. He doesn't have any trouble keeping up with all of us."

"I love your theology. It's so simple."

"It has to be simple because I'm simple."

The conversation soon turned to Clayton's recovery. "I want to thank you for taking care of me, Seana. I know I was a bad patient, but you pulled me through." He reached out and took her hand, half expecting her to draw it back, but she did not. She was watching him curiously, and he lifted her hand and kissed it. Her lips changed then, as did her eyes, as he continued to hold her hand. He couldn't help but admire her red hair that glowed as the fading light slid across its surface. He allowed his gaze to follow her thick hair down to the smooth roundness of her shoulders and the graceful curves of her body.

"Aren't you going to shove me in the water for taking liberties with you?"

"No, I'm not." She withdrew her hand. "I do have a rule, though, that I established a long time ago."

"A rule? What kind of rule?"

"My rule is that I don't get involved with any man who has other commitments."

"Well, I don't have any commitments."

"Yes you do."

Clayton told her about his visit with Sarah. After giving her the brief highlights, he said, "So, you see, I don't have any commitments." He turned away and watched the tiny bugs that were skittering across the surface of the water. He said quietly, "And it doesn't look like I'm going to have anything like that for a long time."

"Why not?"

"For one thing, I may wind up being broke. We're on the brink of losing the family business. I'm sure you've heard about it."

"I have heard that your father's having a difficult time."

"And I haven't been any help up to now, but I'm going to try to be from now on. But I'll be too poor to have a sweetheart. I'll be too poor to have a fiancée. So I guess you're safe."

"I'm used to not having any money," Seana said with humor stirring her voice. "And since you don't have a sweetheart or a fiancée, I think we might work something out."

Clayton straightened and turned to her with astonishment and was glad to see that she was smiling. "Does that mean I might take a little liberty?"

"You're a fainthearted one, you are," she said. "Any other man would have done something about it if I had told him such a thing."

Her laugh stirred Clayton, and he didn't hesitate to put his arms around her and kiss her firmly. She stayed with him, her lips soft and yielding but returning a pressure of their own. He held her in his arms after the kiss, soaking in her loveliness and strength.

Suddenly a giggle burst from her and she pushed away. "I gave you baths for weeks, and in all that time you never once tried to kiss me."

Her humor was contagious.

"I was afraid you'd break my other arm."

"You might have been right about that! But now, since you're no longer involved with Sarah, you can ask my father if you can come courting. That means you can sit on the porch with us until he decides if you are a fit man to see his daughter."

"All right. I'll do that." He started to say more but turned his head at the sound of an approaching car. He got to his feet when he saw who it was. "It's Sis and Temple. Come on. Let's go welcome them back."

The two moved across the lawn to greet the returning honeymooners. As the newlyweds got out of the car, Sharon was radiant as she cried, "Look who's out and about! The patient on his feet with his nurse."

"Marriage agrees with you, sis. You look absolutely beautiful." He shook Temple's hand and said, "How's the groom?"

"I've got him trained," Sharon said. "Give me a year, and he'll be perfect."

Temple laughed and shook his head. "She's right about that. I'm just a big toy to her."

"How are the folks? And how are you?" Sharon asked.

"I'm better every day. I have a good nurse here. She quit working for me, but I'm making plans to go over to her place now and then to get cheered up."

Sharon raised her eyebrows. "Sounds interesting! And how are things at the office?"

"Well," Clayton said thoughtfully, "the truth is we're poor and bound to get poorer."

Sharon shook her head. "No we won't. The Winslows will come through. We always have."

CHAPTER TWENTY-FIVE

A Fitting Finale

★ ★ ★

Leland and Lucille were thrilled to see Sharon so happy. The days when they had been so anxious for her to marry in high society seemed long ago and already were becoming a dim memory. Both of them had seen the joy in their daughter, and if it had not been for their pressing financial problems, their contentment would have been complete. Neither of them had questioned Sharon on the matter of finances, but they both had assumed that Sharon would have to support their new son-in-law.

On the third day after Sharon and Temple had arrived back from their honeymoon, the entire family sat down together at breakfast. The table was covered with platters of sausage, ham, eggs, potato casserole, biscuits, and fresh fruit, and as they started to eat, Leland said, "Well, today's the day."

"The day for what, Dad?" Sharon asked. She was sitting next to Temple, and both Lucille and Leland noticed that she occasionally reached over to touch him as if to be sure he was real.

"This is the day we meet with the loan committee at the

bank and make our plea. I don't want to get your hopes up. Clayton and I will do the best we can, but Daniel Wright has pretty well warned me not to expect to get the loan."

"You never know about committees," Temple said before putting a morsel of ham in his mouth. "I never knew a committee to do anything smart or wise yet."

Leland grinned at his new son-in-law. "I expect you're right about that, and this one probably won't prove any exception."

"What time is the meeting?" Lucille asked.

"At ten o'clock. We'll have to leave shortly after breakfast."

"I'm going with you," Lucille announced.

Leland was surprised. She had never made any attempt to go to any of his business meetings, but he knew she wanted to give him moral support. "That'll be good. Maybe they'll see my poor wife and feel sorry for me—sorry enough to give us several million dollars!"

"Why don't we go too, Sharon?" Temple said, the corners of his lips turned upward in a smile. "When they see you've got a worthless son-in-law to support, they'll have to feel sorry for you."

"I doubt it." Leland shrugged.

"Maybe we ought to put on ragged clothes and look hungry," Clayton put in.

"I guess we could do that," Leland said with a smile.

"Seana says we're going to pull through this," Clayton added. "That woman's got more faith than anyone I know."

"I say we're going to make it too," Sharon said. "Let's put on our best clothes and go in there and face that committee like we own the world."

Leland slapped the table with his palm, making the dishes rattle. "By george, let's do it! We'll show them the Winslows are nobody to trifle with."

★　★　★

The bank president's secretary met Leland and his group as they entered the lobby. "Come this way, Mr. Winslow. Mr. Wright and the committee are dealing with another matter that's taking longer than they anticipated, but it won't be long, I'm sure."

"Thank you very much."

The party followed the secretary, all of them dressed up except for Temple, who wore a pair of jeans and a red-checked shirt that drew everyone's attention. His Stetson was still perched on his head. Sharon had rebuked him for not taking it off in the bank and for not dressing up more, but he had said, "Clothes don't make the man, sweetheart. They're not going to give money because your dad's son-in-law is wearing a pretty suit."

As they waited in chairs outside the conference room, Leland turned to face Lucille. "If this goes badly, I guess I can always go back to where I was when we first got married. I didn't have anything when I met you—and it looks like we'll be starting over again."

Lucille smiled encouragingly. "We can do it again, Leland."

Temple suddenly got up and said, "I've got to make a phone call. I'll be right back."

Sharon watched him with surprise and wondered who in the world he would be calling. There was no time to think about it for long, though, because the secretary came back and said, "If you would come this way, the committee is ready."

Leland let the ladies go first; then he and Clayton followed. When they entered the large conference room, he saw that the committee, comprised of five men all dressed in nearly identical black suits, were sitting along one side of the table. *They look like roosting buzzards,* Leland thought but smiled and spoke to Daniel Wright, the president, who was at the end of the table. "Good morning, Daniel."

"Good morning, Leland. I see you've brought your family with you."

"Yes, I believe you know my wife, Lucille, and my daughter, Sharon Smith. Her husband has gone to use the phone. He ought to be back in a moment."

Wright welcomed them, but it was obvious to everyone that he was nervous. "I've asked the committee to reconsider your request for a loan," he said, "and now, perhaps, you would like to voice your appeal, Leland."

Leland stood up. "I think you all know my record. You have all the papers and the financial history of Winslow Industries. I can't add anything to that. We've had hard times, as others have had, but I am confident that with your help we can weather this storm." He spoke a few more words but found himself staring at stony faces. Deciding it was hopeless, he thanked the committee for their time and sat down.

The chairman of the committee, a short, heavyset man with small eyes and a double chin, spoke up in a rather clinical voice. "Naturally we would like to help you, Mr. Winslow. You have been a faithful depositor and customer at First National for many years." He went on for some time, but everyone in the room could see what was coming. "Things are so uncertain these days that we have curtailed a great many of our activities. I'm sorry, but for the last time, we're going to have to refuse the loan."

Leland showed no emotion. "Thank you for your time, gentlemen," he said courteously. "I'm sorry that we couldn't do business."

At that moment Temple walked in through the door. He was still wearing his Stetson, and he looked decidedly out of place in his cowboy outfit and suntanned face. "Did you get everything settled, Leland?"

Leland did not have time to answer, for Daniel Wright interrupted. "Temple Smith!" he exclaimed, and when Leland glanced at him, he saw that Wright's face was suffused with astonishment. "What in the world are *you* doing here?"

The whole Winslow clan now looked up with equal

astonishment. "Do you two know each other?" Leland asked.

"Know each other!" Daniel said. "Why, we go way back. I can't believe you're here."

"It's me all right, Dan. How are you?"

"I'm just fine. But you haven't told me yet what you're doing here. You seem to know these people," he said, waving his hand toward the Winslows.

Temple thumbed his Stetson back. "I'm here with my family, Dan. I talked Sharon into marrying me, so I guess you'd have to say I'm part Winslow now. What have you decided about the loan?"

"They turned us down, Temple," Sharon said, still trying to get over the surprise reunion of these two men. She couldn't fathom how Temple would know Mr. Wright.

"It's just as well," Temple said with a broad grin. "I've been talking to Jefferson over at Chase National." He turned to Leland. "They're waitin' for us over there, Leland. The loan will be set up right away."

"Wait a minute!" Daniel exclaimed. "Don't be in such a hurry, Temple. You always were an impulsive fellow."

He glanced down the table at the members of his committee and said, "I'm sure the committee will want to reconsider. We didn't know you were involved in this." He looked directly at Temple and said, "You're signing the note at Chase, aren't you?"

"Yep. Sure am."

"Well, let me tell you right now: whatever rate of interest they've offered, we'll cut it by half a percent."

"Make that three-quarters."

"Done!" Daniel said instantly. The committee members all looked at one another and shrugged. "Now, Leland, I'm so happy this has worked out this way. If you'll come back tomorrow, we'll have the papers ready."

All of the Winslows were staring at Temple, and Leland voiced their question. "Who *are* you?"

"Why, I'm your son-in-law, Leland."

Daniel jumped in. "You mean you don't know who your own son-in-law is?"

"I know he's Temple Smith," Leland said.

"But don't you know he owns Okla Oil Company—and a lot more besides?"

Leland stifled an exclamation.

"Let's get out of here," Temple said, taking Sharon's arm. "We'll be back tomorrow, Dan, to sign the papers. Come along, sweetheart." Pale with shock, Sharon left with Temple, followed by the other stunned Winslows. As soon as they were outside the bank, Sharon turned to him while her parents and Clayton huddled around them. "I don't understand this. You own an oil company?"

"He owns Okla Oil Company," Leland said in a strained voice.

"It's like this," Temple said. "I started out working on rigs when I was sixteen years old and pretty much worked myself to death for nothing. A few years ago I bought some wildcat stock and struck it rich. It was fun for a while, and then one day I got tired of the rat race. I hired a man to run the company, and I've had fun just bummin' around trying to serve the Lord in small ways since then."

Sharon was at a loss for words, and then suddenly she began to giggle, which soon turned into a laugh.

"What in the world are you laughing at?" Temple asked.

"I'm laughing because I gave you money to buy gas to go home and see your mother."

Leland stuck out his hand to shake Temple's. "Here I had resigned myself to being saddled with a poor, worthless son-in-law. Looks like I'll have to give up on that expectation."

"You may have one yet. You know how the oil business is."

Clayton shook his hand too. "I'll have to be nicer to you now that I know how important you are."

"You shore will," Temple said in his Oklahoma drawl

and grinned. "Anyone wanna go get a hamburger? I'm
starved!"

★ ★ ★

Sharon sat at the dressing table that night brushing her
hair that came down well below her shoulders. She was
studying Temple in the mirror, who was seated on the bed
watching her. He rose from the bed and came over and took
the brush. She had learned on their honeymoon that he
loved to watch her brush her hair and at times even took
over the job. "Let me do that," he said. He began to brush
her hair slowly, and it gave her an odd feeling to have this
tall, strong man performing such a lowly service. "I think I
would have made a good lady's maid," he said, "at least for
this lady."

She rose and turned to face him. "I feel like such a fool."

"Look, Sharon, I didn't set out to deceive you, but it
troubled me that your family was so set on your marrying a
rich man."

"I think Mother and Dad are cured of that. They don't
have any more daughters to marry off anyway."

"I just wanted to be sure you loved me for me and not
for what I had."

Sharon smiled wryly. "Here I've been worried about
your marrying me for money, and now the shoe is on the
other foot."

Temple put the brush down on the table and ran his
hand over her hair. "You have beautiful hair," he said quietly.

"I wish I were more beautiful—and a better wife."

"Impossible!" Temple said emphatically. "I don't know
where God will lead us, but with you in my arms, I know
we'll make some beautiful music together!"

She laughed and tilted her chin up to kiss him.

"We've got a lot of living to do, Sharon Smith. And we're

not kids anymore, so let's make every minute count!" He glanced at the bed and winked at her.

Sharon pulled his head down and kissed him thoroughly, whispering, "We will, Temple—oh, we will!"

A Heartwarming New Series From Lauraine Snelling!
Ruby and Opal Torvald's estranged father has left them an inheritance. Leaving the comfort of New York for the unknown wilds of Dakotah Territory, the sisters soon discover what he left is something quite different from a gold claim. With nowhere to turn and a scandal brewing, Ruby and Opal face a journey that is lighthearted, heartwarming, and inspiring.

Ruby
Pearl

Historical Sagas You'll Love!

A Biblical Saga of Jesus' Heritage
Master storyteller Gilbert Morris turns his imagination to the Jewish ancestry of Jesus of Nazareth. The result is an exciting series with riveting, action-packed adventures that will entertain, enlighten, and challenge readers to look anew at early heroes of the faith.

Heart of a Lion–Noah
The Gate of Heaven–Jacob
No Woman So Fair–Abraham and Sarah